ROSELAND

CHRIS WOLSEY

DEDICATION

To Veronica and Avis: daughters of Porthleven
and sisters for circa 90 years.

THANKS

My thanks are due to George Dubrik for creating the two maps, to Dane at Ebook Launch for the cover and to John Hutt for his professional edit. This book is richer for their efforts.

CHAPTER 1

Land holds memories and secrets. Into the soil of Cornubia is etched the lives of those who have gone before us. Their voices resonate from the ground if we can listen. In my way I have been their guardian.

The great lord Yusuf travelled north from Massilia along the Rhodanus river before turning west along the Liger to the Gallic port of Condivicnum. As "nobilis decurio" for the Roman imperium he had travelled the route many times. His goods of Gallic wine, fish oil from Spain, fine Samian cups and bowls were now loaded on to his five merchant vessels. Each was large, able to carry three thousand amphorae of trade goods, with high prow and stern against unruly waves. On each the great sail was unfurled against the central mast. The smaller canvas at the prow was readied and the steersman stood between the two great flat oars he would use to guide the ship out of the harbour.

Yusuf looked across to his ward in the line of men hauling and coiling the hemp ropes on to the wooden deck. Eashoa was a strong lad, in his twelfth year, willing for any challenge and intelligent enough to learn. The men liked and respected him, and not only because he was the grandnephew of an important man.

'My lord?'

'Yes, captain. Start our journey.'

Commands were given and the great barques slowly gained speed as they left the safety of their anchorage. Yusuf reflected, as minister for mines he was skilled in his profession but he was no mariner. This Phoenician from Tarsus had the expertise to reach the clouds and cliffs of their destination. He would be the master as they sailed north west, before they would ride the winds east around Armorica and north again to the Isles of Cassiterides.

The great Atlantic Sea was kind over the next week. With favourable winds the steersman milked four or more knots day after day. He stood on top of their cabin at the rear of the deck and plied the ropes that controlled the rudder oars either side. Eashoa was usually with him, even in inclement weather. The boy was a natural, instinctively feeling changes in wind and sea, as he maintained a steady course under the captain's watchful gaze. He delighted in the arcane knowledge that guided the mariners across endless water beyond sight of land. Each day he turned the sand glass every thirty minutes while on deck to measure time and progress: with the master's guidance he used the cross-staff to read the angle between the sun's height and the horizon so their position could be plotted; and so taken was the captain that he explained charts and star maps to Eashoa's avid brain. At nightfall the boy ate with his great uncle and pointed out distant squalls in the setting sun, the detailed habits of birds learnt from the crew, and shared that joy of life that Yusuf was steadily losing to matters of state.

In the Gallic channel the waters changed: the dark blue Atlantic gave way to paler, milky ripples over the rock shelf that led to the northern seas. Wave directions became fickle according to the winds reflected off distant shores. On the morning that Eashoa's young eyes spied land the sky filled with cloud, and freakish squalls soaked them all. Now their captain drew on his maritime heritage as the Phoenicians steered through diminishing visibility over the stirring green deep.

'By the mark 25 fathoms. Sand.'

Yusuf listened to the monotonous voices of men with sounding weights calling the depth, and from inspection of the wax on their bases the sea bed: 'rock', 'fine stone', 'mud' or 'sand'. The strong current was dragging them east towards the narrowing of land between Gaul and the Brythons. Their course was first set northerly toward Karrek Loos y'n Koos, the "Grey Rock", a port in the woodlands and rich farmland that ringed its great southern-facing bay. But their destination was The Lake, a safe haven reached by a winding river in the eastern part of the bay, through the green vale to the great Lake itself. There they would trade for the tin and lead ingots so vital to the Roman army.

'By the mark 18 fathoms. Fine stone.'

It was late summer, with time enough before the winter tempests, but this weather was unseasonal. The captain's instructions to his crew became more measured, curt, as he studied the darkening, turbulence. His steersman battled the increasing undercurrent stirred by winds that now opposed it. As the murky white shroud thickened the cornu, bronze signal horns, sounded from the other four ships. Yusuf mused whether the fleet would turn south to wait for better weather. But soon that option closed. Winds from the south west drove in from the Atlantic. It seemed almost immediately massive swells rolled the shallow-bottomed ships towards the shore.

'By the deep 10 to 12. Clean, stone.'

The captain's horn signalled to tack against them into safer water away from the breakers crashing into rocks too close in the mist. Each master at the helm wrestled his vessel south but was dragged east. He prayed to his gods to save them from the precipitous cliffs of the Ocrinium Promontory that loomed in the fog.

Yusuf and his grandnephew peered through the mirk towards the sound of the lead ship. It had no choice but to try for the safety of that river. A shaft of sunlight pierced the swirling mists and for a moment both saw the barque, the river mouth and The Lake. A green paradise of carefully tended orchards lined the route to The Lake itself and beyond. But then all was shrouded again before a gigantic crack cut through the roar of the surf. Shifting tides had lifted the entrance bar into a treacherous barrier. In a moment of clear sight they saw the ship ground high on the pulsating gravel and a steering oar sheer in two. Helpless cries were soon followed by timber rupturing and terracotta vessels shattering on the swirling shingle beach. Yusuf gave silent prayer for the seamen lost.

'By the mark 8. Clean.'

But the others were no safer. In vain mariners shouted the depths of their markers pulled up from the side. Soon the tidal race and short heavy waves drove another vessel into a submerged reef many leagues from the black, fissured stone of the headland. Fractured cries were quickly lost in the maelstrom. Close by a third vessel rounded the promontory and looked to the quieter waters of the Cerrion River. But a mile off shore they spied the boiling sea sweep over seaweed-coated rocks. Their submerged neighbours tore the ship's side open. In seconds the men were twirling mannequins in a heaving carpet of shattered boards and ballooning canvas.

Yusuf stood on the cabin roof; his left arm gripped a railing, his right encircled Eashoa. In the chaos of thought, a fortune in ships and lost cargo, the agonised cries of men, he felt the calm of his charge. The lad absorbed the power of Nature as though studying the delicate colours of a new fish. The horn sounded again. The captain had made a desperate choice. In moments the steersmen of both ships turned their vessels downwind. The great sails snapped into place and men steadied their feet against the surge in speed. Clearly this was a fraught measure to gain the safety of Rock Anchorage.

As they coursed into the broad expanse of white crests whipped by the crying wind they passed the rocky fortifications of Pen Dinas on their left before the sixty feet high cliffs of Rhos appeared full ahead. Soon the cornu signalled again and sails were partially reefed on both ships. Ocrinium Promontory, the grave of three ships, started to protect them from the worst of the storm. There was cause for hope. But neither ship took depths, crewmen rested; some shut their eyes in prayer. The awful sound of grinding keel and splintering wood was almost simultaneous. The prow of their partner rose up on a great black rock and sank too quickly to think of turning to help. Yusuf saw their own nemesis was a shoal closer to that mighty rock face of Rhos. For a moment they grounded but the next surge floated them off and the craft rode the wave further into the estuary, taking on water rapidly.

Precious cargo was thrown overboard and crewmen pushed spare canvas into the gaping hole. They all searched this peninsula for a safer anchorage than the crag receding to their right into the darkness. The captain steered towards a wide inlet but the currents and blustery winds drove the vessel past its entrance.

'Look,' Eashoa called, and pointed towards the tree-lined banks ahead. It was a light, flickering through flailing branches.

The ailing craft was sluggish now, lower in the water. The captain made the only choice he could and navigated towards the beacon. Surging swells drove the vessel in as the steersman fought to keep away from whatever peril was just beneath. As the light came closer they could see it moved and around a corner were several more lanterns showing a clear path towards a sandy shore. They all gripped whatever there was and waited for the inevitable. The crippled barque beached heavily but stayed upright. Strangers from land then braved that awful night and rode out in small boats to take every man of Yusuf's party to safety. More drenched figures with flaring torches guided them along narrow woodland paths away from the storm into simple wood and thatch dwellings.

Beside the hearth, in dry homespun clothes, Yusuf ate the scalding stew of oats with mussels, some fish and a few discernible vegetables. Each man gave thanks for their miraculous rescue. In the flickering firelight at the centre of the room he studied the peaceful brow of his young companion in sleep, before he joined the slumber of those around him.

§

'Confounded wind,' Meredith heard Jeremy say as he strode twenty paces ahead of her. He didn't notice her pigeon steps struggle unequally in the November gale.

Tintagel causeway was not the nicest place to be in a winter storm straight off the Atlantic, she thought. Despite the wet weather clothing her elfin body was soaked, down to the silver bob of hair sticking to her scalp under the sou'wester hat.

She looked down the three hundred feet of crumbling cliff to the boiling black and grey ocean below; the shingle beach beside Merlin's Cave churned into what resembled the action of her washing machine. With the wind came dollops of natural soap suds, the scum blown in sheets from the crests of monster waves in the darkening afternoon light.

She saw Jeremy wobble as a ferocious gust hit him on the narrowest point of the causeway which was the only access to the "island". The lichen-covered ruins of Arthur's fortress glistened in the driving rain. A split second later the same blast knocked the feet from under her and she tumbled into the rock and tufty grass onto her left side.

'Jeremy! Jeremy!' she shouted into the fury. 'I'm going back. The wind's too strong.'

He turned and realised she'd said something.

She saw him wave his arm backwards.

'You run along, dear. I won't be long.'

She'd been dismissed.

'You're ignoring biology, Jeremy,' she grumbled. 'We could do with a bit of Darwin here!'

There was no point in telling him what a rude sod he had been lately, she thought. Instead she got up, wiped off some of the mud, and braced herself to keep her feet against the blustery squalls thumping her back.

Meredith shouted, 'You're such a —!' but stopped, in case anyone was listening.

Ten minutes and several stumbles later she was in the car with a cup of scalding sweet tea from the Thermos flask.

As the hot fluid followed her throat down to her warming stomach she looked in the driver's mirror. A minor wardrobe crisis had happened, but then Jeremy would probably not notice if she was wearing nothing at all. Then she sat back and contemplated other things. Over the next hour her mind roamed through where Jeremy's passion for King Arthur had taken them. It was the driving force of his life, but it was unrequited. For decades Jeremy had been the Cornish authority on the life of Arthur, the legends but more particularly the real evidence for his existence, however scanty that was.

But, he would not like her to say it, he had failed and he was old. Also he was ill. Having lived with him for several prison sentences she knew him too well. Lately he was eating less and complained of belly ache, when his stomach had always been bullet proof. I wish he'd stop scratching his arms too, she thought. There was clearly something wrong and he was too cussid to go and see about it. Well soon he would have no choice. She did not look forward to the confrontation. In fact conflict in any form terrified her. She sipped more tea and stopped shivering. Despite his foibles she'd stuck with him. Soon she would be the one to tell him to see a doctor. A blast of wind buffeted the Morris Minor Traveller. She thought of Jeremy on the bleak headland above the raging sea.

'I know I've seen it here somewhere,' Jeremy said to the tempest. He clambered amongst the foundations of the castle studying the rubble interior. This was the remains of Arthur's castle as the tourists knew it: romantic cliff-top setting, a mysterious tunnel to Merlin's cave below, the birthplace of the boy Arthur. But these ruins were 12th century Norman at the earliest, six hundred years too late.

Dr Ralegh Radford's excavations in the 1930s had uncovered monastic remains from the 7th possibly even 6th century AD. These were no longer visible, and he, Jeremy Pascoe, did not believe the finds belonged to a group of monks. Poring through the excavation reports there was too much pottery of a quality that not even extravagant men of the cloth would ever covet. He knew Radford's interpretation was wrong and he was going to prove it.

Jeremy was cold, sodden to his skin, and aching everywhere. Generally the weather would not have bothered him; this was what Cornish archaeology was like. He had to find it soon. Meredith would not appreciate that their jaunt on such a foul day came to naught. The wind knocked him flat again, so he tumbled over another pile of Plantagenet stone and grazed his shin on the uneven rubbly surface.

'Damn and blast.'

But then he saw it. His fall had been serendipitous. The dislodged tuft revealed a quarter of red brick. Its profile was of one end, showing the width and the clay used in its manufacture. It was unmistakeably Roman. His theory might hold water yet. He looked up at the sky and the gallons of it pouring onto his head. There had once been a Roman defensive structure here, on a remarkable natural site. Maybe there was an Iron Age promontory fort before it, although he doubted if there was precious little proof that had not fallen into the sea centuries ago. But most importantly a native warlord of Arthur's stature would not have ignored such a perfect protective position. If the Romans built here then probably so did he. But his links with their culture were disputed. His era was surrounded by the crumbling remains of Roman Britannia, barely a century from their departure. As a warrior surely he would draw from the expertise of the greatest fighting machine the world had ever known to that time. But this was speculation. The Roman brick was fact.

He was glad to get back to the car. Meredith handed him the hot cup.

'You're wet through, Jeremy.'

'Mm.'

'What you need is a piping hot bath and a good rub with Vicks.'

'Mm.' He would not object to that, he thought, wriggling in his seat to ease a sore back. He started the car for the long drive home in the gloom.

As the weather thrashed the slate tiles and lashed the window glass of their three-story terrace house overlooking Falmouth harbour and Carrick Roads, Jeremy struggled with a fever. At midnight the doctor told him his temperature was 100.9 °F and noticed yellowing beneath Jeremy's eyelids. The GP lifted his pyjama shirt and found swelling in the lower abdomen. In the morning there was no change. Tests in Falmouth hospital over the next few days revealed the worst: advanced Pancreatic Cancer.

'How long?' Meredith asked the specialist.

'It depends very much on the individual but life expectancy is generally three to six months.'

§

'How do you know about Yusuf's journey, Justin?' Arthur asked me.

'I was told it by my father.'

He was always questioning for the truth in what men said. I, in my turn, could read much in a person's face or body movements. When I described the storm both spoke volumes of words. Arthur was a fearless warrior but some past event had given him a dread of open water. I answered his queries as at our first meeting, months before, when he had ridden ahead of his guard.

My task in this world was to give succour to those who dug for the black ore in Cornubia. Many times my father and I would be called to a help a boy maimed by a fall of rock, a woman cut by tools for breaking stone or men made old before their time with lungs full of dust or poisoned with the arsenic that came with the mineral. Always we were welcome.

Pestis was sweeping the land and the miners were most vulnerable due to their contact with traders from the south. Our community stretched to aid all who asked. I was sent to the north east where I ministered to the children of these people. The signs were clear: white spots inside the mouth, a red rash spreading over their small bodies and the fever. In truth there was little I could do beyond giving sweet liquid, and herbs to bring down the infection. After weeks of struggle, where some lived and others died through chest fluid or boiling brain, I was going home.

Some of the menfolk gave me escort on the open road south. But we were slow, much slower than a larger band of horsemen gaining on us from behind. A tall young man was at its head. Truthfully I held no great concern. It was easy to see that a thin, fair-haired youth was no threat to them. But the miners were uneasy as we waited by the roadside and the warriors encircled us.

'Hail,priest. Where are you headed?' Arthur called.

'Lannsiek, half a day's ride from here, my lord.'

Arthur pulled up his mount and looked, first at me: at my eyes for a time, measuring my worth; and then at the leather satchels on my mount and the mule behind. When he saw books and bags of potions he smiled respect.

'What do you call yourself?'

'Justin, son of Justinian, lately of Armorica but called to service in Rhos, sire.' His eyes wandered over my slight body, trained by books and not the sword, and the pale blue eyes in a clean-shaven face like my father. His gaze paused for a time on my flaxen hair shaved high on the forehead like others of my faith.

'I am Arthur, ill-conceived son of Uther Pendragon. I know your homeland well.'

We fell into step on the open moorland path. Soon my escort turned back to their homes. My safety was now Arthur's concern.

'Merlin holds great store by such things,' nodding towards my baggage. 'Do you know the Druids' ways?'

'Not well but I believe we can find common ground between us.'

He laughed. 'I wonder. He is wary of the teachings from Gaul.'

Myrddin Sylvestris, "of the woods", or Myrddin of Carmarthen, the old Roman sea fortress of Moridunum, Merlin, however he chooses to be known, was Arthur's mentor and companion. Despite their differences of disposition they had one great need in common: they were bastard sons of two brothers, Uther and Ambrosius, the champions of the Britons against the Saxons, now that Vortigern was gone. Both knew my homeland, Armorica, but Merlin was a scholar not a warrior.

From the day we met I saw little care for his appearance or dress: no razor had ever touched his hair or face; the heavy woollen toga and Roman army sandals were for frequent travel. His speech was mostly distracted, halting as if his mind was in several places at once. Often he would chew beard or hair in a frenzy of thought. But he was immensely inventive: as he aged he created curved glass lenses in a wooden frame for seeing and dead men's teeth set in a resin bond for eating. His tricks charmed children and men alike. I was to feel Merlin's passion in debate. It took a time for us to find that on which we agreed.

As we rode I learnt that Arthur had left the court of King Mark, at Fowydh, that morning. He was glad to be gone.

'Uther warned me of the intrigue, the harsh tongues against my birth. But it is my cousin's fear that drives his mistrust of me: that and too many lies from those who advise him.'

He looked at me with such intensity when he said. 'But I will rise above their petty squabbles. When Uther and Ambrosius are too feeble to carry the fight the lords will look to me to save them from the Saxon raiders.'

Over the hours of our journey Arthur chose to confide in me. His quarrel with his cousin King Mark rankled more because they had grown up as friends. Often separated by distance, as Arthur trained in Armorica or was guided by Merlin, they were like brothers whenever they met. Mark was groomed for kingship, with tutors and a courtly life. What they shared was a love of the wild country between their fortresses where they coursed birds of prey and rode hard. Gradually Arthur's physical attributes outshone his cousin's but Mark could not give in. The horse's fall into rocks left Mark broken, despite Merlin's great skills over many years. Mark became bitter. Arthur's sorrow was wasted as the jealousy increased with Arthur's rise to greatness.

When we rode to my home and down to the water's edge he rested his horses for a short time. Up on the hill we shared our water and bread. For the first of many times we sat on the bracken and watched the tide come into this small cove. For he always felt the peace of this place. When he left our community I knew we were friends.

'God speed, Arthur.'

He waved. 'The deep peace of the Great Spirit to you, Justin.'

His safe haven was at Deadman's Point, a few hours' ride away. Uther maintained this sanctuary for his son. But Uther's court when he was not campaigning, which was rare, was at Tintagel on the north coast, where Igraine sat as his wife. Arthur's sister, Anna, shared the palace with Morgana, the daughter of Lord Gorlois and Arthur's mother.

'Uther was besotted with Gorlois' wife. The lord died in the battle over her but not before she was seduced by Uther. I am the result of that lust. A speedy marriage to Igraine gave me legitimacy but not the nobles' respect.'

Gorlois' supporters were always a threat. Uther protected Arthur, but his training was constant, first in Armorica with the Sarmatian warriors, now with his personal guard along the cliffs of Rhos.

Merlin taught him a great deal more. At any time he and young Arthur would walk away from protection into the wild lands of Rhos or along the forested creeks of the River Fala.

'What do you see, Arthur? What do you hear, smell, taste in the wind?'

In time questions were fewer and in his silence Merlin observed the change. Arthur quietened his mind. Difficulties of training, Uther, whatever of the future and the past, were gone as he disappeared into the Natural world. Arthur became of the present and what was around him. His senses silenced thought. Instead he studied the myriad pebbles on the beach, the hidden life of the forest and the fish swimming in the shallows.

One day Merlin dozed on the roots of a tree overhanging a tidal creek. Young Arthur studied crab tracks in the mud leading to the water, and then the tiny creatures coming in with the tide. He put his head under and with eyes open he was another being alongside them. For a long time he was in their world upside down looking upwards at the sky, so peacefully. But then he spluttered for breath. The advancing sea had swallowed the mud that imprisoned his feet. His nose was barely above water, and then not. He used his strength: his legs pulled, his arms thrashed but there was no release. Then he went quiet, and thought; very LOUDLY. Merlin woke.

'That is a skill, Arthur, which Druids take a lifetime to learn. You are an apt pupil.'

Most of all Arthur had an affinity with the birds of the air. As he looked so he felt that he was that feathered hunter surveying his domain, the air currents and the details of terrain below. For hours he was every sensuous thing in this space. In time he learnt to control this imaginative dream.

'Soon you will not need to try. The magic will happen,' said Merlin. In his heart he desperately wanted Arthur to take a different path to Uther when he faced the Warrior's Burden.

Arthur rode beside me as his questions about Yusuf and Eashoa flowed. My mission on that day and others was to aid the miners and traders, from the near port of Lannvowsedh to the farthest reaches of Cornubia. Medicine and counsel were for the sick and forlorn.

Many times I would send their children to collect seawater. This I boiled and let cool and later would apply it to wounds. These would be packed with seaweed for my father told me it was rich in Iodine, a cleanser. Miner's damaged eyes I would flush with this water and cover from the light. Bones broken were strapped with branches and twine. Sometimes the quiet was severed by screams as I pulled collar bones and knees back into place before strapping. Later when I conversed with Merlin we agreed on most treatments but if his knowledge was greater I humbly accepted it into my repertoire.

At times my skills of language helped the tinners trade with Armorica and Gaul. Arthur had cause to use that ability too. We often met on the high pathways across the peninsula.

This day it was my task to satisfy Arthur's thirst for knowledge.

'Justinian, my father, told me the stories when I was old enough to understand. He and the elders of the house wanted me to realise that we had come to a special place full of healing.'

Arthur rode silently, ever the great bear compared to my slight build. At twelve years old he was groomed to be a warrior: tall, dark, his hair plait proudly long and his muscles hardened by constant preparation. I was destined to be a man of peace, an unlikely friend except for our shared memories.

He understood the need for healing, we both did. When our grandfathers were young the might of Rome was tested on all fronts. Britannia's imperial legions could not stop the Irish from raiding the west, and the Picts and Saxons the east. For a time Maximus ruled Britons and Gauls until ambition led him onto Emperor Theodosius' sword. The emperor's son Honorius left us to anarchy after his henchman Stilicho took most of the legions to fight the Alan and Vandal hordes crossing the Rhenus River. What troops were left elected Constantine to lead them, before he too was cut down by those loyal to

Honorius. At last the emperor made clear that these islands would face the raiders alone.

Arthur's ancestors had worked peacefully in the villas of middle Britannia, near Calleva Atrebatum on the Port Way. Imperial edict demanded that farmers bore no arms. They had never known war, had no skills in its arts. Talk in the markets was of troubles on the Rhenus River but the Roman army would deal with that. Then the invaders came to the rich farmlands of central Britannia. Many supported Vortigern when he tried to appease the warriors, since any price is better than war. But the slaughter in the Saxon Terror was vast, a scar in Arthur's memory that would never heal. Ambrosius and Uther were children, the only survivors of their family, when they were spirited away to safety in Armorica. They joined so many Britons seeking refuge there that its name changed to Britanny.

My family were slaughtered by Visigoth raiders who came to my home in great ships. My father hid me from the pillage but the sounds still haunt, the smells of death and burning still touch my soul. Justinian and I were aided to recovery by the Breton Fathers. Our new life of caring for others began when we were sent here.

Now, as boys at the start of manhood, Arthur and I had come across the water to this wild land of Cornubia. My life of compassion had begun. Arthur's destiny was war so that others might know peace. He would not appease the Saxons, Angles or any other invader. He had felt the results of Vortigern's weakness.

When Arthur halted the troop at a ruined native fort overlooking Rock Anchorage, he nodded to Merlin to test his skills first. Merlin sat astride a white mare to one side of the rest. On his leather gauntlet was a white Tawny Owl, hooded like the other birds of prey on men's wrists. But his was to limit hearing not sight as with the falcon.

He dismounted. When the bird's movement stopped he removed the cover and murmured in the Brythonic speech. The creature studied its surrounds testily before taking flight at its chosen time. Merlin watched it adopt a hovering pose a little way above and beyond him. He withdrew a red cloth weighty with meat and decorated with partridge feathers. Soon the low hum of the lure swung around Merlin's head turned into a screeching roar louder than the waves thrashing the cliffs below us. Merlin looked upwards and continued the swing, his burly short arms and stocky torso perspiring with the effort. Then he let go. The lure soared high in an arc fifty paces long towards a patch of coarse grass.

I saw those with falcons impatient with Merlin's odd choice of hunter. But none dared show it openly. The owl now began a long shallow glide, building up speed soundlessly. If my eyes left its flight I would never have known its presence. It struck the prize a man's height from the earth, its talons cradling in a grip of death that no living prey would have survived. Merlin looked at Arthur, who smiled and touched his heart. The owl was allowed to eat its fill with more strange words of encouragement. Now it was Arthur's turn.

On his gloved right arm was a female Goshawk. He whispered soothing sounds to her as he lifted the hood from her head. Tsarati, the "hunter", shook her feathers so that the bells on her legs tinkled. Arthur continued to croon and stroke its head. This creature lived and breathed with him. He took a piece of raw meat from his pocket, bit into it and shared it, mouth to mouth. Then he untied the straps. With a simple lift she was aloft, high and straight, before she circled the sheer cliffs above the pounding waves of the Atlantic sea. Then she hovered, watching Arthur's every action. The creature saw him reach inside the covered basket and remove the dove cradled in both his hands. For months he had trained Tsarati with a lure, a cloth pouch containing a raw morsel. Today her prey was live.

Arthur called in whistles, he and the bird alone in their wild space, his mind in Tsarati's, two hunters in unison. Deftly he plucked three tail feathers and thrust the dove skywards. Able to fly but unstable it dared to strike out towards the open waters of Rock Anchorage. Tsarati was motionless before she dropped into a vertical dive, precisely calculating the wounded bird's line of flight. In seconds the hunter became a straight arrow streaking down and down. She pierced the dove with pinpoint accuracy, the bird's demise instantaneous. With her talons gripping its inert neck she alighted near the old Roman beacon.

Arthur's horse was in full gallop while the bird streaked down. As Tsarati landed he pulled up and dismounted beside her.

'Good girl. Good. Good.' And then many words in the Sarmatian tongue as they plucked the feathers together, he taking a bite out of the raw flesh and then offering it to Tsarati to do the same. He and she were one in the wild moment that took away dross and helped in the healing of his soul.

As we rode back from the open common and down through the wooded lanes to the port he asked me more about Yusuf's journey.

§

Jeremy's nephew, Philip Trevasco, stood in the International Arrivals section of Terminal Three at Heathrow Airport. It was 6am and still black outside. Only a few months ago he had been doing the same thing in Nicosia airport, a tiny cousin to this vast hall. He was waiting for Rosalind Bernaud, his Aussie girlfriend. He could safely say that, having survived a baptism of fire in Iran and then resurrecting that passion between them in Cyprus: they were an "item". But then her ardour was so unpredictable that he was never completely safe in such pronouncements.

There was no mistaking that blonde mane, green eyes in gently tanned face, slim but sensuous body wrapped up in a brown Dryasabone jacket, walking towards him. The Flying Kangaroo had delivered the beautiful package from the far off land of Oz yet again.

'Hi. Good flight?' He'd said something like that last time.

'Yep. No Zorba to bounce us around,' looking out through the plate glass streaming with rivulets, 'but your weather looks a bit ordinary.'

He made the mistake of going to kiss her but she turned and his lips met her cheek. Damn, I forgot that, he thought. No public show of affection. Oh well. There would be private time.

He loaded her rucksack onto a trolley and he collected his from the locker at the side of the hall. At the turnstile he handed her a train ticket and then a Tube ticket. The trip across London was punctuated by squeezing through narrow spaces with ungainly bags and standing crushed between commuters while eyeing their belongings in the luggage space. As they came up the elevators out of the stale air of the Underground they entered the vast glass and steel concourse of Paddington Station, that miracle of engineering by Isambard Kingdom Brunel.

Philip's timing was good. They had ten minutes to absorb the ornate tracery of this Victorian Gothic aircraft hangar with the light at the end of the glass tunnel. Then it was nearly five hours of rocking warmth to Truro as he watched Ros doze after the long flight. One British Rail coffee was enough. She joined him in a black tea on the premise that it was nearly impossible to make a mess of that. It was marginally better.

Vistas of British green pasture alternated with rugged coast in Devon and finally Cornwall. The weather was lighter, with patches of sun, and definitely kinder. She approved. At Truro the atmosphere was rural, a near empty station platform for the train to The Dell in Falmouth. She had caught up on sleep.

'I think I could get to like this place.'

Ros was less impressed with the walk up to Clarence Terrace from the station.

'Any chance of a taxi next time?'

Fair comment, he thought. It just didn't cross his mind.

But the last bit was a gentle decline, past the Orient Hotel with outside tables and signs advertising beers she had never heard of: Doombar, Skinners and Cornish Knockers, to the tiny walled garden at the front of a tall terrace house.

'Come on in,' said Meredith as she shepherded them through the high glass porch. In the towering hall before the two flights of stairs the smells of carpet, cleanliness and musty pictures climbed up the wall into impossible spider web country. Meredith's petite figure, in white blouse and knee-length grey woollen skirt, led the way.

Meredith opened the door to another flight of stairs. 'Philip asked for the attic. I think he made a good choice.' Her bright eyes behind practical glasses radiated warmth.

Thanks Meredith, she thought. The anticipation might give her energy for the last few steps.

She dropped her rucksack and sat on the end of the bed. Out of the floor behind her was the stairwell they'd come up. In the left hand corner was a tiny bathroom and toilet. Her eyes followed the angles of the roof towards the window. The bed was parallel to it and she'd gravitated to the view. It was worth the climb. Their vista was high above Falmouth harbour: in the docks to her right they were refitting huge cargo ships; in the foreground yachts played tag in that vast expanse of water called Carrick Roads; to her left was the green farmland promontory of Trefussis and a labyrinth of creeks which led up the Fal River to Truro; in the centre distance was the Roseland Peninsula and its quaint harbour town of St Mawes. Yes she could learn to enjoy this place.

His shower was perfunctory so Ros could luxuriate away the journey. When she came down to the tiny kitchen she squeezed in beside Philip at the red laminate table and absorbed another view of St Mawes in the late afternoon sunlight. Thirty years before this place had resonated with the sounds and sights of war. It felt like they had only just left. Jeremy perched precariously opposite her, his walking stick propped beside his chair. His thinning hair stretched across an impressive dome which balanced on a smallish, unfit frame. His manner was severe, his strength limited by the rapid onslaught of his illness, but he still dominated the room. Meredith turned off the news on Jeremy's radio and passed Rosalind a small glass of Amontillado sherry.

'Thanks.' She sipped and listened to Jeremy.

'So what do you know about King Arthur, lad?' The tone was authoritative, with some doubt that Philip had it in him to complete the task. Jeremy had watched him grow up, at a distance. The studious, gangly kid had turned into a tall, slim student, with rather long black hair of this era. To Jeremy's surprise he had attracted an antipodean soul of interesting beauty. Maybe Jeremy was too close to the child to see her attraction for him but Philip had done rather well for himself. She might just have honed his intellectual talents with a bit of self-confidence.

§

Arthur held the reins loose as he listened to my story.

'In the bright, sunlit morning Yusuf found his grandnephew studying the structure they had spent the night in; the clay lining which kept out the damp from the flat bench cut into uneven ground. Poles supported the roof beams, which were covered in tied bundles of reeds, and outside the wattle and clay interior walls was loose stone held together with more clay. Ingeniously a shallow trench caught rain dripping off the roof and guided the water away.

A short distance off-shore the Phoenician captain and steersman inspected the destruction. By various means they communicated easily with local craftsmen who gestured where suitable timber might be found to repair the vessel.

Yusuf and Eashoa were met by the leaders of this community. In the converse it became apparent that these people had traded with Syria Palaestina for many generations. Some of them were descendants of migrants who arrived in ships such as these. Yusuf was informed that the task would take months, so great was the damage to the substructure. Already teams of men with ropes were ready to drag the great ship out of the water.

"Marmore, "Great Lord", May we show you the workings of our trade?"

As decurio Yusuf already knew a great deal but a look from his young companion was enough. In a short time they were travelling out of their refuge across the open water of this magnificent harbour of Rock Anchorage. Their transport was a flat-bottomed vessel lined with oak planks caulked with waxed linen thread. Its high bow and stern were a match for the heavy seas all on board knew too well. The leather sails drove them west towards another creek, wider than the one they left, which carved a passage deep into the land mass behind the Ocrinium Promontory. At the dockside of Trelivel they saw many ships loaded with black ore: tin mostly, but lead and copper in lesser quantities, ready for export with the right wind and tide. All around were signs of industry, from the red silt flowing in the river, to the discarded ore and slag laid on the road that they now walked upon.

The way rose steadily to open moorland, wind-blasted granite only fit for common grazing of sheep and a few cattle. They passed wagons loaded with ore bound for the furnaces. From this elevated view they could see much of the coast, the creeks and open water they climbed away from, and the rugged cliffs that they now saw anew. Soon they came upon the mine their hosts wished to show them.

Women and girls, the Bal maidens, crushed the ore by manual labour. Hidden by piles of debris was the Bal, a slanted shaft. Deep within it was a series of ladders from ledge to ledge down into the blackness. Their guide was a short, muscular man with a necklace of unlit candles, and one protruding in a device beyond his nose. At each level boys pushed barrows out of the workings to load into buckets to be hauled out by ropes, or even by some who carried the ore up the ladders on their shoulders. The tunnels to the tin lodes were narrow, at the start the width of two men and the height of one. Soon it was only the width of one who stooped with a barrow, a little wider in the middle to avoid his knuckles grazing the rock. Down at the face, for the seams often ran diagonally in an incline, they saw a narrow band of white rock gleaming between the blackness of the granite. This was the goal of their toil, the tin or stannum of the Romans or kassiteros as it was known to the Greeks who named these islands the Cassiterides. Over this land were a myriad of holes like this one.

On the surface the broken rock was washed for impurities before entering the conical furnaces. Air guided in from one side raised the heat. Yusuf smelt the sulphur and saw the crystalline particles of arsenikon, deadly arsenic, coalesce along the channels for its collection. More heat and skimming the liquid surface gained greater purity but the metal still remained black. Their hosts complained of the "Wolf" that ate into their wealth. If they could remove the hard Lupi Spuma or "Wolf's Froth" then their ingots would be nearly pure. Yusuf now chose to reveal the additional purpose of his visit.

In Massilia the answer had been found. With Yusuf's help their hosts roasted the impure metal with limestone. Acid separated and combined with the soda and the "Froth" broke down. The black mineral was now smelted again so that with gently rising heat, since tin melts at a lower temperature than the rest, the white metal flowed into crucibles. These were stirred with wet green sticks to remove the final contaminants. Eashoa delighted in the process which turned stone into liquid which funnelled into four-pronged moulds to cool into the metal ingots to be shipped to Rome.

During their travels over the next weeks his great uncle often watched him talking with these mining people, particularly the young. They would escape their cramped two room dwellings and join him in the apple orchards leading down to The Lake. This was the green paradise they had glimpsed through the swirling fog. His stories of the East were matched with theirs of the North so that they found common ground. They were drawn to him. He was a born teacher.

Soon it was time for the voyage around the western extremity of this land north east to Ynys Wydryn. The south westerly winds drove the smaller barque up the Sabrina estuary. Eashoa stood with the steersman as he negotiated the rising tide into the narrows. For much of the time its waters were glass, until the great wave roared up the contracting funnel to catch the unwary. Again Yusuf marvelled at Eashoa's fearlessness. While Yusuf's men loaded lead bars, Eashoa gained the trust of those he met amongst the apples and other fruits surrounding the glassy waters of the island town. It was a peaceful time.

But Yusuf's business was completed, his great ship loaded and ready. Eashoa looked out over the mighty harbour of Rock Anchorage from the cliff top that had so nearly destroyed them. I think he knew that his steps would never return to this happy isle. His destiny lay elsewhere.

Many years later Yusuf returned, aged by tragedy but full of wisdom to share with his old companions in Cornubia. He travelled the length of the land sharing his knowledge and healing. In Rhos, where he and Eashoa had been saved, he built a shrine and a place of learning, which I know so well. But his final years were spent in a simple dwelling beside the lakes of Ynys Wydryn among his trusted friends.

This is my knowledge because I am Justin, soon to be the Iustus here in Rhos, now that my father is called to minister in the land of the

Cymbrogi across the northern water. I am one in a long line of those appointed by Yusuf. It is our mission to keep a light burning on that fateful clifftop and to do what is just for those we serve.'

I looked towards Arthur, the great bear who was my friend. In my mind I knew that my other task was to serve him. Our destinies, great and small, were intertwined when he came to Rhos.

§

Philip had always been 'lad' and the term stung. Like Peter Pan it was if he had never grown up in Jeremy's eyes. Philip realised now that Meredith, not Jeremy, had invited them. Surely under his disbelief there was hidden some hope of their success? But Jeremy had no intention of letting go the reins just yet.

'Not very much actually, beyond the legends: the Round Table, his Knights, Excalibur and Merlin, of course. I'm sure you will enlighten us, Jeremy,' he said pointedly, tapping Ros' knee with his.

'That would take much too long.' But Jeremy then proceeded to precis and criticise Geoffrey of Monmouth's fanciful account in his 12th Century "History of the Kings of Britain" and finish off with Thomas Malory's "Le Morte d'Arthur" from the late 15th century.

'That book has beautiful copper-plate engravings of Arthurian characters and legends,' Meredith said. But she could read the polite glaze creeping over Rosalind's eyelids.

'Jeremy would be happy to show you his etchings, Ros.'

Ros looked at Meredith. There was no hint of intended humour. Ros chose to interpret the comment as the books in his library.

Meredith lifted blistering hot plates from the oven warming tray with bare hands, filled each dish with mashed potato, sausage, onion, peas and carrots, and laid them out, Jeremy's first.

Ros saw that his had noticeably less on it and wished she could swap. How could Meredith bear the heat without oven mittens? She also noticed that Jeremy prickled: sharing a lifetime's work was not easy but there was no choice.

'Beyond the folk lore what real evidence have you for Arthur's existence, Jeremy?' Philip asked. Or should he call him Uncle as he had always done. Surely this was different. They'd been asked to use their skills to solve a problem. It should be a meeting of equals.

'My books and notes will show you that Arthur was not just legend. He was real, a war leader,' he paused for breath 'who united the Britons against the Saxon invaders in the Post Roman period.'

'Was he based in Cornwall?' Ros asked.

'Yes.'

'Not Wales,' Jeremy continued 'or Scotland, or Winchester, but here. Cornwall might be seen now as a backwater in the south west corner but it was a major centre of Britain in Arthur's time.'

'What about Glastonbury?' Philip asked. He vaguely remembered that Arthur and Guinevere were supposed to be buried in the Abbey.

'No. In 1184 fire destroyed the Abbey and in 1191 the so called graves of Arthur and Guinevere were found, and were lost again in the Reformation. That and the Holy Grail buried under the Abbey were stories invented to bring in pilgrim money to rebuild.'

Meredith put down her glass of "gassy pop", her lemonade, and stepped in to help. 'Jeremy believes the answers lie in Cornwall. Over the years we have visited lots of places claiming to be Camelot, such as South Cadbury and Camelford. But Tintagel seems to have the best claim, in spite of the fanciful fibs told to tourists. Then there are his many battle sites, including the final one with Mordred at Camlann. We used several school holidays for that one: the places in Wales, Hadrian's Wall in Scotland, Cadbury and of course Slaughter Bridge here in Cornwall. That one seems to have the best claim.'

'Promontory forts, Meredith' Jeremy prompted.

'Yes, we've visited boat loads of them, in stunning locations too.'

'What's your role, Meredith?' Ros asked. She was sure she was not just chief cook and bottle washer. The signs of traditional marriage were there: he was the bread winner and she the home maker; his food was put on the table at his chosen time; and Meredith deferred to his superior knowledge. Ros was not a fan. This was the seventies for goodness sake.

'I help with the records.' Meredith saw the enquiring look on Rosalind's face.

'Come on, I'll show you.'

She led Ros downstairs and opened the door. When Meredith switched on the light Ros saw a large room with a huge bay window. In day time Ros guessed it would be flooded with sunshine. Ros was transfixed, and a little jealous. Meredith's studio was stacked with paintings, oil and watercolour, of Cornish landscape scenes. Completed pictures six deep propped against the walls. On one side was a shelf of art books that Ros was drawn to but saved for another time. Primed canvases were carefully arranged with tidy boxes of materials, brushes and palettes. In the middle of the room was her easel, angled to catch that special Cornish light from the window. There was a three quarters finished painting of some ruined walls on a precipitous cliff overlooking a vast ocean and more massive sky. It was labelled "Promontory Fort at Dodmans Point, Roseland".

Ros absorbed what she could without impolite rummaging. Each painting was a precise record of the remains, almost photographic, but with an atmospheric flourish to match the superb backdrops. On the back she noticed detailed references to finds and coded links to what she guessed was an exhaustive card index in Jeremy's library. For the first time Ros wondered if this was her destiny if she and Philip could make sense of living together. She was impressed by Meredith's talent and her distinctive version of traditional landscapes. It had a gentle touch that matched her character. Ros had to get Philip to look at them some time for his archaeological opinion.

Meredith stayed quiet while Ros took it all in. Instead she studied Ros. She could see that Philip had chosen a real beauty: early twenties, slim, striking green eyes against blonde sun-streaked hair. Rosalind was intelligent, a match in wits to Philip. Meredith was forty years on from them but enjoyed the excitement that sparked between the pair. Good luck to you both, she thought.

'I understand why you asked Philip to help but why me?' Ros asked.

'Philip didn't say much about you, really. He tends to keep his own council, even with us. But he did mention your photography and painting. And,' she paused. Would it hurt Philip if she said it? Probably not? Besides she admired Ros' Australian directness. She deserved a clear answer. 'He hinted that you had an uncanny ability to link with the past in some way. He wasn't specific, of course. That's not him. So I thought you might make a good team, given Jeremy's situation.'

An hour later the girls returned. Philip had been asking questions strategically to fill in his enormous gaps of all things Arthurian.

'So you would like Ros and I to visit the Cornish sites, study the archaeology, excavate if there is time, and generally use our expertise to corroborate your work.'

'Yes.'

But he could see that there was something else. Meredith was itching to say it but waited for Jeremy. Ros asked the question.

'What else do you want us to do, Jeremy?'

'Glastonbury claimed Arthur's grave and the Grail of Christ. I don't accept that.'

They waited for his lungs to recover after a coughing fit.

'I believe they are both here, in Cornwall!'

It took a moment or two for the real task to sink in.

'You want us to find King Arthur's Grave and the site of the Holy Grail?' said Philip incredulously.

'Yes.'

Piece of cake, Ros thought flippantly but refrained from saying it. Jeremy was deadly serious. Oops, that was a bit too close to the mark. She looked at Meredith. There was dignity and pleading mixed in her gentle eyes. This was Jeremy's dying wish.

'A tall order, Jeremy,' they said together with as much confidence as they could muster.

CHAPTER 2

Trelivel was an ancient town on an inlet of the great waters of Rock Anchorage. Across that broad expanse of protected sea the cliffs and creeks of Rhos were just visible. A mariner could spend weeks navigating all the channels that fed that mighty harbour. The town was busy with mining, smelting of the black ore and ships loading the shining ingots. On this day a new breed of merchants arrived in the port. My friends called me to be interpreter. From their dress of skins and furs I surmised them to be a Gallic tribe newly settled in Armorica.

After a repast of fish, bread and ale the tables were cleared. Samples of gold jewellery set with precious stones or inlaid with enamel panels of many colours were laid out. The shiny winged ingots were studied and weighed by our guests, as the miners ran practiced fingers and eyes over the bracelets and rings. I watched men's faces and read for honesty in their intentions. For only with trust could a long relationship develop. I was not sure.

But that afternoon arrangements were sealed and that first ship lifted anchor and made headway down the river and out of sight beyond Pen Dinas. As light faded the family of two children I had nursed through the Pestis gave me shelter and shared a vegetable pie with heads of fish facing skywards.

There was a knocking on the stout door. My host ushered his wife and children behind the curtain of the back room. I then called out. It was Arthur with a dozen men.

'You are not safe, any of you. Their ships are coming back, many of them. Leave now, Justin.' He had seen everything from Rhos: their crossing, the single ship leaving the harbour, but the fleet hidden behind Pen Dinas headland.

'What of these people?' I pleaded.

He looked at small faces peering around the curtain, the man's defenceless fear, and looked at me. 'We are not enough, Justin. You can see that. Our flight is all that will save us.'

Outside there was a single deep note from a Frankish carnyx, a battle horn, and the screams began. Through the doorway the sky was alight. His companions were restless. Arthur had arrived too late.

'Commiz on,' our frantic host beckoned.

We followed him as he herded his family back up the hill behind the village. Arthur's guards were right behind. Their horses and the solitary groom were ahead. The mayhem and slaughter followed. We were seen but ignored for easier pickings. Arthur argued with his warriors but what were our few to so many? In the narrow lanes mounted troopers, however skilful, would be picked off by these Salian Franks hidden in Gallic clothing. My childhood nightmares flowed down my face in salty rivers.

Still our host ran and we followed. Out of sight of the town we were joined by others, all struggling with the misery of their present survival and the horrible deaths of those they loved. Soon we entered the warren of tunnels dug into the hillsides. Candles were cradled ahead of us by those who knew the way. Arthur's men split in two, one group to a grove by the river with their mounts, the other our rear guard. And there in the damp and darkness we slumped down and waited for the terror to end. Arthur was silent and impassive for a long time.

'Do you not feel for these people?' I said in irritation. 'What if it was your wife, your children?'

'Two generations ago it was my ancestor's,' he said quietly.

I looked into his eyes and realised how wrong I was. He had not forgotten.

'Their time will come,' he said. 'That is my role.'

I laid my hand on his arm. 'Sorry.' But his body seethed with anger. 'Make your task retribution,' I said, 'protection for the defenceless, not vengeance. That will only destroy you.'

'But what is your part, Justin? What can a man of peace do against such violence?'

During those long hours of night I told him again of our ways: the counsel of the hurt, the aid to the sick, the teaching of the young, so that all were stronger to face the tribulations of this world and had hope for a better. This time my words settled on fertile ground.

'If these men were of my belief they would not murder and pillage their fellow men. And your role would be obsolete.'

He smiled. 'We work towards the same goal.'

Looking back it was clear that Arthur had long been torn between the old faith of Merlin and the new. This belief had been in Britain since before the Emperor Constantine. Arthur's grandparents, the miners and my community had all accepted Christianity. I believe one night spent in the tunnels of Trelivel was enough for him to decide.

Late next day we wandered through the carnage and destruction. So many naked and pillaged bodies, mutilated children, littered the slowly burning embers of the once busy town. This time my face was dry but my mind cried out. The slaughter was senseless, not a battle between equals but a carnage of innocents. Neither of us would ever forget. But it was Arthur who nursed and nursed an idea which became a solution.

§

Over months into years Arthur now served in the teulu, the personal guard of Uther, his father. Uther's brother Ambrosius, Supreme King, had been bloodied in Gaul by King Euric and a mighty army of Visigoths. He barely survived his wounds so Uther now took the mantle of defender of the Britons.

One day a visitor came to our community.

'Justin,' the boy whispered after he had caught his breath from running. 'A Druid comes here, and with warriors. What shall we do?'

'We will greet him, of course.' The wide-eyed young tinner, his leg much recovered from the rock that crushed it, followed me at a distance.

Merlin swung down and left his horse with his escort, four of Arthur's most trusted companions. He met me in the luxuriant garden of sweet-smelling shrubs, shady trees and broad leaved palms which surrounded my cell and the small school for the tinners' children. Only this morning I had buried one of my charges, another result of insufficient food and a gut malady.

We sat together at a high point on the bare slope and watched the gentle ripples enter the bay. 'What can you do for them, Justin?' Merlin said.

'I can help.' I thought of what lay behind the question. 'The tinners know that.'

'Yes, but your destiny lies elsewhere. Arthur has spoken of you. He has the greater need, of both of us.'

I rested my arm on the wooden spade and followed his eyes to the water, which led to the broad expanse of Rock Anchorage. My words in the cave at Trelivel had born fruit. On the wind-blasted centre of Rhos I remembered his disdain for his father and the deep loss of family that matched my own. He had forgotten nothing and had a dream to end the suffering. Was my mission here, among these good people? Or was it helping my friend however I could, in his greater undertaking?

'Asking for my aid is not an easy task for you,' I said.

Merlin smiled. 'True. But this mission needs the best we can give. What he will achieve will change both our worlds.'

I passed on my duties to others in the community and the tinners escorted me to Tintagel. As I crossed the great ditch I could see warriors preparing for another sortie, against a Saxon raiding party in the east of Dumnonia.

On that day I saw Uther mounted up, advising his son before his first battle. Arthur was restless under his father's gaze, but not more so than Merlin close by. There was a disturbance in the Druid's manner that matched rumours about his past. It was said that some terrible slaughter had unhinged him for a time. His hands fidgeted, his mount danced to his mood, and his eyes were a long way off.

Then Uther become silent. He could not watch his son take the same risks that he had taken. Instead Uther rode closer, clasped Arthur to his chest, and turned his steed towards the left flank. Uther knew his son would make more errors if he watched and worried. He would have done the same. Leadership in battle was about confidence, about being in the right place in one's mind. Uther had given his advice. Now it was for Arthur to make his own mistakes.

Arthur led the right flank and Uther the left. God, or the gods according to Merlin, looked after both. The victory was theirs. Arthur soon became "Master of Horse", second only to Uther himself. Again and again word would come of a pirate raid, whether Pict or Irish. Uther's arrival drove away the scavengers but rarely saved the people from the fate of Trelivel. Orphaned children were always left to the winds of life. The lords of the western lands, Reghed, Elmet, Gwynedd and Dumnonia ,cared little for coastal villages of farmers and fishermen. Their teulu remained safe behind strong walls, not to be frittered on minor skirmishes. Let the war leader exhaust himself and his men on such trifles.

At times I despaired of my role in Arthur's world of war and savagery. Then I would return to my ministry with the tinners.

Brythonic lands of the west were bleeding. Their lords were disunited, more interested in squabbling with their neighbours than facing common enemies. Meanwhile the wolves of the sea preyed on the defenceless. Each summer, when the grain seed was planted, raiders would cross the Gallic Sea and pillage what they could. For them the life of a warrior, for all its risks, was far superior to the drudgery of eternally farming small plots on poor soils. What they plundered, slaves and minerals amongst the loot, relieved the burden for their wives and children. After the autumn raids their stories of great deeds lit up the long winter nights.

Arthur came back to Rhos a man, a proud warrior who had seen too much. And he brought a gift.

'Merlin said that you needed a tree where you sat with him. Where shall we plant it?'

I took him to the same spot that he knew; for we had often watched the tide from its grassy slope. We dug the hole and planted the sapling, a Yew Tree. I fetched water from the spring to provide its first drink.

'An interesting choice,' I said as we sat and rested beside the damp earth.

'To me it is a source of bows for future archers. For Merlin it is a sacred tree.' He looked at the view for a while. 'For us it will be shade in this peaceful place.'

§

'The miners bring wealth but the lords do not protect them,' I said as we rode towards Tintagel on the high roads going north.

'As a lord with land and title I could, but I am heir to neither. I am not King Mark or a Prince of Reghed,' said Arthur.

'In Dumnonia cities, farmers, even the churches keep the militia supplied,' I said.

'But Cornubia has always been a poor land to crop. The sea provides more,' he said. His face changed, 'Except for its wealth within.' He pulled up his mount and looked towards the sea. The answer had come. 'The miners can provide the means for their survival.'

His solution was simple. If the tinners gave a tithe to Arthur, a tenth of what they earned, he would build his own teulu, a force of warriors loyal only to him. It would be a mighty assembly of horsemen for their speedy aid. With financial help the old forts on the headlands could be refortified, the beacon towers made ready. The tunnels would be perfected into final places of refuge.

'What of the sea, Arthur?' I asked.

'I have pondered that. As my horsemen guard the land so a fleet must protect from the sea.'

'I think I have an answer, Arthur.' But the choice would be difficult.

I spoke to the elders and they too had heard of a renegade leader of many ships anchored off the north coast at Heyl, the "estuary". Tewdric, the admiral of the Visigoth fleet, asked for sanctuary from his enemies.

It was mid-day when Arthur and his guard rode across the narrow land bridge into the first ring of Tintagel fortress. Under a leaden sky the sea crashed dark breakers into the harbour beach below. A misty rain enveloped us as we crossed the courtyard towards the great central hall. Beside a smouldering fire sat Merlin opposite Uther, who was sprawled on a long couch. Tendrils of smoke wound to the covered vent in the roof and were immediately whisked away by the high winds outside.

Uther was muscular with lanky limbs and thinning grey-black hair. The wide trousers and fine tunic were soiled with food, as was the red cloak loosely draped over his shoulders. A full pewter goblet rested close to his right hand, the jug of red wine half empty. The reddened ivory queen on Uther's side of the chess board seemed pensive, separated from her disgruntled king and guarded by a lonely knight and three pawns. From the remaining pieces between the two men it was clear that Uther was playing badly and Merlin was trying not to win.

'Come, Arthur, and your spiritual friend, Bacchus beckons,' Uther said as he nodded towards the carafe.

Uther was slurred of speech but lucid in reminiscence.

'You fought well that day, Arthur, by all accounts,' he said.

'As did you, father. You were like a madman from what I was told.'

Uther laughed. 'It was easier to severe a few heads than think of what you were up to. You will understand one day when you have a son.'

As our goblets remained barely touched and Uther's was steadily replenished Arthur explained his plan for Cornubia. I studied his father's battle-scarred arms, sagging cheekbones and bloody eyes. Was it years of war that brought his malaise, or bitterness that injury had taken away the lust that bore Arthur? Impotence must have been such a cruel irony after a lifetime of sinful liaisons punctuated by the delights of battle. For the rest he functioned with a little food and a constant flow of wine, beer and strong spirit.

Merlin was bored. Now he appeared much older than Arthur. Already there was more white than red in his long hair and whiskery beard. His clothes were the simple woollen tunic and shawl of a proud Druid. His features were bronzed by weather and his blue eyes danced with intuition.

We were both peacemakers. His education surpassed mine, in Greek philosophy, in the ethical choices that men faced, but this made him more tolerant of different beliefs.

'There are many ways to the same place, Justin. Yours is only one,' he said to me sometimes during our discussions.

On this occasion our eyes met, curiosity and contest to be kept for later. Arthur's plan was more important. Merlin saw the maturity but without the guile that distinguished his father.

'You care too much about these people, Arthur,' said Uther. 'They will betray you like everyone else some day.'

Arthur frowned. 'The lords and Saxons might but not these folk.'

I would have commented on 'their innate goodness' if it was my place to speak; and said to Uther 'you have been poisoned by war' if I dared.

'Do as you plan, Arthur. With a teulu of your own you are safer against the lords. I will support you.'

When drink released Uther into sleep Merlin joined us on the ramparts looking north to the horizon of long, lazy breakers over a bronzed sunset sea.

'I see the decline in my father,' Arthur said to Merlin.

'Yes. But Ambrosius is closer to the otherworld. Soon the reins will be yours. Will you be as good a "Supreme King" as they, Arthur?'

'I have no liking for kings or petty Brythonic chieftains. Dux Bellorum, "Leader in War", will suit me well as a title.' He left the rest of the question unanswered.

§

A day later we three waited on the sand beside the great bay that the Heyl River fed. A little way off a line of fifty ships of war was arrayed to impress us. From that formidable display of might came two smaller craft rowed towards us. Our small guard was uneasy. When the vessels beached twice our number positioned themselves either side of their leader. Each was dressed in padded trousers and jerkin, leather shoulder cover and helmet, lance, spear and sword visible, their composite bow loaded with arrow and ready. A well-built, tall man in middle years, dressed as his guards but more richly so, walked confidently through the water towards us.

'Greetings, great lord Tewdric, Admiral of the Visigoth fleet,' I said in his language, on behalf of Arthur. I pushed away the image that someone of his generation perpetrated that awful sack of our village.

'Greetings lord Artorius, Master of Horse,' I translated back. 'Your reputation as a warrior precedes you.'

Once seated at the table on stools, Arthur tasted the food and drink first and then offered a goblet. Both groups of guards relaxed but remained alert.

Tewdric's massive chest shook in laughter. 'I like your manner, sir' he said with a slow, magisterial pace. He then drank deeply and placed the vessel on the table like a piece on Uther's chess board.

Arthur did the same: raising his glass in silent toast and standing the piece beside his guest's. Tewdric's intelligent eyes studied Arthur's, who held his gaze. The older man drew in a deep breath, sat back and indicated with a gesture of his right hand for Arthur to begin.

I again marvelled at Arthur's grasp of the heart of negotiation. Merlin's eyes said the same. Arthur spoke for Uther and Ambrosius, Supreme Kings, as well as for himself. Tewdric was master of the sea, Arthur and his companions controlled the land. Each had the power to hurt, to deny what the other wanted. Tewdric wanted a haven for his warriors and their womenfolk, safe from predators on land, as Arthur wished from the sea. For mutual benefit they agreed to travel the road forward together. Documents were drawn up and I was involved in their translation. But really the deal was done on that day with a handshake.

'Our task is to remedy the confusion left by others,' Arthur said.

'And to look after those who matter to us,' Tewdric replied.

In my mind I could only agree. Was it possible that others might act like Arthur some day?

Tewdric's sailors and their families settled the land either side of the Heyl estuary. Very soon they proved their worth. By strange irony the Salian Franks, having gained easy loot once, returned. Their target was Deveryon, a port for the miners of tin and copper from Rhyd-ruth, eight miles inland.

The enemy lay at anchor hidden by low forest just outside the rivulet. Twelve ships of Frankish warriors, each with sword, spear, knife and throwing axe, waited for nightfall. But their progress had been watched from the southern cliffs of Rhos, into Rock Anchorage and beyond Trelivet. Hillside beacons on the coast and inland carried the word to Tewdric in hours. Some of his fleet were docked at Grey Rock, one of the ports in the southern bay beyond the Ocrinium peninsula. A cohort of Arthur's cavalry, fully three hundred strong, set out from Deadman's Point. Inside the town women and children were dispatched upstream to hide amongst the thick forest of Wet Valley. Some menfolk carried on with their business, the rest waited indoors armed as best they could. Merlin and I were left on a hillside above the creek with torch sticks up-ended in a bowl of pitch. If any of the enemy broke through to threaten the hiding place of the womenfolk we were to signal by lighting the brands from the hidden fire. Then Merlin and the menfolk would guide their families into the mines. Over time this knowledge of the by-ways of the tinners, across moorland to north and south coasts, and underground too, we shared with Arthur.

At dusk the first keel slid up on to the sand. Its warriors raced towards the dock and its warehouses. The second horde poured up the street throwing incendiary poles on to the thatched rooves. A third, fourth and fifth followed. A throwing axe sliced through a solid oak door, a spear sped through an unshuttered window. The dwellings were empty.

The raiders looked at each other but the lure of plunder was greater than their wariness. As the ships were emptied of all but a few guards the town's menfolk appeared at the top of the main street. Farm implements and staves were no match for what faced them. The roar from the Franks might have been heard in Trelivel as they charged forward.

Now it was Arthur's turn. His horses had been trained to stand deathly still. Light from the fires glistened off the myriad of steel plates stitched to leather and hung over the horse's sides, neck, breast and head. As the human tide reached twenty paces from the ragged line, Arthur's horsemen closed in from behind. There was no need for battle horn or cornu: stealth and speed were so much more effective. Now with laughing courage and curdling shrieks this band galloped down on the raiders. Those at the rear saw them and some turned to face them. But then the miners stepped aside as the remaining cavalry, led by Arthur himself, stood ready to charge headlong into the Frankish front.

I saw my friend as I had never seen him. In chainmail armour, the red dragon pennant lifted high over his upright lance, the look on Arthur's face was terrible. Then he lowered his face shield and spear, advanced and became a warrior in full flight. The red plume on his helmet danced to the beat of his horse's tread. The ground shook with the pounding of so many hooves. This was the retribution for the innocents of Trelivel. I struggled with the brutal vision. As the Franks had run pell-mell up the street there had been no need to form a shield wall. Now the outstretched lances picked off their targets like pigs at the hunt. The Franks barely had time to let fly a single axe. As the fighters at the front realised their plight they turned into those behind them, so that many fell in the melee without aiming a blow in defence. The carnage was pitiless. I saw Arthur pin men left and right until his momentum was slowed. Then his sword hacked shoulders and necks so that his horse's chest was dripping red. So many bodies were shattered by hooves crashing down as their riders carved a bloody passage through. Any enemy left wounded was dispatched swiftly with club and mattock by the following miners. Those warriors who fled towards their ships were run down by the Arthurian lancers. A few managed to join their compatriots as they raised sail but in the panic most were finished off in the shallows. I watched the lapping tide glow red in the burning light.

Out of the harbour five ships reached the waters of the creek, where they faced the fifteen craft of Tewdric's mariners. Two of the Visigoth number hung a rope between vessels to cut off any escape to the open water of Rock Anchorage. The Frankish ships were so undermanned they were doomed from the start. Tewdric stood on the steering deck of the lead ship like a giant from a Germanic legend. When the boarding ladder was secure he rushed across with his warriors. His delight in crushing blows of slaughter was clear even from my vantage point. No quarter was given or asked for.

I turned away from the butchery. However right the cause surely conflict was wrong.

Merlin read the language of my face.

'What would you have Arthur do, turn the other cheek?'

'My father taught me the doctrine of "Ius Bellum", a "just war". Against a grave wrong violence is the only answer. But theory and practice are different things.' I wrestled with the thought: how could force be the product of love for one's neighbour?

Merlin stood quietly watching the nuances of the expanse of water beyond the creek. I believe he was remembering the times he had walked between massed ranks of Brythonic warriors baying for blood. With a raised hand he had commanded silence from those minds fixed on gory revenge. His words were of peace, the thoughts of their loved ones, a reasoned alternative to senseless slaughter. For some leaders the spell over their minds was broken. They turned away. But at other times his arguments were lost and his eyes were drowned in the tragedy that followed.

'As men of peace we can influence. But Arthur's courage is greater. He accepts danger and suffering to change his world for the better. Our counsel might save innocents or spare hostages, but Arthur's need of our friendship is greater. Think of Uther.'

Yes, war destroyed the victor as well as his victims. Uther's mind was poisoned by images he could not remove even in sleep. In daylight a little wine constantly made the day bearable enough for him to exist.

'These men will return as warriors in another life. Maybe their eternal souls will be closer to a good life.'

'There we differ, Merlin. Those who do good things are rewarded in Heaven, for ever. Those who do evil are punished.'

'What an interesting thought; a reward for living a good life. How much better it would be to live well without a bribe or a threat!'

We left our lofty perch and again I was assailed by the groans and smells of the dying and deceased. Merlin and I moved among the injured and gave aid where we could. Our inclination was to help warriors of both sides but the mining families prevented that and systematically looted the enemy dead. Ships were loaded with the corpses, which were thrown overboard in Rock Anchorage.

Arthur looked to his men and only briefly acknowledged the gushing thanks of these people. When Tewdric docked the two great men clasped each other as laughing brothers. The deal was done and proven. Over the next days and weeks word traversed Cornubia and across the Gallic channel. Arthur had drawn blood.

For a time I went back to my ministry to these warm people. My presence, as one who had known suffering, aided those who had lost, so that their anguish was not alone and in some way decreased. But my mind was uneasy. Arthur went back to punishing raiding parties and Merlin to protecting his friend however he could. My destiny had changed and I could not resist. The miners understood. Word came that Ambrosius had succumbed to poison from an unknown enemy. But most believed it to be the work of Vortigern's son, Paschent, King of Builth. Now the mantle belonged to Uther alone to lead the battle against the Saxons. When Merlin and Arthur rode across the causeway and bridge into Tintagel's defences I joined them. Inside the fortress Uther was alone with morose thoughts. Merlin enlightened us as we approached his quarters.

§

The girl in front of me is expendable, not really there as something living. I remember the time when wenching and battle went hand in hand, that manly urge to conquer. Now I can have whatever I want but the lust is not there. I gesture for her to robe and be gone. I see fear that she has displeased me and relief to be away from my calloused hands.

'I bred warriors,' I shout aloud. Then I watch lines of ants on the floor, single file, carrying crumbs, line upon line. 'We needed fighters and I created them.'

Time is a fickle mistress. In battle seconds are long and yet too brief. Then there is the tedium of sitting in front of a log fire; alone, uninterested, waiting for the wine to take effect.

'Ah Igraine: such beauty!' I pause in a sudden uptake of breath, entirely captivated by the vision. I remember her loveliness in our union, the culmination of so many dreams. It is good that Arthur was the result. Lust is such a base word, so limited, inadequate, beyond the female imagination to grasp its power. For Igraine totally absorbed my being. I could not eat or sleep. Time stopped. From the moment I saw her beside Gorlois at the feast I knew. Merlin was reluctant but eventually agreed. Igraine became sick and we entered the castle as the Druid and his assistant. Whatever herbal potion he prescribed made her a willing mare to my stallion. A copy of Gorlois' ring on my finger and shaved cheeks were enough. After we left she spoke to her handmaiden of Gorlois' visit to her chamber, even though Merlin and I knew that her husband was already dead upon the battlefield.

But at a certain point in a man's time everything closes. The fire in my belly is dead. And so with battle? For a time Ambrosius and I held back the Saxons, Jutes, and Picts. My brother and I have given peace to so many. Maybe future generations will remember what Uther Pendragon did.

'To keep them safe I poisoned my mind with dreams beyond their comprehension. Why do these women resist my advances? It becomes the battle all over again. Please me! A gift for my gift! A simple trade really.'

My lips drip with another slurp of wine. Pigs and goats, human or otherwise, did they understand the price?

'The cost of greatness is carrying the burden of being responsible. Yes I did it, for good or ill. Blame me or laud me. It was a life above the filth. I have no regrets.'

My face creases in a smile. A moment ago I thought of Igraine, now as aged as the crones she sits with. I will find death in battle and not face grinding oblivion as I slide into dotage.

'I will die when I least expect but at a moment of my choosing.' I laugh too loud, alone.

§

When Arthur, Merlin and I walked into the stone room lit only by firelight Uther was slumped on the couch. The cracks in his face and the plump of his belly rippled in the crackling light. Merlin covered his comatose form with a robe and we left. The Saxons under Hengist's son, Octa, could wait.

In the icy breeze of morning Arthur said, 'Father, you are too ill to fight. Let others lead for you.'

But Uther was immovable. The day that Uther led his army towards Verulamium Arthur received word from Tewdric to block a sizeable force of Irish who'd broken through his maritime defence wall.

'Great Spirit, grant thy protection, strength and understanding; in the love of all existence, and in your love, Mother of all.' Merlin's words to Uther earned a smile.

'May the love of God keep and protect you.' Mine received a curse. But I knew my role as we joined Arthur's horsemen on their journey west.

§

That afternoon Arthur's riders stopped the pillage of Din Pentir, an old fort overlooking the entrance to Dowr Kammel. The newly rebuilt stonework bought time for the villagers to hold off the marauders until Arthur's arrival. As always surprise caught the intruders as a rabble. Merlin and I watched the familiar slaughter of men who'd left the ripening grain of their homelands in search of plunder and would not return to their loved ones.

But a group of twenty fighters under the leadership of a stout, red-haired chieftain crouched among outlying rocks that broke Arthur's cavalry advantage. They would have to fight these men hand to hand.

Merlin walked forward and stood between the two groups of bloodied men.

Arthur had no need to raise a hand in Merlin's defence, any more than did the chieftain. All respected the authority of the Druid.

'Come, Great Leader. You have fought well. But now think of your kith and kin. What will your wives and children do without their men to provide for them?' Merlin said to the leader in his own tongue.

'And you Artorius, Master of the Horse, son of Uther, Supreme King of the Britons, will you preserve the lives of these valiant men? If they lay down their arms and swear allegiance to you alone, will you grant them pardon?'

Merlin waited until the din of war became quiet. In the silence Arthur spoke.

'I grant the lives of these brave men if they will serve me faithfully.'

In this way Arthur's forces grew. Men were granted land for their families to settle. In return, like Tewdric, they paid loyally in blood for Arthur's cause.

That occasion lifted my spirits. As we ministered to the sick and dying I knew that there was another role for peaceful men in the arena of war. But there was to be no such mercy given to the Saxons. As we rode to join Uther he already faced his enemy in battle. This "Half-Dead King", as the Saxons called him, sat on his horse at the head of his armoured cavalry.

In front of him was a line of his infantry, militia men recruited from all the nearby towns threatened by this latest Saxon incursion. They had all suffered at the hands of the Saxon Terror and smarted for revenge. To the sides were bands of archers ready to soften up the Saxon "boar-head" of mighty infantry that confronted them, the wedge-shaped formation led by Octa himself.

Uther swayed in the saddle but those closest steadied and supported him. The two sides taunted each other and shouted obscenities across the divide. Knowing that time and strength was not his to own Uther gave the signal: the deep-throated barrage of carnyx horns bellowed across the valley. The militia line slowly moved forward as the Saxon boar-head did the same. Archers loosed their shafts into the Saxon ranks so that a steady number of bodies were trampled underfoot, only to be replaced immediately to hold the tight formation. Beyond his hatred Uther could only admire their military prowess as formidable infantry. The first axes flew through the air and cleaved into the wood and hide shields of his line with devastating effect.

The ranks were closing. The Saxon front sped into a run, their shield wall still tight. The impact was monstrous. Nothing could stop that wedge breaking through Uther's front line and second and into the third. Bowmen loosed arrow after arrow into the side flanks of the Saxons until they too were steadily cut down.

The gods are kind, Uther thought as Arthur's force sped in from behind and lined up on his left flank.

'Greetings father, Uther Pendragon, Supreme King of the Britons.'

'Welcome, Arthur, Master of Horse.' Those around roared their applause.

Uther gave the signal. His cavalry split into two cohorts, he leading the right, Arthur the left. As the Saxons cut and sliced the Brythonic infantry gave ground but did not break and run. Men were fired to win or die rather than let these pagans continue their rampage west through what was left of their homeland. Saxon and Briton saw nothing beyond their individual death struggle until Uther's dragon pennants lowered and lances smashed into the unprotected sides of the boar-head. Uther was magnificent, like a great ox ploughing a furrow through the enemy. He felt no pain and no fear. He was in the lap of his gods so that he was invincible: free, lithe, able to draw on all that was inside him without reserve. Men of the third and fourth lines of the Saxons turned their shields to face the cavalrymen but by then Uther's swords and spears were carving bloody tracks through their ranks to meet Arthur and his compatriots on the other side. From somewhere Uther found strength and fought bravely with his companions.

By late afternoon the battle was already won. Merlin and I trawled the field for those we could help. The dead were being looted for valuable swords and armour and the stories of brave exploits were being composed around camp fires. All around us ravens and crows feasted on torn flesh.

But Uther's wish to die bravely in combat, his time of choosing, was not to be. In the morning he drank from a spring near the battlefield. The Saxons had poisoned it so that his death was lingering. There was time for me, summoned by Uther himself, to pronounce my blessings without opposition and for Merlin to escort his journey into the afterlife.

Merlin's guidance for Arthur was now infinitely more important. As Supreme King Uther's death left a vacuum of power that the quarrelsome lords would fill. The chaos began on the battlefield as leaders squabbled over their rightful share of the spoils, according to their perceived rank. Arthur would have intervened but Merlin stayed his arm.

'They are not yet ready and you must be prepared. A little magic maybe,' Merlin said smiling cryptically. Merlin used his power to call a meeting for four months hence. All would come by the Druid's authority but also through fear that whatever chanced they must be a part of it. Our troop left the camp to its quarrelling and rode north-east to Choir Gaur or Stanheng as it was known to the Saxons. There, in that holy place of souls, Merlin interred Uther beside his brother Ambrosius within the circle of ancient stones. On the way back to Rhos Merlin gave me a task that I was uniquely suited for. The miners trusted me and owed a great deal to Arthur, now and into their future. Arthur and Tewdric defended Cornubia. I spent the time with the miners and their families. Merlin went west on his own quest. At the allotted time we came together at The Lake.

§

In the fertile valley leading to The Lake, Nimue and her companions tended the ancient apple trees. Sacred mistletoe hung in garlands throughout the avenues of fruit. Intricate faces of a deity known as the Green Man stared down from vantage points in trees and rock. In their belief he was the regenerator of Natural growth, rising in spring, made fertile in summer and in autumn entering the death of winter. This was a hallowed Druid place where potions cured all manner of ills of the people of Cornubia. Despite our differences of belief my respect was gained with the pain-relieving properties of pounded Willow wood and vinegar. This powerful drought relieved the agony of those with injury or internal illness. But Merlin, for he frequented this place often, had many such herbal remedies produced in this idyllic and blessed setting. His skills were great and Nimue was avid for his learning. As she charmed him with her affections he would return besotted to share more. After weeks of preparation by the Ladies of the Lake the sacred apple brew was ready for the great ceremony.

On the morning of the day lords great and small from Cornubia, Dumnonia and beyond gathered amongst the apple trees beside The Lake. Each of them was plied with goblets of the fermented juice by acolytes of the female Druids who ruled this place. By the water's edge was a great stone carved in ancient times by the giants, as was believed. Around it was a circle of branches, leaves and flowers of the orchard. Merlin stood beside the stone altar resplendent in white tunic tied at the waist with a golden belt and clasp. He appeared to ignore all but Arthur, dressed in black, with silver chain mail and a blue cloak emblazoned with the red dragon. I stood with Merlin and waited for his magic on this glorious spring day.

He raised a hand and across the lake glided three low punts, each rowed by four maidens dressed in white. Their gentle movements cut a precise path across the still water until they rested at the centre of the lake. Merlin now intoned the spirits of earth and air and fire and water. As his forehead bent forward in reverence an arm rose from the lake. All the guests gasped in wonder. In its slender white fingers was a mighty sword, its pommel encrusted with rare gems, within its scabbard engraved with ancient Ogham symbols of his faith. As we watched one of the maidens of the first boat clasped the sword and laid it across the palms of her companion as the glistening limb retreated into the depths. Then her companions rowed into the shallows where Merlin chanted Brythonic verse to accept it on behalf of Arthur. Mesmerised we saw the three vessels and their unearthly occupants row to the far side of the lake and disappear into the sudden mist.

The sword was indeed a wonder, given to me by the tinners who drew upon their ancient heritage of master blacksmiths from the East. It had been cast in a stone mould, its two leaves separated at precisely the right time to retain its great strength and beauty. On its blade were the Runic spells decreed by Merlin. Nimue, chief of the Ladies of the Lake, had been the first maiden to clasp the sword. Morgana, Arthur's half-sister, was the second. Nimue and Merlin had devised the precise dosage of the Henbane leaves. Soaked in the apple wine it produced the required magic.

Merlin gently laid the sword on the stone altar. Then he picked up the ram's horn inlaid with silver dragons and blew a long low note. The reply came from across The Lake. In minutes a squadron of horsemen in full battle dress rode into view. They remained perfectly still as a small armada of larger craft pushed into The Lake. With the sound of oars slicing and bow waves rushing the court of Lyonesse escorted the King and Queen and their adopted daughter, Guinevere, across the water.

As the first craft grated on the shingle edge we marvelled at the virginal, flaxen-haired beauty that stepped on to land. Her dress was of the Brythonic style: long in sleeve, flowing white linen to her Roman sandals, bound with silver cords at her middle, her hair plaited intricately at the back but flowing to her waist. She was fifteen, the same age as Arthur.

She and her father walked slowly through Avalon, the avenue of ancient apple trees, their branches entwined like arms above Guinevere's head. From my vantage point the gnarled trunks seemed to sprout from the depths, a mirage I knew but strangely enchanting. I thought of the marvel that Merlin had wrought. Lyonesse was a small kingdom, alone and vulnerable to the princes of Cornubia and Dumnonia. Arthur was Master of Horse, with great prospects but a tainted son with a lesser right to a kingdom of his own. Guinevere gave him that right.

Arthur stood waiting at the end of this "vale of apples", Affalon as it was once known, outside the circle. He looked back at Merlin. I saw the trust. He would do what was required. When all were ready Merlin called.

'Let there be peace in the east, in the south, in the west and in the north.'

Arthur then entered the ring and waited beside the altar. In his hand was a wreath of apple blossom to match the loop. Guinevere now entered, arm in arm with her father Cador; grey, large and genial. When she reached Merlin she stopped and let loose her father's hand. As Cador stepped back Arthur placed the wreath upon her head as though a crown for his princess. She in turn lifted her garland with two hands and placed it on Arthur's head. The mighty sword lay on the stone altar in front of them.

'Let peace rule in all worlds.'

Merlin took the hands of the couple and bound them together with white cord. 'May all witness this handfasting. May the ancestors of both houses be in harmony. May they accept the events of today, and the blood union of Arthur and Guinevere.'

'As the moon waxes and wanes, as day becomes night and day again, so all things in life are within the circle. This is our existence: the rocks, the soil and the pebbles on the shore contain the stories of our lives.'

'Will you Arthur love and honour Guinevere when gales blow cold?'

'I will.'

'Will you Guinevere love and honour Arthur when passions wane?'

'I will.'

I stood beside them as they broke bread and poured mead on to the earth of their ancestors, before they served each other.

Merlin then stepped to one side and I replaced him at the altar; for the people of Lyonesse, as many others present, had taken up the Christian faith. Our second ceremony was simple as so much good had been said in the first. Arthur and Guinevere pledged their troth to each other.

'I, Arthur, take thee Guinevere for my wedded wife, to have and to hold from this day, for fouler and fairer, for richer or poorer, in illness and in health, to love and to cherish, till death do us part, according to God's holy ordinance.'

After Guinevere's reply I blessed the rings, those visible symbols that bound each other as the cloth cords had done. After our prayers Merlin opened the circle. He had one more task.

'My lords, all here present, you have witnessed this marriage. Arthur, Master of Horse, son of Uther Pendragon, once Supreme King of the Britons, is wed to Guinevere, Princess of the ancient lineage of Lyonesse.'

Arthur stepped forward to the stone altar, drew the sword from its scabbard and raised it high. I marvelled at the art of the metallurgists of Cornubia. It was magnificent.

'The spirits of The Lake have decreed that Arthur wields the fabled Excalibur,' Merlin's voice boomed. 'In the battles to come he will cleave a path through the multitudes of our enemies. He is your Dux Bellorum, your Leader in War, Arthur the Pendragon. Show your allegiance.'

None dared resist but as they filed past their young leader I saw their eyes betray other thoughts.

CHAPTER 3

Philip awoke to the piercing cries of seagulls wheeling over neighbouring rooves in search of plastic bags and open bins to raid. The steady clang of steel on steel from the docks and horns from the ferries gave the impression of a lively start to a new work day. He rubbed his eyes. Sleep had been disturbed by dream scenarios that all ended in embarrassing failure. Each started with happy optimism but slowly disintegrated into a multitude of petty problems that separated them from their goal. The task Jeremy and Meredith had set seemed impossible.

Ros was stood by the window, engrossed in the view, unaware of the lovely silhouette she presented in the eastern light.

His feet sidestepped creaky boards to stand behind her. He hugged her waist and nuzzled her neck. Then he scratched her back, first through the material of her Snoopy nightshirt, then under it, drawing patterns between her shoulder blades. She moved a little so his touch was accurate to the itch. Ros did not object when his fingers roamed to encircle her breasts and play with the nipples until they rose in unison. Still she absorbed the sunlit view across the harbour to St Mawes and the Roseland peninsula. When the fingers of his right hand strayed down the cheeks of her rump she turned her neck.

'Not in front of the natives, Philip,' she said quietly.

'They'd need exceptional eyesight and a good set of binoculars,' he rationalised.

'Maybe,' as she led him back to bed where they made love under the shafts of that translucent Cornish light.

'By the way that big parcel came by train yesterday. Meredith told me the courier put it in the back of the garage,' she said after they sat up and she had wrapped the sheet around them.

'Good. If Jeremy can spare his car we can add some aerial surveys.'

'We?'

'Yes I need a good photographer,' he said.

'I heard that line once before, in Iran, and look what that led to.' She pictured the hang glider and then pushed away her deep fear of heights.

'Me?' He was chancing his arm in the mellow glow that exuded from his body.

Ros gave a mock smile. Flattery would not be coaxed so easily.

He followed her downstairs. As Philip passed the open door to the next room, the lounge, he glimpsed the LP record player and Jeremy immersed in Debussy. His eyes were shut. As the belch rose Jeremy cradled his belly but no pain registered on his face.

On the kitchen table were fresh bread rolls, "splits", from the local bakery, strawberry jam, marmalade, a mug of black tea for him and very hot Nescafe for her.

Meredith had done well as usual, he thought. Her teenage years working at The Atlantic View had given her cook's hands and the skills of a chef. Through the window he studied the half-sized rubbish lorry moving slowly down the street, a runner ahead turning in the wing mirrors of the two lines of parked cars. As the bins were upended into the back the driver trickled by the untouched paintwork with millimetres to spare.

Meredith retrieved a glass bowl of Cornish Clotted Cream from the fridge and placed it beside the splits. The yellow caking reminded Philip of fresh soft cheese. The look on Rosalind's face was polite and priceless.

'Don't you have clotted cream for breakfast in Australia?' he said, smiling.

'No, but it's an interesting thought.' She spread a dollop with some jam on the bread. It was different, hugely filling but she'd cope.

When the sun disappeared and the wind-blasted rain drummed on the windows it was easy for them to spend the morning in Jeremy's library. It was in a tidy alcove under the attic stairs: horizontal lines of books arranged by topic; a desk with Jeremy's Remington portable typewriter, a vase of pens, and homemade notepads cut and stapled from waste paper. Behind two photos of their grownup sons was one of Meredith's paintings, "Tintagel in a Winter Storm".

In the first hour they realised that amongst the wild claims, contradictions and passionately held semi-truths was a core of substance. They could understand Jeremy's conviction that Arthur was a real person under the legends. Then they each gravitated to their interests, almost on masculine and feminine lines.

Philip tried to piece together the collapse of Roman rule in Britain, what came next and how an Arthur might fight the Saxons. Would he copy Rome and add some of the Celtic fury that Caesar had faced fifty years before Christ? By mid-day he knew of Emperor Honorius' instruction to the Britons in 410AD to defend themselves as best they could from the raiders: Irish, Scots, Picts, Saxons and those who smelled easy pickings in an apparently defenceless land. Here in Cornwall, the land of the Dumnonii and the Cornovii, the Roman presence was less entrenched than the rich agricultural heartland of England. And that was it: there was less that the Romans wanted here. Minerals of course, but the uplands were poor scrubland fit only for common grazing, the coves and estuarine valleys isolated, woody and almost impenetrable. There were roads but no Watling Street here, just age-old access by sea. And in the ensuing Dark Ages, a time of incessant war and revolt, mystery and legend thrived in this place of isolation, where the Tamar River cut off Cornubia, in Latin, or Kernow, in Cornish, from the rest of Britain.

Because the Romans were largely disinterested their remains were limited: a Roman fort at Tregear near Nanstallon; a few Roman milestones, one near Tintagel, another close to the hill fort of Carn

Brea near Redruth, and another two near St Michael's Mount in the south.

And what of Arthur? His battles were spread so far apart that his reach was beyond any infantry, however well trained. Therefore Arthur had to have led cavalry. One speculative link with the Sarmatian horsemen from the Ukrainian steppes was possible. After centuries of raiding the Danube region Emperor Marcus Aurelius had defeated them in 170AD. Instead of execution they enlisted as auxiliaries, 5,500 men and their families, and were stationed along Hadrian's Wall. Here the descendants of those formidable Scythians that the Classical Greek Historian Herodotus wrote about had kept out the barbarians, the Picts and the Scots that now raided with impunity. That was until they met Arthur. Was there a connection?

It was mid-day. He was being swamped by possibles, so that it was far too easy to join the dots to make up a permutation that fitted some preconceived theory. It didn't seem the stuff of serious scientific enquiry. But at least he was building a picture, creating reasonable hypotheses that could be tested.

Because Cornwall was more linked by sea than land could Arthur have had a navy? How else could he have defended the coasts of a piece of land where one day was all it took to walk from north to south, sea to sea? When he thought of sea horses he knew it was time for a pause.

Ros also took a break and walked past the kitchen where Meredith was preparing the mid-day meal. Jeremy watched from the red Formica table as she lined up the scruffy ends of the carrots and beans.

'Are you going to cut those off?' he snapped.

'No, I'm going to give them to you just as they are,' she replied without looking up.

Ros kept walking. She was drawn to Meredith's studio but that was for another day. Back in the library certain characters attracted her attention: Merlin of course, Tristan and Isolde's doomed love affair, and Guinevere. If she followed Jeremy's ruthless process of discarding all but the facts then with Merlin there was no evidence left. Was he a wild man from Wales? Was there substance in the story that he helped

Uther Pendragon to cuckold Lord Girlois in Tintagel with his wife, Igraine? The result was Arthur. It was a messy story, just like Tristan, King Mark of Cornwall's nephew, given the task of bringing Isolde, Mark's future bride, back from Ireland but falling in love with her instead. So much subterfuge before their affair was discovered and then everything turned into tragedy. Both stories seemed sordid, creations from a later time of medieval courtly love. Would Guinevere have dallied with Sir Lancelot, or he with her, in Arthur's Camelot? Ros had an aunt called Jennifer, the modern translation. But the mental picture of her didn't match this exotic legend.

But two lines of enquiry appeared. Was Merlin a Druid, the old order, in the period of Celtic Christian missionaries? She was not religious. It was not evidence based. She could accept ghosts before she could believe in a God. Living was for experience and what you could do for family and friends, but she did not condemn those who had a faith. Despite her beliefs the clash of Druid and Christian, their ideas about the Cosmos argued between erudite, passionate thinkers, would have been a delight to witness.

The other was Guinevere: her nature and her homeland. As a Celtic princess was she constrained by the mores of a thousand years later? Ros had promoted the idea with Philip that a culture's level of civilisation could be gauged by how much freedom and equality their womenfolk exercised. After their time in Muslim Iran the thought of Guinevere being in free contact with courtiers was something to ponder. The lady also came from Lyonesse, a fabled land swallowed by the ocean just like Atlantis. The evidence for that, by Jeremy's yardstick, was in Mounts Bay with its forest of drowned tree stumps at low tide near St Michael's Mount.

Was Tintagel Camelot? In those troubled times, the thousand years of the Middle Ages, no enlightened rule was possible without impressive fortresses.

'Promontory forts,' she said to Philip when he parked a cup of coffee by her hand.

'Yes,' he said, between sips of scalding hot black tea.

Meredith had no objection to Ros showing Philip her studio. He absorbed the paintings, less from an artistic viewpoint but more as an imaginative photographic record. Back in the library he found a traced outline map of Cornwall with coded links to all the promontory forts that Jeremy and Meredith had visited. Military precision was the thought that stuck in his mind.

Back in the lounge they both looked out of the window. That view of the harbour and beyond was magnetic. The sun beckoned through parting clouds.

'Do you feel like a walk?' she asked.

'Why not?'

'Don't forget your Mackintoshes,' Meredith called up the stairs. 'We don't want you coming back like wet shags!'

Ros draped her Dryasabone over her arm and Philip grabbed his anorak.

Outside, Clarence Terrace became a blustery tunnel between houses and low garden walls as they turned left and down towards the near vertical stairs of Jacob's Ladder. The last of its one hundred and eleven granite steps opened out to The Moor, the old marketplace. It was a jumbled mix of architecture: imposing Greek columns and porticos side by side with fifties concrete supermarkets and Tandoori chicken outlets in converted terrace houses. Philip would have to ask Jeremy and Meredith about war-time Falmouth some time.

On the Prince of Wales pier the ferry was waiting. Its high fo'csle was below the level of the stone wharf at low tide. The bottom three steps down were slimy with green weed.

'Min' step, me luvva,' as the seaman steadied Ros's hand when she stepped onto the deck.

She looked at the be-whiskered, leathery face with train tracks radiating from his eyes and mouth. Bloodshot eyeballs and three missing front teeth completed the picture. I don't think so, she thought.

'Only a term of endearment, not a proposition,' Philip said grinning.

They sat outside near the front as the vessel zigzagged through moored yachts. The merchant ships being repaired dwarfed their tiny chugging craft. In the open water of Carrick Roads the waves and wind combined in a chill spray over the prow of the vessel. But ahead the Tudor castle, to the left of the Percuil River, and St Anthony's Lighthouse to the right gave them focus for the twenty minute trip across.

At the top of the steps of the stone jetty she absorbed the architecture of St Mawes: a postcard fishing village, something from a Cornish Gingerbread tin. A few small boats proved it was a working fishing harbour, but the multitude of expensive yachts displayed the playground of the rich. No wonder locals could not afford to buy a house in their own county, Ros thought, remembering Philip's conversation on the train. The summer cottages owned by "emmets", outsiders from London and elsewhere, meant that so many villages were empty of all but apparitions in winter. Scenic beauty was a curse for many of these people.

Philip looked across the river to St Anthony's village. 'When does the Place Ferry leave?' he asked a fisherman weaving nets.

''Arry'll cummiz on dreckly,' nodding towards the Tudor Castle Hotel.

They sat on the stone bollards on the harbour edge and watched the water beyond the boats moored in the mud. Harry's mate continued interleaving the nylon thread without pause, the net spilling over his oily woollen jumper and black wellington boots.

As Harry ambled from a lane beside the Hotel his customers trickled back to the wharf and filed down the steps to the rowboat with a big motor and twelve seats.

'Cummiz on do,' Harry called, his hand out for the fare. 'Like Brown's cows amblin,' he muttered audibly. With no "luvva's" hand the eight people clambered in, those inside helping newcomers across to the far seats.

'E's like a crab goyne jail,' Harry said to the last man in.

Then Harry unhitched the hawser and turned up the throttle from the standing wheel at the back of the boat.

''Arry 'ee crizzlin' like a badger,' Ros distinctly heard her neighbour say above the sound of the motor. But in minutes they were idling at Toddy's Steps, a rocky outcrop at the entrance to Place Creek.

'Na' ee be car'ful. Dawn't ee be cows 'andlin muskets.'

Ros looked at tubby feet in impractical shoes slipping along the stepping stones to the wooded shore and enjoyed "'Arry's" picturesque turn of phrase. Nobody dared ask him when he was coming back.

The lovely fawn stone of Place Manor glowed in the afternoon sun. It reminded her of something French, pointed arches above lots of small windows. Yet the stone was older than the 18th century. According to Philip's guidebook it came from the St Anthony monastery destroyed in Henry V111's Reformation. Interestingly one of its tasks had been to keep a light on the headland until the forerunner to the present lighthouse was built. But the building was closed for the winter. It would have been good to walk its atmosphere, feel its history, but it was not crucial. He knew there was more to come.

He held her hand walking through the Cornish lane between head-high vegetated stone walls, the trees forming an arch above them. A side turn took them into the old Church, Victorian on a 12th century plan: nautical, full of Spry family plaques and references. It was clear that the restorations hid so many more ancient memories. At the south door Philip and Ros stopped at two rows of carvings, a religious story that was not clear to him. Ros should have been looking but was not interested and walked out. She reminded him of a Beagle with a scent.

To Philip the walk along the headland towards the lighthouse was glorious: a huge sky full of fast-moving clouds, high above the blue water of Carrick Roads with Pendennis Castle, Henry's bigger cousin to St Mawes Castle in the distance, and Falmouth town beyond. With their strategic control of the protected harbour these forts must have been built on earlier fortifications.

He was explaining Henry's defences against the Spanish but Ros was drifting. After a while he stopped talking. It was happening again. Did he hate her "gift"? Not really but he worried and felt the loss when her mind was in two places. All he could do was be with her.

'Is it a person?'

'Not sure,' she said, still far away. She was absorbed into the scenery, along the path through open grazing land towards the hexagonal whitewashed block of St Anthony's Lighthouse with the conservatory of glass on top. Near the World War Two remnants of a gun emplacement her feelings soared. When she looked down towards the rocks and black outcrops sliding into depths of blue green clarity she felt her mood plummet.

'Can I help?' Seconds later he said, 'Can you describe it?'

'Not really, to both: elation, dejection, fear, and yet peace. It doesn't make sense. For now that is. But the peace: I'm not really worried. It will fall into place eventually.'

They followed an intrepid couple in walking boots, each with two sticks and all the right clothing, as the weather closed in. On the slipway of Place Manor they watched 'Arry negotiate the swell. He said something and one of the hikers hitched the rope to the bollard. Six of them climbed in. 'Arry' matched the weather, which was surly. On the next stage, a choppy trip back to Falmouth harbour, they huddled inside the covered back as the ship wallowed in rollers created by contrary winds. As one wave blasted across the front of the cabin and slid down the side windows a man's voice rose above the noise.

'"A good sword and a trusty hand!

A merry heart and true!

King James's men shall understand

What Cornish lads can do!"

Two more joined him when a wind squall screamed and thumped the side.

'"We'll cross the Tamar, land to land:

The Severn is no stay:

With one and all, and hand in hand;

And who shall bid us nay?"'

As the little ferry rolled and thrashed up the rollers and down the troughs, so that the lights of Falmouth seemed to approach and recede, they all joined in the chorus:

"'And have they fixed the where and when?

And shall Trelawny die?

Here's twenty thousand Cornish men

Will know the reason why!'"

They all sang the words above the rage outside, including Ros with Philip's help. Until the Lizard headland, and the harbour structures, broke the wind's power.

Where else would they go on such a foul night than the pub? It was the Charles the First in Market Street, along the front towards the docks. Ros surveyed the clientele from the snug, cushioned seats in the alcove window to the street. Two yachties propped up the right end of the shiny timber bar, left toes on the brass footrest, the froth from half pints of Guinness coating their top lip. Most were locals: jumpers and jeans, regulars, with the faces of too many spirits. Or maybe it was what was in the glasses Philip slopped on the table, Scrumpy?

'Cheers.'

She sipped the apple Cider. 'Nice.' But after three mouthfuls she could feel its strength. A few more of these and she'd be legless. But it loosened her thoughts.

'It's more than one person; like overlapping memories attached to the place. But I'm content to wait. All will be revealed,' she said, making light of it all. Her body warmed. No wonder the British pub was all important.

Philip was first to notice the six seamen at a table in the left corner, behind the blackened post beneath the Tudor beam roof. As he had seen before Rosalind's beauty was a magnet to men, like a candle to moths.

'Nice bit of pork crackling by the window,' was a compliment that Ros heard.

57

'Give me twenty minutes with that one,' was the thick Slavic reply.

'I wouldn't spare the rod either,' was mild compared to what followed.

It was Philip defending Ros from Muslim males again, here in his own patch. 'Time to move on?'

'Good suggestion.' She nodded towards the door beyond the bottled lust at the bar.

As he got up first Philip distinctly heard, 'Ye knaw ee's useless as tits ona boar pig.' Ros felt their eyes probing her chest as she followed him.

Outside they turned up their collars against the cold wind with a smattering of sleet. Ros hooked through Philip's arm as they continued along the front into Church Street. He was looking for a right turn up steps towards Clarence Terrace. As they steered into an alley a dozen teens in hoods, tight jeans and leather jackets stepped out from either side of the path. Their faces were visible by the glow of their cigarettes. Philip pulled her closer and cracked his knuckles.

'Go' a light, mate?' as one stood in Philip's path, dropping cigarette ash on his workman's boots.

'Don't smoke, thanks,' Philip said as his buddy on the opposite side scraped his steel toe-cap close to Ros.

Philip projected energy and power over her like an umbrella. He saw fence palings propped against the walls and half empty flagons of rough cider that stunk around them. A knuckle duster gleamed off a far street light. He felt their aggression in the air and in their fidgety feet; they were almost salivating.

'Keep walking,' he said to Ros as his encircling arm guided her up towards the steps.

'But,' she said and paused for a split second.

'GO.'

She took a few steps.

'FAST,' as he faced the figures emerging from the shadows.

'What ee goyne do boy?' the boss sneered.

'Goyne weaker'n taddy water,' his second spat.

Philip studied them: where they were to his left and right, the confident leader, the rutting stag opposite who wanted his place, the jackals of the pack two paces behind ready to swarm in. Ros was up the first flight of steps to the platform, turning to check but still going.

It crossed his mind that he did not need to be in a primitive place, that the streets of his own country went back to the primeval swamp too. Anyone could die just as easily here.

She knew he could look after himself but was still frightened.

By whatever means he read her fear and knew to trust her feelings.

'Too slow te carry cold dinner.' 'Nawthen te write 'ome 'bout.' The followers were adding their two pennyworths.

His Tae Kwon Do instructor's words surfaced.

'There's no answer to a wack behind the ears with a bit of four by two.'

'Cummiz on!' the hounds bayed.

Philip turned enough to see in his side vision that Ros was at the top of the second flight of steps.

'Shut yer bal,' he bellowed. He crunched his knuckles again, spread his legs akimbo, straightened his neck left and right and narrowed his eyes. Open enough to pre-empt a rush, sufficiently shut to find that clear space in his mind.

The gang was not sure. No one was game to make the first move.

He stayed in that lucid detachment for several seconds. As he opened his eyes wide he stepped forward. Then he spun around and raced up the steps to join Ros.

'Ee's slipprier than a snail.'

'RUN, Ros,' as he took two steps at a time, loping up like a gazelle in full flight.

'Have to lose the fags, boys,' he mumbled as the gang were left to shout obscenities.

For the sheer fun, or relief, they ran up the whole way. As they turned the key in the porch door they were laughing and puffing in equal measure. Inside the attic room she wrapped her arms around his waist.

'Better part of valour, lover boy.'

'So I'm not so daft?' he chanced.

She kissed him and stripped off for a shower. While the water steamed, and Ros repeated some of Trelawney, Philip opened the envelope Meredith left.

"The team is working at Tintagel tomorrow. You and Ros should take our places.

Love Meredith."

Once clean and after some cheese and biscuits that Meredith had left in the fridge Philip spent the next hour teaching Ros self-defence. Maybe their experience tonight had something to do with it but she was a star pupil.

'Step forward. Hold my shoulders, right leg behind me and push.' He went down hard.

In the lounge downstairs Jeremy opened his eyes from Bach and looked upwards.

'Horizontal folk dancing?'

'Shush, just dancing,' replied Meredith, putting down her Jean Plaidy, "The Captive Queens of Scots". Although she did hope that the activity upstairs was more horizontal. That was a lovely time, she mused, when frustration/love was channelled into something rather beautiful and warm. She missed that. Gradually it had become lost in work, raising kids, paying the mortgage. So that when it was all over "horizontal" meant sleep and "goodnight dear" from single beds. Life was not fair; it escaped you when you least noticed. Good luck, she thought, enjoy your dreams because you've no idea how long they will last.

Philip bear-hugged Rosalind from behind, but she dropped low between his arms and elbowed hard towards his groin. Philip flinched but she stopped short accurately. To his instructions about jabs to the nose, kicks to the shins: 'Piece of cake!'

After learning to fall half a dozen more times she got a fit of the giggles. It was time to "hit the sack" as Ros would say. Curled up with the rain thrashing the window, the harbour lights dancing in the rivulets, he showed her Meredith's letter and asked her about those feelings again.

'It was a person, in fact several, as I said, their experiences interleaved into the landscape in some way. But I might need your help this time. There's something different, beyond my experience. I know it's big and that I am out of my depth.'

He frowned.

'But I'm not frightened of any of them.'

'Easier than the Comtesse?'

'No, but yes.'

He turned out the light.

CHAPTER 4

The logs in the fireplace flared with the damp winds coming down through the vent in the roof. It was a wild night of searching gusts and crushing waves outside. Arthur sat on the sheep-skin covered, wooden seat scratching Taranau, "Thunder", behind his ears. The shaggy, grey wolfhound leaned against his knees. Arthur's mind rambled towards the next campaign against the latest Saxon incursion. Word from Gurgust Lethum, king of the northern kingdom of Elmet, was that Colgren and a large band of Angles were besieging the old city of Lindum. On Merlin's map it was clear that the roads the Romans built, what he called the Fosse Way from Isca in Dumnonia, and Ermine Street from Londinium, met at Lindum and went north to Goddodin. The small garrison was all that prevented the invaders from splitting the Brythonic kingdoms in two. In days from now he would draw blood again, in his own right now that Uther and Ambrosius were gone. His band of lancers would travel north along the Fosse Way and meet with the forces of Elmet and levies from Powys and Gwynedd. Would they meet him with their infantry as demanded by custom? There was always reluctance. How deep would the pirate crews have bitten into the heartland of the north by the time all was ready? He pushed some thoughts away: beyond a plan and proper preparation there was no purpose in worrying the problem like Taranau would a hare.

Then he absorbed Guinevere's form, her lithe body framed by rivers of hair, the flowing linen dress flickering in the firelight. She leant forward as she concentrated on the piece of fabric within a circle of raffia. He watched the finishing touches applied to the red dragon stitched on to a blue background. Tomorrow it would replace the pennant on his lance that wind and wear had shredded.

Two months ago they had met as strangers and married according to dynastic custom. Merlin had chosen and who was he to question that judgement. That first night the feasting went on into the morning hours. Bonfires were lit all over Cornubia and Dumnonia and were kept burning for three days to secure this auspicious event.

The elders of the ancient tinners' town of Hellys provided the bridal chamber. Before dawn the two of them had escaped to the apple orchards lining the river down to The Lake. There they told their stories. Guinevere had grown up in protected peace, oblivious to the suffering beyond the palace walls. The Saxon settlements were a long way away. There had been raids but stout walls and an unenquiring mind was enough. Poets, minstrels and learned men were always welcomed by Cador, her adoring father. His daughter had been schooled well in the gentler arts. Merlin had tutored Arthur in many things, as others had schooled him in the arts of war. But he felt boorish in comparison.

When he led her across the causeway into the courtyard of Tintagel it was clear in her eyes that this was a stark, unadorned bastion of defence that he had inherited on the death of Uther. It was not enough for her.

That night in their bedchamber he had admired her beauty as she undressed before him and then slid under the bear skin coverlet. He quickly did the same and held her shoulders to keep her warm as waves and wind thrashed the headland. But he continued to hold her as images of Trelivel, and all the brutal pillage of raids he had seen since, bombarded his mind. How could Uther slaughter and wench in equal measure?

Now he awoke when a wooden shutter flexed at the end of a long breaker of wind. Rising through waves of sleep he composed himself. It was near morning and today he would lead his teulu north against the Saxon raiders again.

Guinevere stirred and curled into his shoulder.

'Is it time?'

'Soon.'

Her arm strayed from his neck to his chest to his belly. He felt the familiar stirrings, not in his control but pleasurable nonetheless. There had been so many false starts: his thoughts of Uther, the bloody meat littering the cobbled streets of Trelivel, the childish ways of his half-sister, Morgana. But Guinevere showed him how easy it was to enjoy her body, her eager murmuring as he penetrated and the embarrassing excess of her climax. Some sort of love was growing between them. With Merlin's advice he might make her happy.

That is if he avoided the stray arrow or an unforeseen sword blow from behind. His survival depended on the favour of Merlin's gods, or the single God if Justin was to be believed; that and his skill on the battlefield. He smiled. You are never more alive than when you are seconds from death. Tsarati would not concern herself with such imaginings. The Goshawk meted out swift judgement to her prey and had no disquiet for her own existence. She was in the moment, the now, as he was in the thick of slaughter; deep in instinct, that miraculous prescience of everything around him. Like the hawk he could see better from the rarefied air. So that peaceful days in Cornubia were dull in comparison.

As dawn's rays streaked the forbidding sky he looked up at her window from the courtyard. Her golden hair shone against the grey stone tower. Around him grooms held the stallions of the troop, his personal teulu paid for by the tinners. It was a hundred strong and growing rapidly as the younger sons of the Brythonic lords arrived hoping for advancement through war. In the wind torchlights fluttered off the chainmail, the engraved bosses of shields and their plumed helmets. Taranau sat unconcerned on the ground beside him, alternately grooming his coat and eyeing the shaggy companions of the other warriors.

Again Arthur studied his knights astride their snorting mounts, the creatures' odour and steam rising from flank and mouth equally. As always each man had checked his four-winged leather saddle and the girth strap tight under the belly. His remounts were loaded with extra provisions and weaponry. On the long ride it was vital that the rider spread his weight to protect the horse's back.

He remembered Merlin's explanation of the saddle. Sarmatian warriors, and the Scythians before them, had devised it but the Romans had perfected it. Through his contacts in Britanny Merlin had learnt of a vital extra added by Attila, the leader of the Huns who had swept through Gaul and threatened Rome itself. The Hun saddle continued the leather-covered, wooden frame down the sides of the animal to accommodate the cavalryman's feet. Gurgust and the other princes were reluctant to adopt this change. But Arthur knew that these stirrups gave stability in a battle charge. On impact with a lance the enemy was impaled, not the mounted warrior thrown off.

The animals' restless feet had begun the rhythm of their journey. How many men would return in a month's time? Had their wives shared their bodies as Guinevere had and for the same reason: a male heir to continue their name?

Guinevere closed the shutters. Arthur mounted and led the band across the walkway and turned south east towards Isca Dumnoniorum. Soon they rode through steady rain but then winds on the high road along the granite backbone dried man and beast. Arthur detached himself from the tedium. He thought of Tsarati and was transformed into her spirit for an indeterminate time, soaring over this rugged land of thicket and scrub tree, soil barely able to support the few sheep and cattle that roamed the moorland. By late afternoon they set up camp outside the eerie ruins of this once great city, Isca Dumnoniorum, a decayed remnant of Roman power. Like the Saxons there were too many ghosts in that decay for anyone to settle again within its crumbling walls. Instead Arthur's band camped under cover of forest, close to water. Soon each man returned with provisions, some extracted from farmers to supplement the basic rations they carried. Much of this was barley for the horses, the standard Roman ration of three and a half pounds a day. Others used their skills with bow and line to bring back rabbit, duck and fish. Around the fire Arthur listened to those eager for glory, telling exaggerated tales of their prowess. A third of his force was untested and not much older than him. He and I chose to say nothing. Only their first battle would enlighten them.

Over four days Arthur admired Roman engineering as we followed the military roads; straight lines over rolling green countryside of scattered forests on ridges and farmland in valleys and plains.

'Roman efficiency,' he mused to me from the saddle. 'Their methods of getting control were not pleasant but their peace was better than chaos.'

He did not need my agreement. We and our families had seen too much.

'But they had a paid, standing army to gain and then keep the peace,' Arthur continued. 'Even with the tinners help how do I do the same with no central resource? The princes provide levies only after the crisis has happened.'

It was not long before we came across the work of the raiders: villages torched, full graveyards and a meagre few to farm what was left. Arthur's memories returned when the braggarts stared wide-eyed and silent as the party rode through the devastated countryside. Soon the living bore tales of another party in the wetlands of the east coast. A day's ride from Lindum Arthur turned the band to meet them.

'Murderous thieves and butchers, all of them. Women, priests, all of them slain without a care at all. There's only one place for these heathens,' said Glyn. He had returned with a cart full of tallow and skins to the spiralling smoke of his village. After hurriedly burying his mutilated wife and two sons he'd turned south on the military road, too shocked and rambling to think. Meeting Arthur gave him purpose.

This Christian has lost Justin's compassion and forgiveness, Arthur mused. Was there a Hell full of these warriors who'd chosen a life of piracy to feed their families, rather than the eternal drudgery of farming?

Glyn led the way through marshland and swamp. Not good country for cavalry was Arthur's first judgement. As others set up camp on a forested hill above the watery plain Arthur, a few companions, and his guide reconnoitred the pathways across this treacherous terrain. Glyn signed that the raiders were just over the next rise. He and Arthur climbed to the lip while the rest waited with the horses. Just as at Deveryon there were a dozen ships pulled up on the shingle bank at the mouth of the river, the Glein according to the guide. In the sea fog rolling in with the afternoon breeze they saw shadowy lines of pirates returning with loot from the plundered villages, Glyn's amongst them.

Back at camp Arthur's men had their backs against trees in the circle around the cooking fires. In the moonlight sentries stood lonely and unseen in shadows, their ears alert to any untoward sound. Arthur's face was lit by the flickering light as he explained.

'Tonight the raiders celebrate. Tomorrow they will leave to either plunder further up the coast or join Colgren at Lindum. We must prevent both.'

On the journey he'd appointed leaders of ten based on experience and loyalty but most of all decency. How could they fight to save vulnerable people if they acted like the savages they battled? Arthur's band would kill to create peace. He had listened to Merlin and I discuss this contradiction. By example he could change people's hearts. Was it an impossible dream? Merlin thought so. Arthur remembered our debate.

'People believe what they want to believe, something bigger than themselves. Why should we disappoint them?' Merlin had seen my disapproval written across my face. 'Surely Justin, we both deal in magic, promises, a soothing draught of what pleases them.'

'Like the draught at Arthur's wedding?'

Merlin had smiled. 'You and I are just different sides of the same coin.'

'A man's faith is more than that. It should not just explain life but make him better.' I was always the optimist. 'It must offer hope for the poor and make the rich generous. Most of all it should question the established order.' As I walked away 'Out of present grief something good must come,' I had said aloud to anyone within earshot.

Glyn's wagon gave Arthur his plan. He split his troop into three. One group would remain in camp with Gareth and Kay. The second led by Lamorak would take a wide traverse down to the beach on the southern side of the ships. Arthur would take the third to the northern beach. For the moment men and animals rested to the sound of celebration along the shore line. Men's cloaks protected them from the damp ground and drizzling rain. Like Arthur many chose to listen to pleasanter sounds of the night: the birds, the rustling creatures, the wind patterns through the trees. It was rest before the test of their mettle.

When the sand glass showed three in the morning the beach was quiet. Arthur waited for Lamorak to mount up, his giant shadow stretched in the rising moonlight. He looked towards Gareth, who raised his arm. Bors and Kay steadied the horses along the long leather tether. Arthur swung on to the back of his horse, Hengroen, and led the third party north. Carefully he guided the stallion's steps along the wind-blasted ridges of tufted grass, each of his party mimicking the hoofprints. Within the hour he was waiting on the shore, the ships' lights barely half a mile away. As before every battle time slowed. His mind became still and in the clarity of thought the plan became real.

An hour later he gave the signal, the single screech of a Barn Owl that Merlin had taught him as a boy. Lamorak's 'hoo, hoo' of a Long-Eared Owl was barely audible but was quickly followed by the 'kewick, kewick' of a female Tawny Owl. Man and horse waited.

The first earthen-ware pot shattered as a dull crump. It was followed by a rain of thuds of ceramic on wooden deck. Soon the first tendrils of flame spread from the burning oil and rose through the reefed sails, a pinpoint of light shining upwards into the breaking cloud. Kay, Glyn and the rest had completed their task and now retreated to camp.

The raiders were overconfident. It was fully two minutes before the first human cry was heard and by then the urns of tallow wax and cloth strips had done their work. There was chaos of running silhouettes and splashes as they leaped overboard. Arthur raised his pennant high, the red dragon on blue, and his men began to canter in close formation. Light from the fiery ships flickered off the steel scales protecting man and beast. He knew Lamorak was doing the same, as those in camp waited on horseback for the two wings to meet.

Most of the pirates had grabbed some weaponry. A life of fighting meant that seaxes, knives short enough to stab and long enough for a poor man's sword, were on every man's belt. Many had time to carry a throwing axe or their shield. Few had retrieved the spears that might have given them a chance. Over the din some heard a sound like thunder. Most only saw the flash of steel and thrash of hoof as the first men were ridden down by the two troops carving a gory channel through bodies and dying men's screams. Soon the southern and northern bands reeled and came in from opposite sides again, lances impaling their targets as they tried to face the nearest horseman. In the melee a small group of men scrambled up the grassy edge and tried to regroup but Gareth's men appeared from the darkness of the forest and rode them down from a third direction. Within minutes there was no contest. Where was their leader? Had he been cut down early or was one of the burning ships his funeral pyre? If Arthur pulled back now and waited for surrender then his enemy could regroup. His own warriors were finite; injury to man or animal left him weaker to face Colgren at Lindum. Either a signal came now or the slaughter would be extermination. There was no signal.

He saw Glyn pulling weapons and helmets from the dead closest to him. His face streamed tears but out of his mouth came obscenities that no Christian, or man of any faith, should utter. Arthur rode over the churned ground and saw that the victory was complete. He turned away and looked north, towards Lindum.

As the hazy dawn glowed his teulu reformed. Those warriors freshly blooded he congratulated. Those who had frozen with fear and hidden Arthur left to accompany Glyn on his journey south. No doubt their story would change by the time they reached their loved ones. Bors and others dealt in threats so that the cowards took their share of loot to safety. There was no room for extra weight on the ride north.

Once on the Fosse Way the forty miles to Lindum took a day. As any true cavalryman would each knight looked after his horse well, with grain in nose bags in the morning and resting in grassy meadows beside easy water whenever they could. All through the day they rode for an hour and refreshed for a quarter of that. Then their mounts were ready for ambush or swift attack. Always they would conserve their own energy. Each man functioned on that finely developed line between awake and asleep.

Late afternoon Lamorak came back with word that Colgren's forces were camped along the Linnius River south of Lindum's walls. In the gently undulating land of low hills and lush pasture Arthur chose to camp on the lower slopes of a hill, out of sight of the marauders on the far side. It was a bowl, a natural amphitheatre, where he could speak. For no one should go into battle without knowing something of the stratagem and sharing in its creation.

Lamorak gave his report. The enemy was camped in the meadows just over the hill. 'King Gurgust's pennant flies above the ramparts,' Lamorak said. 'His militia line the walls.'

'Then we must provide some entertainment,' said Arthur. He saw a look in Gareth's eyes. Already his men trusted him to be right but there were limits to what they could endure.

'Tomorrow.'

When the plan was clear Bors picked Geraint to join him on the first watch on top of the rise. Three more pairs would replace them so that no man faced the coming fight without sleep.

Before sunset Arthur joined Bors on the lip of the hill. The grassy flood plain would be treacherous. But he could see the patches of secure terrain before the gloom obscured them. Back in camp Arthur continued to ponder the plan: surprise but in daylight. Again a force split into three seemed fortuitous; despite his numbers being vastly inferior to the host encamped by the city. He would leave an exit for the enemy. His men could always mow down a fleeing rabble afterwards.

§

Colgren's guards stared blearily into the watery sunlight breaking through the haze. They reported a small force of cavalry coming over the rise just south of the camp. In disbelief they saw Arthur and twenty horsemen, in full armour and in perfect formation, slowly advance on the camp.

Colgren was of the old school when single champions fought in front of their respective armies. He admired bravery. He studied Arthur, seated on mighty Hoengroen, and listened to his younger warriors with better eyesight describe this tall youngster with black pigtail who stopped his horse and now looked at Colgren.

'He shows no fear, my lord,' said Hengist, his most trusted companion.

Colgren paused to see what this intruder would do. Arthur did nothing.

§

Arthur's inner mind was with Tsarati, high above the plain. Lindum's ramparts were full to brimming, Gurgust amongst them. The king was a shoulder and head above his subjects. His blue eyes in white parchment skin penetrated the distance as though searching for Arthur's thoughts. Arthur was Tsarati, seeing his prey, hovering, calculating distance, absorbing his quarry within his eyes. He was of the moment, a wild creature facing life and death equally. The seconds were glorious.

From the hill Bors saw that the Angle leader was amused and careless. He heard Colgren's shout.

'Take your men and play with our friend.'

'Who will join me in a little sport?' Hengist called. The roar was deafening. With no attempt at formation the fastest warriors raced to be first to face this youth, still as immobile on his horse as his few companions. Others followed in the hope of amusement and maybe a helmet or some other loot.

Arthur waited. He raised his dragon pennant high and yet remained still. For the signal was not for his immediate companions. He lowered the lance by a quarter and the line gently moved forward. Another quarter and they cantered. Arthur revelled in the discipline of his comrades, knee to knee, now laughing with excitement at the coming fray. Colgren's rabble only had eyes for Arthur's troop. Arthur saw the moment when Colgren glimpsed Lamorak's men riding hard from the right out of the cover of the knoll. In full gallop Arthur watched Hengist' dismay as Bors and his lancers rode hard down from the high ground and veer to Arthur's left. The camp was in turmoil. Men ran to their weapons, the few cavalrymen too late for their horses. Others shouted in vain to form ranks before the horsemen could cut through the infantry line and thunder through the camp.

Arthur was in the thickest of the melee, first pig-sticking; the force of his ride lifting the warrior off the ground before Arthur deftly pulled out the steel and slammed into the next and the next. Once through the line he and his warriors turned and slashed backs, shoulders and heads in great sweeps of their swords. This was what they had practised so many times and now dealt instinctively. Armoured horses rose above the tumult and crashed their hooves down on their prey. Others turned and took bites out of the enemy. Some pounded through and over warriors who could not raise their spears fast enough to pierce the animals' bellies and were crushed with their seax blades still in their belts. Hengist stood his ground as Arthur turned his horse towards him. Pause was death, Arthur thought; that ever present stray spear or sword stroke from the back. Hengroen's flashing bulk drove through the falling figures in their path and then spun in front of the warrior, whose arms were raised with spear and long seax. Horse and man were one, as Arthur's spear deflected Hengist's and his sword sliced down through shoulder and arm. Hengist's chest erupted in blood as he fell under Hoengroen's enormous hooves.

Colgren was flanked by his closest guard as the knights scattered running men and camp followers, cutting them down with abandon as the rest ran towards the cover of forest and swamp.

Arthur's men were superb horsemen, knowing that to follow risked horse and man being cut down in churned quagmire or ambushed in tight thickets where cavalry had no advantage. Instead the three troops slashed and cut easy targets before Arthur's signal, a single note from the short cornu hanging from his side. Then, as a man, they left their quarry and rode towards the open gates of Lindum.

Lindum's supplies were scanty through the siege but swelled from hidden caches in the surrounding countryside to provide the great feast held that night. I watched Arthur's men eat and drink with the best of them. Merlin joined us after the battle but the injuries he and I patched were slight. Each man celebrated being alive after two successful encounters in as many days. Arthur's prowess was sung and his reputation grew.

In the morning the militia infantry of Elmet joined Arthur's cavalry as they advanced towards a ford over the Linnius where Gurgust's scouts said Colgren had halted.

I was with Arthur as again he studied the terrain. It was a narrow crossing for men at waist height. Colgren's forces were in tight formation on the other side. It was too deep for his cavalry to force through. This was to be an infantry battle while he watched for his chance to follow if Gurgust's men gained the far ground.

The next day was one of brutal attrition. Brython and Angle fought bravely. Where the raider had experience, a hardened force whose life was marauding, Brythonic farmers had hatred and revenge. To give in was to dishonour the loved ones who had been lost. The waters ran red. Arthur listened to the curdling screams of the dying; the desperate blows before senses closed for the last time. He could understand his father a little more. How could you shut your eyes and not see the same savagery night after night? When Arthur was a boy Uther would never tell him about battles lost and won. There was never jovial play, only angry replies that broke the bond between son and his father.

'I envy your choice in life, Justin. Yours is the easier burden' Arthur said.

After another day, when renewed courage and determination came to naught, Gurgust and Arthur broke camp and went their separate ways. Winter was close. Better to return to homes and begin the affray again in spring. Maybe now the Brythonic lords would provide more troops.

§

As Arthur led his tired warriors into the courtyard Guinevere looked radiant in a long flowing dress, her hair plaited at the back but flowing to her waist. Arthur looked first at her and then at us. She looked as lovely as on their wedding day, but with a little more. Our eyes could not hide it. Guinevere was newly with child. She had never looked more joyful.

The weather in Cornubia was mild compared to the north. There was time for the first part of Merlin's plan. Our party and baggage were accompanied by the most select of Arthur's knights: the eleven who joined Arthur at the Round Table, devised by Merlin but wrought by Cador's most able craftsmen. Of the more than three hundred knights of his teulu Arthur's paladins were Lancelot, Percival, Gareth, Bedivere, Kay, Galahad, Bors, Gawain, Tristan of Lyonesse, Lamorak and Mordred.

Our progress from Tintagel south across the Cornubian high lands followed the tinners' ways down towards Grey Rock and the great southern bay. It was leisurely and finished for the night in the apple orchards beside The Lake. Simple structures had been erected according to Merlin's instructions. For once Arthur needed no plan. He and Guinevere strolled amongst the groves rekindling lost moments. He ate the apple she gave him, as she did his, as their arms intertwined like that first handfast in Avalon.

On the second day the party rode through a forest of Oak interspersed with Alder and Hazel trees with the sound of waves to the south-west until they came to Pennsans. They followed the wooded valley up to the town; its wealth derived from copper and tin, and encamped within the old stone fort overlooking the bay. Guinevere was happy because she was so close to her land, Lyonesse.

It was hard to keep the pace unhurried along the high pathways past tin mines and spoil heaps where livestock grazed and yellow fields of grain curved down to the edge of the sea. Guinevere could see her home, "The City of Lions", on a rise in the fertile plain below them. A little after mid-day our party entered an avenue of stone guardians which led into the palace, their stern feline eyes looking back towards Cornubia. The tiny population threw flowers: daffodils, narcissus and gentians, so that the road was a sea of yellow, white, and pink. Cador and Esylt looked resplendent with the colours of the flora mirrored in their silk gowns.

During the evening festivities I watched Arthur. He smiled for Guinevere, was as gracious as he knew how to his hosts, but occupied a place that no one, except Tsarati maybe, could reach. He was a man of war incapable of savouring the delights of peace. Yet his whole life was spent attaining it for others. Guinevere noticed but had no more power to change his thoughts than did the rest, with the possible exception of Merlin and me.

On the final evening I strolled with Merlin along the city ramparts as the sun turned sea into liquid gold. Merlin was pensive and my instinct was to accompany him. In the time that I had known him I had surmised that his brilliance was tempered with brooding melancholy, often changing in the space of a few hours. When not on campaign with Arthur, Merlin's efforts here and his projects elsewhere were exhausting. Now he was strangely distant, ignoring my words so that silence was the best option.

His wide eyes bored into the sea as though to see beneath it. Body and breath shuddered.

'What? What do you see?' I whispered as I steadied his shoulders.

He could not speak. His body was not his own, for minute after minute, until his collapse. Only afterwards could he describe the apocalyptic vision that his gift of second sight had shown him.

'Lyonesse is doomed to be swallowed by the sea. Great waves will come from the south-west. Leviathans higher than these ramparts will engulf the forests, the rich farmland and the pleasant towns, all that Cador's people have worked so hard for. The City of Lions and its people will be just a distant memory. The bells of their churches will only ring in wild tempest beneath the turbulent sea.' His look was of untold sadness. 'Guinevere must never know this, Justin.'

§

When the first balmy days of spring came Arthur's teulu rode north once more. Through her open shutters Guinevere saw them leave. Her face was pensive, that of a wife watching her husband go to war. I was told that later she gave prayers to the gods of Merlin. In the chapel adjacent to my small cell she also shed tears for the Virgin and her Son.

The journey to Lindum was slowed by a band of Tewdric's Visigoth infantry, partly funded by the tinners. Tewdric's presence at Heyl while Arthur carried out his duties as Dux Bellorum was vital to everyone's survival. As we rode sun and wind conspired with the budding natural world. Merlin and Arthur shared the sights and sounds as they had in

Arthur's youth. I listened and learnt and enjoyed their companionship. A day's march from our goal we were met by cavalry from Gwynedd and Reghed. Arthur's exploits had graced the feasting tables of all the Brythonic lords, including those of King Cunedda of Gwynedd and King Urien of Reghed. Their sons, Llywelyn and Ceredig respectively, would lead their troops. These kingdoms were closest to the wrath of Colgren if our mission failed.

The Angle king was easy to find at the far side of the same ford over the Linnius River. His forces were swelled by more Angles and Saxons eager for plunder. Colgren's word fame was good. He had withstood the forces of Elmet and the Dragonlord Arthur the previous year. This time they would not just hold back the Brythons but would sweep them out of the rest of this land.

Gurgust marched his infantry, along with levies from Eboracum and other cities within Colgren's reach, to the ford. Arthur rode his troop, followed by those of Llywelyn and Ceredig, to an open field nearby. As horses grazed in a circle, an inner ring of men listened to Arthur's stratagem.

'A year ago I watched many good men die at this crossing. However we curse the Saxons and their like they are great warriors. We will not watch another slaughter of worthy men. This time they can be beaten.'

He explained the plan. 'Ceredig, will you and your warriors stand where I stood a year ago and wait until the Saxon shieldwall crumbles?'

Ceredig bristled. He had come to fight not guard the road to the womenfolk of Lindum.

'It is a hard task because it requires patience. Like you I itch to slice a Saxon head from its neck. There is no more important task than this. Without your line of cavalry the Saxons will sweep Gurgust's infantry into the deeps. Your presence holds their line and buys us time. Can you do it?'

Ceredig reluctantly agreed. Arthur had succeeded before and he had no better plan.

Before dawn I absorbed the sounds of a waking army: ablutions, smoking fires, lowing of cattle bleeding a little into cups from the nicks in their throats, the lusty slurps of warriors gaining vigour from the blood, horses whinnying and human curses, and the silence of men about to die.

On a grey morning as rain squalls drove in from the sea the drums and carnyx horns of both sides began. Gurgust's infantry on the near side of the Linnius River were backed and flanked by the line of Ceredig's cavalry. Either side of the infantry were small knots of Elmet archers. Behind the men of Elmet was Ulphilas, the "wolf", a son of Tewdric leading his Visigoths as a rear guard if the front line broke. Opposite, across the water, was the impenetrable shieldwall of the Angles and Saxons. Both sides traded insults: their enemy's parentage, their mothers, their wives, their weakness and fear. Then began the wild screams perfected in battle to create courage in the owner and fear in the opponent. Arrows flew and men dropped, to be replaced immediately from behind. Ceredig remained motionless as the men of Elmet advanced across the water, knee then waist deep, before the clammering thuds as shields drove into each other. Then with spear, short sword and seax the killing began. The shouts to frighten became the screams of the gutted. Ceredig and his men watched blood trails spiral down the river. The thunderous noise took away every thought other than survival. For minutes and more minutes the horsemen watched. Their mounts fidgeted and the men stepped them forward and back to hold the line.

But out of the tumult the pitch of screams changed. The Saxon front lines were as before but to left and right, beyond Ceredig's vision, foot soldiers were trying to turn to face a new enemy. Arthur and Llywelyn had struck. There could be no other explanation.

This was Ulphilas' cue to action. His men advanced across the bloody mess of water and bodies. Their fearsome yells gave extra strength to the front line that they now pushed. Slowly the Saxon shieldwall bowed in and split.

Ceredig was jubilant. His will had held his men together. Now they were free to vent their rage. Arthur's teulu had charged the Saxon and Angle right flank, Llywelyn the left. As lances and swords carved trenches into unprotected sides the centre could no longer hold and replace the forward lines. Soon Ceredig's horsemen completed the circle of cavalry. Colgren's forces broke and survivors ran towards the estuary and the safety of their stronghold.

But in the rout was the personal bodyguard of Colgren. At a bend in the river horns blared and the fleeing enemy massed again where the river protected their two flanks and back. The shieldwall was restored.

Arthur blew his horn. Gurgust and Ulphilas understood but in the din of battle it took time to restore order to their own infantry. As they slaughtered stragglers most were drawn to the shieldwall. In the melee Arthur felt control ebbing. This was where chance could take a victory and shatter it into a defeat.

His horn blew again. Arthur, Ceredig and Llywelyn gathered their troops about them and waited. The shieldwall was holding against all that Gurgust, Ulphilas and the militia could hurl against it. The tide turned and the Brythons broke, a few then a breaching dyke of men rushing back towards Arthur. Arthur himself then rode forward, stood high in the saddle and drew Excalibur from its scabbard. The fleeing men saw the magical sword and its owner. There was only one place of safety. In front of Arthur the infantry line formed, men of Elmet, Visigoth, side by side, waiting for the enemy to clash again.

Saxon and Angle could smell Brythonic defeat. They were running en masse. This was their chance of real victory, plunder, loot and land for their families to follow. The advance was almost orderly but it was not what Colgren wanted. As they moved away from the river their flanks were no longer protected. As he shouted across the water the battle slipped from his hands. His supreme infantry, the crème of warriors, was not in his control.

Arthur waited until the Saxons blundered into the infantry wall. Then he gave the signal that the men of Ceredig and Llywelyn expected. Horsemen from Gwynedd reared their horses left and those of Reghed to the right, as did Arthur, circling wide to cut off any chance of retreat to the rear, towards the river bend. In an hour the slaughter was complete. It was a miraculous stroke of luck if any raider escaped. In the aftermath Colgren's body was found in the river shallows, drowned, a sword cut to the back.

§

It was a slow journey home, loaded with loot, lauded by ordinary people as a saviour, praised by Brythonic lords who muttered about upstarts under their breath. I rode with Arthur. His mood was sombre but content. We compared our upbringing in Armorica: mine of books, herbal remedies, contemplation, reading the needs of the poor; his daily exercise for strength, flexibility and the welding of horse and man in battle.

'So we could reach to the ground to pick up a sword or strike an enemy.' He showed me by reaching down to pick up a stick beside the road. 'We could ride at speed side by side and hold our formation. Our lances could strike targets accurately, our horses could brave cold and water as we did, and each of us could defend with sword against twenty around us on horseback. In time we felt no discomfort and no fear.'

'You speak of turning the other cheek, Justin, but that did not work for those we lost in the holocaust. I cannot do the same. But continuous war is not the answer either. It must be for a good purpose, for a better change.'

There I could agree. If there was such an idea as a Just War then Arthur tried hard to master it. For much of the journey Arthur entered that Natural space that Merlin had shown. I did not disturb him.

Half a day before Isca he was met by Merlin on the Fosse Way. This was the task that had kept him away from most of the campaign. He led Arthur and his knights across lesser roads to a new home, a mighty plateau encompassing eighteen acres, with fortification of four ramparts and ditches, at the centre of which was a magnificent hall of over sixty feet by thirty feet.

'What is this place?' Arthur asked.

'Local people call it Camelot.'

At the open door stood Guinevere, for whom Merlin had created this palace. Arthur thought back to her eyes when she first saw Tintagel. He had asked for Merlin's help in pleasing her. This was his answer.

While he was away Guinevere had always used her authority to run his household and defend his fortress. In Camelot his strength was supplemented by her subtlety and finesse. She was queen of a court equal to anything in Lyonesse.

As grooms took horses and wives their men Arthur met Guinevere inside the Great Hall. She looked diminutive in its vast chamber. Her body was still extended under the loose gown and her face was gaunt. He looked to Merlin but he had stepped away. Without words she held his hand and led him to their chamber. In a tiny cot was a days' old boy, premature but perfectly formed, his features the best of the father and the mother. Arthur gently clasped his tiny hand. It was cold in death.

Guinevere studied Arthur's face. Never again did she want to see such loss written so clearly. Arthur would have a living son. That was her duty to him as his queen.

CHAPTER 5

The bedside alarm sounded: repetitive buzzes like an angry wasp. Ros reached over Philip's comatose form and shut it up. It was 6am and still black, with the dock lights shining up like a hidden Christmas tree. He's hogging the blankets again, she thought. She lay back to gather her jangled senses. It seemed strange to be in darkness so late on a dig day. Hot shower water on her face helped to wake her up. He snuck a kiss as she stepped out and him in.

Downstairs the coffee and toast smelt great. She was getting used to yellow butter and tart Robinsons' marmalade. Ros described to Meredith the motley crew they'd met on the steps.

'I wouldn't trust that lot as far as I could spit, and I can't spit very far.' Then Meredith mouthed "Peter Piper picked a peck of pickled pepper", like a spitting sound, counting the syllables on her left hand. She held the teapot and poured with her right. Jeremy chose to wait until Philip came down to open his mouth.

'Now, lad, here's how to get to Tintagel.'

He gave Philip typed instructions based on his AA maps. As he passed over the keys to the Morris Traveller Jeremy said, 'Now look after the old girl.' He refrained from telling Philip how to drive it.

Ros was handed a magazine packed with loose pieces of typed and hand-written paper. It was the Cornish Archaeology Journal with its lead article on the excavations at Tintagel Castle.

'Thanks.'

Jeremy nodded.

Philip changed the subject and maybe Jeremy's tone.

'What was Falmouth like in the war, Meredith?'

She put down the dish towel. 'Well I can't tell you too much because I grew up in Porthleven on the Lizard. There was rationing of course until well after the war finished. I don't think I saw a banana until I was married. And at night time we saw the German planes coming over to bomb the docks at Falmouth. But Jeremy can tell you more, can't you?'

'I remember the oil store going up with a direct hit one night. That lit up the whole sky. We spent an awful lot of time in the Anderson Shelter in the back garden here: damp, uncomfortable place.'

'Were you old enough to help in the war effort?'

'When there was an air raid on I cycled around the streets in the blackout and reported back on any damage.'

'Sounds dangerous to me,' said Ros.

'I suppose it was but you didn't think about it. Once I found where the bomb landed by falling into the crater.' He paused for breath and to watch his captive audience. 'But I climbed out with only a few scrapes. The warden thought I was sleeping somewhere because I was late.'

'I remember the evacuation of Dunkirk,' said Meredith. 'Anybody with a fishing boat went across to pick the troops off the beaches. Mother gave quite a few of them tea and sandwiches when they got back. Night after night the boats went over. One moment they would be fixing up some decking and then it was all hands on deck. Trawlers and all manner of craft slowly motored out of Porthleven harbour, to be joined by others from Penzance and St Ives and all along the coast. Those who made it back were jammed with people.'

'We looked after our own,' she added with a lump in her throat.

'It was May 1940,' interjected Jeremy. 'The entire British Expeditionary Force was in a German noose, but Vice-Admiral Ramsay's team under Dover Castle organised navy and commercial ships to pick up men at the Dunkirk docks and at a derelict pier. The beaches were too shallow for the destroyers so those little craft were used to ferry men out to the big ships. All the time they were being bombed by Stukas and the rest,' he extracted from his encyclopaedic memory. 'But Meredith was right about little ships going across at night and collecting as many as they could fit in. In nine days from the 26th May to the 3rd June over 330,000 British and French troops were rescued but most of their weaponry was left behind'.

'I remember the Americans everywhere just before D-Day,' Meredith mused. 'We were old enough to understand more then. They were practising for the landing; big friendly men who missed home. The kids got chewing gum and local girls nylons. They had so much more than our soldiers.'

'Carrick Roads and all the creeks up to Truro were full of hidden ships,' said Jeremy. 'King Harry Ferry had government spies and bigwigs stationed there. The beaches were either concreted to load landing craft or were full of barbed wire, anti-tank cubes and pill boxes to repel any assault. And there must have been a good number of submarines under there too.'

'Everybody did what they could to help,' Meredith continued along her own thought process. 'The Dunkirk spirit: I can do my bit and save someone.' After a pause, 'Churchill bluffed Adolf with his cardboard guns to ward off the invasion.'

'A bit like Arthur's fire beacons on the hills? Both were saving Britain from annihilation.' Ros was picking up Meredith's wavelength.

Jeremy nodded, as though he hadn't thought of it in that way before.

'Everybody got lost with all the road signs switched around. But nobody went far because fuel was rationed. Jeremy courted me on his motorbike. He used to do fifty miles to the dozen in that smelly old thing.'

'My own special blend of alcohol distilled from potato peelings: Falmouth to Porthleven and back, via Gweek and Helston, on one pint of mixture.' Jeremy smiled and winced together.

§

Meredith waved as Philip and Ros walked up the back garden path to the garage door. All this talk of the war had taken her mind back, to a time before. She and Tamarisk had been sent off to play for the day while their mother worked the hotel, the Atlantic View. Times were good before the war and business was busy. As usual they had wandered along the beach to Loe Bar before returning to the rock pool beside the stone harbour wall. It was her favourite place.

'Don't go near the cliff edge and don't go into the sea,' her mother told Tamarisk. She was older, seven, and in charge. But paddling in the shallow hollow, full of little crabs and tiny fish left by the tide, was different. It was sunny and calm, a lovely day.

'You stay here, Meredith. I'll get the pasties,' instructed Tamarisk in her grownup voice.

Meredith watched her climb the rocks to the pier and hurry along the harbour road to Mrs Nancarrow's shop by the inner harbour. Then Meredith went back to laying on the edge and putting her head just above the water to follow the crabs in their shells scuttling between seaweed and sea urchins into their hidey holes. Then she would suck in a big breath and blow bubbles around her open eyes.

§

The breakers swelled and broke lazily on the rock shelf. Tamarisk raced the pattern as they flowed through the outer harbour and stopped at the dry mud of the inner entrance. She fiddled with the coins as she waited for the six people ahead of her to be served. It took ages.

'Tha'll be sixpence, me dear,' the lady with floury white arms said.

When she came out the boats in the inner harbour had been lifted from the mud and were sliding on their ropes as the water receded. How did that happen? That's not right, Tamarisk thought. She ran back along the harbour wall as fast as she could, the hot pasties under her jumper bouncing and burning her tummy.

§

The shushing of the waves and the sun on her back made Meredith sleepy. The placid pool of glistening water was like her goldfish bowl. After the Helston Fair she and Tamarisk always came home with a bright orange fish each swimming around the clear plastic bags. As she dozed it became quiet. The whack of the breaker turned her like a spinning top and pushed her over the ledge into the pool. She curled up like a baby and was tumbled backwards in the foam: her bottom thumped into rock, then her right side, then a third hit to her left thigh, a fourth into her right shoulder so that her forehead grazed the sharp stone, and the fifth that flattened her onto the bottom. Her dress stuck to her as she lay like a starfish on the sand. She remembered opening her eyes wide open and the water was suddenly so white and swirly she couldn't see which way was up. It went on for such a long time. She was frightened and opened her mouth to scream.

'Don't Meredith,' the kind voice inside her head said. In the snowy blur she saw him, an olive-skinned boy with warm brown eyes.

'You're safe,' he said as he held her small hand. She recalled smiling at him as the current tried to drag her out to sea. Then she relaxed and trusted him. His hand was so strong but he didn't hurt. When she was sitting on the edge of the shallow pool like before, Elvan went. She didn't know why but she had always known his name.

'I'm all right, Tamarisk,' she said as her sister dabbed the hanky on her scratched forehead. As they sat in the sun and Meredith dried out, Tamarisk suddenly cried.

'I won't tell, Tamarisk. I will never tell,' Meredith said as they squeezed each other close.

§

Inside the garage Ros made sense of the double wooden doors out to the back lane. She counted fifteen repairs with fruit box slats. Philip got into the Morris Minor Traveller. He looked at the fake wooden dashboard with speedometer clock in between two glove boxes, the four pull-out buttons and the key ignition between them. He pulled out the choke and turned the key. After two tries it bit and Philip slowly pushed in the choke so it didn't stall or flood. Both of them were sure that Jeremy was listening.

Ros waited in the lane as Philip pressed down the clutch, then accelerator to a dull roar, and pushed the gear stick into first. As he let down the hand brake between the leather bucket seats he kept the accelerator at the same height above the floor and gently raised the clutch. With a tiny hint of hopping the car was in the lane and idling while Ros negotiated the doors into closed.

In the dull grey light before dawn he peeled right into the narrow alley, the width of one car and a bit, and then on to Clarence Terrace. The tail and front indicator lights flickered off the damp rough-stone walls. Philip weaved through the cars on Arwenack St down to Swanpool and right into Woodlane and on to Dracaena Avenue. Out on the A39 they passed the turn to Newquay and drove on through Wadebridge. It was good to get used to narrow Cornish roads again without too much traffic.

Ros held a torch and intermittently read out Jeremy's directions and salient facts about Tintagel from the Journal. She watched Philip orchestrate the three pedals that rose from the floor into synchronicity, without "kangaroo hopping" or stalling. His feet brought back a rare memory, of a church organist's toes cajoling the bellows to produce just the right note.

'Tintagel: 12th century castle ruins on "The Island", which is really a peninsula accessible by a narrow causeway. Three hundred feet below is Merlin's Cave under the headland, supposedly with a tunnel up to the castle. Some remnants of a Celtic promontory fort, aka Meredith, and later remains of the Cornovii, a tribe present in Arthur's time. Once called Belerion by the Classical Greeks this part of the country became Cornubia, the western part of Dumnonia. The modern name Cornwall probably comes from "Cornu" meaning "horn", the shape of the land, combined with the Saxon word "wealas" meaning "foreigner". They also called it West Wales to distinguish it from the Welsh in the north.'

Just beyond Camelford he took the B3263 into Tintagel. Philip pulled up in the tourist carpark and reefed on the hand brake. Habit made him find a rock to jam under a back tyre, just in case. That sort of drop would do more than scratch Jeremy's paintwork.

§

Jeremy went back to the delights of Debussy. Meredith checked to see that she'd given him his breakfast tablets. She was keenly aware that she was left looking after Jeremy while Philip and Ros were having fun at Tintagel. A magical place, she thought. As she picked up the next shirt to iron her mind drifted easily to her two boys.

Peter loved cooking and gardening. He was always under her feet. She was for ever showing him new birds and flowers. He was a decent little artist too. Sam, well he loved fiddling with machines. In the back garden Jeremy would show him how the collection of miniature steam engines he had built worked. The boy would heat up the boiler with a gas burner until Jeremy pointed to the first engine. Jeremy would take the lighter out of the boy's hands and Sam would turn on the valve to make the pistons begin to rise and fall. Then he would try the next and the next, to start up as many machines as the steam pipes would allow. It was a delight if he could nurse one more into life by turning the flywheel with his little hands. Christmases putting together Lego and Meccano all ended when they set their Eleven Plus exam to go to Grammar School. Jeremy insisted that they go to the best boarding school they could afford with their two modest incomes.

'Toughen them up with a good education to face the world,' he said.

Jeremy often talked about schooling, how it fitted into the gene pool generation after generation.

'A father engineer, the mother an artist, they produce an interior designer or a plumber or someone who mends cars. Education lifts people out of poverty, gives them chances and changes the genetic code down through their descendants. That's why we give them the best whatever it costs.'

'Of course they will fly the nest some time just like in Nature. We are the enablers, nothing more.'

Meredith was not so sure. Not that she had much education with the war. The only teachers left were too old or infirm to fight. She remembered the pot of glue on the desk, made from water and precious flour, and sticking bits of magazine into her notepad. Mr Prynne would be outside the open door with the butt of his cigarette between shaking nicotine fingers staring out to sea. That was on the days when she and Tamarisk went to school. Not too many did in war-time.

Why didn't you talk to me, Jeremy? We shared the work with the house, the money, the garden why not the kids? I think I was fed a herring on that one, and not even a red one.

She put away the ironing board and sat down with her Jean Plaidy, "Katharine, the Virgin Widow". After a page she thought of those short holidays together as the boys grew away from them with a new world of influences. We did our best. It all went so quickly. Could we have done better? She tried again with the book but the claustrophobia of the tale was catching.

You dwell on the early bits, she thought: the courting and then marriage in St Bartolemews Church in Porthleven. She recollected saving coupons to make a one-tier wedding cake, and that her uncles were in uniform and their friends in the air cadets. It was so difficult to get the fabric for her dress but family had given their ration vouchers so her mother had just enough to make it. Twenty four guests came and reception lunch was brawn sandwiches, the cake and a little sherry Jeremy's best man had found somewhere.

Those early years seemed to be all passion, trials and arguments.

'So many in society sit on the backs of the rest of us,' Jeremy said. 'The rich and powerful have the chance to write, create, sculpt and never need to earn a quid. The Socialists make sure that the bludgers never need to spend the best years of their lives earning money to feed the family. It's only those with the Protestant Work Ethic that carry them both. How does society choose the right path when both groups play the system?'

He was always so earnest and serious. Over the years they had rearranged their personalities around each other, her bending to him really. They were buried under debt but were always optimistic. Remarkably the submersible kept bobbing up again. But then something was lost on the way that she only discovered when the boys left home for good: one to a job in Holland, the other in Nigeria.

By then Tamarisk's husband, always following the work, had reached Scotland. Their yearly trips to see each other got harder. Then Jeremy said it was too far. Meredith could still see her sister's face at the pavement waving goodbye. That magical meeting of eyes was hard to catch with words on the telephone.

'You were a long way from your loved ones too, Saint Elvan. I know, you always taught me not to waste time by longing for something you can't have. But it's hard not to some times.'

Arthur became more important than family. But children are our inheritance, our legacy to the world, she felt like yelling. There was so much more to give, adult to adult, if only we saw them more often. She calmed herself with a couple of slow breaths. But he's a good man really. He never raised a hand to me or the children. Now the only way to share his world was with Arthur. Otherwise I'd never see him. The art brings a bit of income. I am content really.

She took another long breath, closed her book and went downstairs to her studio. After the curtains were drawn she lifted the dust cover from her latest oil painting: Carn Brea. Underneath the medieval castle near Redruth were the remains of another hillfort. As she prepared her paints she looked forward to showing the result to Ros and Philip on their return. After an hour she made tea for Jeremy, who was sleeping in his chair, and took hers back to the studio. There, she thought, I'm ready to face whatever comes next.

§

As they approached the Ministry of Public Buildings and Works sign in the dreary light Ros felt the skin on her face tighten in the blustery wind across the headland. Philip talked his way past the kiosk attendant and they clambered down the steps and across the crumbling causeway that rose up to the Castle ruins on the Island. Meredith had waxed lyrical about the site but Ros felt she had understated. If King Arthur's presence was anywhere then surely it was here, on this wild, atmospheric promontory.

Philip looked beyond the distinctively medieval ring wall fragments climbing up the slope to the foundation walls that Dr Ralegh Radford had revealed in the 1930s. The United Kingdom was full of National Trust monuments that looked like this. From the Journal and Jeremy's notes it seemed that the outline was fairly accurate. It was uninspiring even to him but the imagination of the average tourist would quickly have moved on to its jaw-dropping location, boosted by legend and Hollywood.

Ahead was a working trench, what looked like a metre wide and ten metres long. Philip looked past the eight volunteers, mostly middle-aged women in hats, corduroy trousers or dungarees, and gloves. He estimated the depth dug was around a foot or thirty centimetres. The ground cover was coarse grass with a profusion of daisies; revealed under it were the foundations of a couple of cross walls and a random scatter of loose stone. Ubiquitous plastic buckets and string lines made him feel at home.

Ros saw the spoil tip, maybe ten barrows' worth and thought of Kara Tepe's massive wind-blown mountains of waste. Any finds for her to draw would be tiny amulets or bone needles, and pottery of course. The typology of the different wares that surfaced as fragments in this heavily eroded site would be the key to dating structures, and ultimately finding the Romans and then of course Arthur. Jeremy's records had been scathing of Radford for not publishing precise stratigraphic plans and sections. But she, and inevitably Philip, could see that there was little depth of soil to be divided into levels. Specific eras of time would be different sections of the site, depending on the random chance of survival against the elements. No doubt Sir Mortimer Wheeler had the patience to find split centimetre depths but most excavators with 1930s techniques would have done what Radford did.

While Philip spoke to one of the volunteers she looked for the view Meredith had chosen for her painting. They were directed to the large figure above a broader trench towards the centre of this massive thirty acre site.

'Hey, how are you doing?' The big man with unruly silver hair and florid complexion stretched out a delicate, freckled hand. 'Mason O'Flaherty.'

Philip returned a firm handshake. 'Philip Trevasco and this is Rosalind Bernaud.'

Mason took her hand more gently and squeezed, instead of the bonecrusher she'd have expected in the Australian Bush.

'Hello.'

'G'day, Rosalinda. You're a long way from home.'

She smiled at the courtesy. 'So are you. Toronto?'

'Vancouver in B. C. New South Wales I presume?'

'Close. Queensland.'

'You two are replacing Jeremy and Meredith. It's a pity about his health. His Arthurian knowledge was helpful.'

Ros read between the careful lines. Jeremy was probably as prickly here, and "his knowledge" probably translated to "know it all". However, he had sold their skills rather well. Mason explained the trench layout and the season's finds to equals. But she could read Philip's expression well enough to know that he felt rather a fraud, given that his knowledge lay elsewhere.

'Radford uncovered the medieval structures but his notes reveal little about the Roman and Post Roman levels. His judgement that the early layers were the frugal remains of a monastery has now been dismissed. In fact there is substantial Roman, Period II, remains throughout the site. Period III, the 5th to the 7th centuries, is also extensive.'

The technical jargon no longer worried her. In fact it was probably the quickest way to impart the summary of what was here. Yes, this was where Meredith had sat with her easel. She paused and then had to catch up with Mason's long strides.

'Over the past two seasons Site C, the series of trenches down the north-eastern slope, has revealed twelve phases of Post Roman material from the early 5th century AD to the late 6th or the start of the 7th century. Post Roman pottery has also been found in the Lower Ward inside the enclosing ditch with a Carbon Date calibrated to between 390 and 430AD. Even the Great Ditch protecting the landward side has Post Roman remains untouched by Radford's work. When he found buildings with serious quantities of Eastern Mediterranean and North African pottery and glass of the fifth to the seventh centuries he wrote about the monkish community here, rather than a significant Dumnonian aristocratic presence.'

Mason walked them down to the Site C terraces. Another seven volunteers scooped soil into buckets with four inch pointing trowels, a tool that was almost welded to Philip's back pocket. Others tied card tags with string around pot rims, bases and recognisable finds.

'Something unusual turns up in the Post Roman period. In Roman Britain trade was via the double route, the maritime and the riverine, the Atlantic and the Rhone/Rhine link. In the Post Roman era imports arrive on the Atlantic side of Britain. In the late 5th and early 6th centuries table ware and glass is traded from the continent, probably France, and is found at aristocratic sites like Tintagel and South Cadbury Hill, as far as Wales and Dumbarton Rock in western Scotland.'

'What was traded in return?' Philip asked.

'Cornish tin, Welsh silver and lead, Irish copper, all driven by Byzantium's need for metals.'

'And Arthur?' Ros asked.

Mason smiled. 'Ah yes, Arthur. Our work has created as many questions as answers. We know that something was going on either side of 500 but what it was and why is not clear. The beach by Merlin's Cave was probably viable as an anchorage for merchant ships. But what created this sudden surge in luxury goods?' Mason's expressive eyebrows and shoulders said the rest.

'So you are here as substitutes?'

'Yes, 'said Philip.

Mason paused deliberately.

Ros saw that he recognised experienced professionals in his field. Were they some variety of academic poachers? What were they really here for? He was waiting them out.

'Jeremy is very ill,' Ros said quietly. 'He has limited time.' She paused again. Mason was a new acquaintance. He was unlikely to believe what she was about to say, but it was best to bite the bullet. 'He has given us an impossible task, two really. He wants us to find Arthur's grave and the hiding place of the Holy Grail.'

Mason's brows and eyes were more expressive than ever. What could he say? Were these two nutcases of the religious variety so common around Mt Ararat looking for Noah's Ark?

'No we are not,' she said. Ros didn't need telepathy to work out that one. 'But we do intend to apply our skills to help Jeremy as much as we can.' Tell the truth and then retrieve the trust.

'We plan to work on site wherever you think we will be most useful,' Philip said, 'as volunteers in a trench or doing a site survey maybe? Jeremy said that he saw a Roman brick here last time he came to visit.' He omitted the fact that he had taken it home with him.

'Ros has photographic skills as well as artistic. Weather permitting we could take some aerial shots of specific features.'

Mason was softening.

'With Jeremy's car we could visit other sites and compare artefacts,' Ros volunteered.

'All right, Phil and Rosalynde. Let's give it a go. I will give you free rein but I'd like you to share your results. Is that a deal?'

Philip and Rosalind looked at each other. She had to say it.

'If we find the sites it would be dangerous to reveal their precise location. Otherwise you would have every nutcase coming out to love them to death.'

He smiled. How well she had read him. 'If you get that far I will accept a little less than the whole truth.' He shook hands with both of them.

'Are you a fly boy, Phil?'

'Not as you think. I can fly a hang glider, tandem so Ros can take the photos.'

'Can you hover?'

'Not exactly, but we are much more static than an aeroplane. And we can fly lower.'

'Now that would be useful,' said Mason. His grin told her that pictures were already arriving in his head.

Philip and Ros visited each of the three areas being worked on: C3 on one of the terraces, T around the castle remains, and the Great Ditch and Lower Ward of the castle area. In the last Philip watched Adrian and Maud, a farmer of early potatoes for the London market, and his manly wife, tracing back what looked suspiciously like a floor level. He itched to help but the space was limited and their work was painstakingly careful. Instead, with their permission, he studied the finds in the plastic cabinet, which protected them against the unpredictable weather, and the pottery sherds in covered buckets. A degraded green bronze buckle, from a shoe probably, was instant proof of an elite who could afford such things. The fragments of fluted glass, some tiny pieces of what was marked as Mosaic pattern, proved the same. In amongst the coarse cooking ware were fragments of Eastern Mediterranean amphorae. He placed his nose against the inside surface of one piece and was sure he could smell olive oil. Was it wishful thinking after all this time?

Ros crouched down beside Avril and Vera, two former members of the Women's Land Army during the Second World War, dressed in dungarees and wellington boots. Jackets kept off the intermittent rain, as did her own Dryasabone but her jeans still steadily soaked it in. Like Philip she went through the finds of local dinner ware with a few pieces of terracotta oil lamp from Cyprus or Palestine and even a bit of Roman Samian cup rim. Unlike Philip she felt the pull of the drop behind her back, with the distant sound of wave surges pouring into Merlin's Cave below them. She became used to the trowel work scraping over reused local stone with fine grit and soil between. In a few hours she was adept at caking the soil to put it in the spoil bucket ready for tipping onto the heap. Her eyes were younger than the Land Girls, of Jeremy and Meredith's vintage, so that she picked out snippets of bone needle and a round pebble with a hole in it that had once been a spindle whorl to stretch wool fibre into twine.

It would have been nice to have had a pint and a ploughman's lunch at the Tides Inn pub in the village. But then it wouldn't have been easy to justify the walk from The Island, and the evener longer walk back after the warmth. So they settled for the site hut that Public Works had provided for them: painted Oregon pine boards with an asphalt felt roof. The rain trickled gently down the window pane on the outside of the cramped space, rapidly warming up with human heat.

'When do you sieve the soil, Mason?' Philip asked gently. He had not seen any such implement.

'Occasionally, when the weather lets us. The soil clags too much.'

'Do you mind if we have a go? There was a device on the Cyprus dig which could separate miniscule finds as well as crop and weed seeds blown in from the surrounding area,' Ros said.

'Be my guest,' said Mason, suitably charmed.

A quick stop at B and Q in Penryn on the way back to Clarence Terrace gave most of what they needed. The forty four gallon drum was a gift from the manager when they explained what they wanted it for. He was another Arthur nut. The drum just fitted into the folded-down back seat of the Traveller, or "the Woody" as Ros called it.

Next day on the headland it was windy with no rain so that the surface layers of the spoil tips dried out. Within hours they were ready for a tarpaulin cover. With Mason's help any new buckets were sieved beside each spoil tip, and the finds recorded for that level. A selection was taken for Philip and Ros' seed machine, a tropical fish tank pump powered by a car battery pushing bubbles through the drum of water. With a regular squirt of Fairy dishwashing liquid the suds were made oily enough to become flocculants, to trap the fine debris and bring it up. With a paint scraper Philip or Ros scooped the scum off the surface, bagged and tagged it, ready for study under a microscope in warmer conditions.

Soon Vera and Avril took over the procedure whenever Ros was called over for in situ photographs or Philip worked with Mason on an intricate hearth or wall feature. One afternoon was spent on a bucket survey of the island. Mason took no offence whatsoever at their success, which boosted the finds tray spectacularly. They were an asset and his ego was not easily bruised.

A trip to South Cadbury Hill produced finds that matched Tintagel, as Ros had half promised. Professor Alcock had excavated this possible Camelot in the late sixties. The hillfort had been occupied in the Bronze Age, the Iron Age, and then the Roman Period. But nothing prepared anyone for the massive refurbishment that took place in the Post Roman era. In the late 5th century this was twice the size of any fort of its day. A cobbled road ran through concentric rings of earth and ditch ramparts. A sixteen feet high Roman wall was fortified with wooden beams and guard towers and slots for archers. Through the wooden gatehouse was the Great Hall. Its crafted wooden structure had what looked like a kitchen to one side, a precaution against fire.

On top of the five hundred feet high mound and its earthen defences Philip studied the National Trust monograph on the site. Ros enjoyed the views of rich English farming countryside for miles in any direction. It was a natural fortress, as good as any promontory fort, even before it was fortified.

The plans showed Roman stone and brick being reused by British workmen using Roman construction knowledge. He showed Ros pictures of finds equivalent to those at Tintagel, expensive pottery tableware and Byzantine glass. In the fine weather they traversed the eighteen acres with a bucket. The sherds, Roman brick and fragments of glass and amphorae reinforced the link to Tintagel.

§

'Barley, oats, bone needles, rodent bones.' Mason passed over small plastic bags with the items found in the surface scum of The Bubbler. Avril and Vera's faces beamed as they stood in the lee of the site hut.

'Anything specific you would like us to photograph tomorrow if we go up?' Philip asked. The forecast was good: mild, dry and warm for the time of year.

'The lower terraces on area C. From the next headland there looks like a pattern, maybe an access to the beach in times of siege. Otherwise I'm sure your judgement will be sufficient unto the day.'

§

In the high-walled garden at the back of the house Meredith had laid out four chairs around the metal table. Jeremy was submerged in The Falmouth Packet.

'There's been another flogging in Saudi Arabia.'

'I'm sure there'll be a backlash about that,' she replied.

Jeremy looked up. 'I often wonder if you do that deliberately.'

'Do what?'

Jeremy went back to his newspaper.

An hour later the four of them sat with biscuits, local ham and Cornish cheeses from a platter. Slim plots of new potatoes and beans grew beside the walls all the way back to Jeremy's shed and the garage behind. Meredith walked across the causeway from the upper floor with the tea. Between them and the lower floor was a sunless area of concrete accessed by steps. Lancelot the tortoise, the garden's permanent resident, happily grazed on a lettuce leaf beside them.

'We couldn't waste this fair weather, could we?' said Meredith, pouring.

'Well, lad, are you winning?' said Jeremy intently.

'Yes, I think we are,' Ros answered for him, feeling the prickles from Philip even before he opened his mouth. 'Don't you agree, Philip?'

'We know a great deal more than we did,' he said. 'South Cadbury and Tintagel were both impressive fortresses in Arthur's day. Mason is a mine of information. Nennius' account of Arthur's twelve battles, their possible sites, and characters like Guinevere-we've discussed them all vigorously.'

'Guinevere bothered me, 'said Ros. 'She's portrayed as an adulterer, probably by church sources later. But really she was a Celtic Princess, marrying for dynastic reasons. No wonder Eleanor of Aquitaine developed the concept of Courtly Love six hundred years later reputedly based on her. Like Eleanor she probably played by her own rules without any disrespect to Arthur.'

Jeremy frowned. He had rarely thought about Guinevere and was even less interested in her. As far as he was concerned she had betrayed Arthur twice, with Lancelot and plotting with Mordred, causing the collapse of Arthur's peace.

'What happened to the garden, Jeremy? It doesn't look complete,' said Philip, moving on. Whatever they admitted to knowing about Arthur Jeremy would tear to pieces just to prove his superiority. It was best to move on to other topics.

'It was bombed during the war,' Meredith said. 'Not quite a bit of Gaudi architecture, is it?' She studied the dark concrete hole with limited daylight for the downstairs windows. 'It's something about something, I suppose.'

'A direct hit to the back of this house and next door,' said Jeremy, without bothering to decipher what his wife had just said. He wriggled to a better position in the chair.

'Afterwards there was not much money to fix anything and even fewer building materials,' Meredith continued. 'So it was hastily finished to avoid compensation. A gift is a gift.'

Ros looked at the causeway and the glass conservatory that butted on to the garden wall. Jeremy's papers were across several tables, with his portable Remington typewriter out of its case in the centre. This was an extension of his and her interests: his time spent with books, hers with paintings, at opposite ends of a sprawling house. Tomato plants in pots were growing well. Two terracotta urns of white and gold daffodils looked like a Meredith touch.

§

'Look after yourselves,' said Meredith next morning. She hugged both of them before they walked up to the garage. Then she shut her eyes and held her hands in prayer. 'Take care of them Elvan, wise friend of my childhood. Thank you.'

Soon the Woody, its roof rack loaded with the rolled hang glider, was ticking over in the narrow road. Philip drove even more carefully on the corners out of Falmouth, for the wind resistance and the extra length out the back. Mason helped him carry its thirty kilo bulk across the causeway and up through the castle ruins. On the flat plateau near area E, where there was most evidence for Arthur's existence, Philip laid out the struts of his hang glider. Ros checked her two cameras, her Pentax ME and the Nikon FM, both SLR for speed and for seeing in the lens exactly what she was taking. She knew that he would not want help assembling the kite and would be in his own world of self-preparation for the flight.

Clipped into their harnesses and with their helmets snuggly fitted he spoke into the microphone. 'Can you hear me, Ros?'

'Loud and clear, maestro.'

She looked north out to sea. Her own mind needed some massaging to overcome her fear. "Suspension of disbelief" she said to herself as a mantra. Just like watching a film and stepping into the story she now took on her role, without the reality. It was difficult but after a few minutes she found that space. With cameras clipped on, side by side with Philip under the great wing of this bird, she looked again out to sea.

'This wind should make us go up rather than out and over, if that makes sense,' he said. He knew it was harder for her to contain her fear if they ran off the edge.

'It does.'

The air rolled in waves, a peak and a trough. He waited to feel the pattern. The breaker went through.

'Ready?'

'Of course.' She focused on the ground in front of her, no obstacles, and then on the horizon.

They ignored the huddled group watching, the volunteers and the tourists. Vera held the back of her hand to her mouth. Avril chewed her finger nails like piano keys. Mason scratched behind his right ear like a big St Bernard.

'RUN!'

The first step against the inertia was colossal. The second moved forward half a step. The third they were still in the trough of wind but could hear the peak coming towards them. Fourth and they had momentum, like paddling a surfboard up the wave to its breaking crest. Fifth her feet dangled while Philip made the sixth step as the wave crashed over them and they rose twenty feet.

Philip slipped into the cocoon almost instantly, manoeuvring the kite to gain height while Ros struggled. Her feet were in the sleeping bag but she could not twist into the horizontal. They were over a hundred feet above and now over the cliff but she still squirmed. Philip held the kite steady and said nothing.

'I can't get straight,' she cursed.

'You have to. Or else we have to land.'

Ros continued to twist and fight the fabric. She had no intention of giving in. All her attention was on getting level so that she did not even see the now one thousand feet of air down to the ocean.

'Got it.' She breathed, relaxed a little, held the bar with both hands, and went back to her suspension of disbelief.

'Good. Ready to bedazzle Mason?'

'Yep. Let's do it.'

Over the next hour Philip worked the thermals off the crumbling escarpments and tried to prove that he could make this machine hover. Ros took photos and guided him.

'Left a bit. Over to the tunnel. Right and back to the Causeway. '

He just did as he was asked and enjoyed the magnificent view. On these early shots they were high enough to see all of north Cornwall and most of the Devon coast. The estuarine labyrinth of the Fal River to the south seemed a nanosecond of time away. And the tinners' ways across the centre granite spine of Cornwall were easy to delineate. Rock outcrops with megalithic dolmens were markers on land and from the air. Above them was the tangle of vapour trails of planes going to Lands End and then turning left to the Continent and south; right and north, out to sea for Ireland and America. It was a glorious sunny day in winter.

'Perfect day for flying, Ros.'

'Mm. I'm not sure you should say that.'

Now they were low, completing the circuit of verticals over each trench area, the Great Ditch and the Castle ruins just beyond the Causeway.

'Time to line up C. Can you work your way down, please?'

He hovered again but watched a band of cloud coming in. The wind was still steady. They were over the second bench. Ros's Nikon clicked again.

'Third, please.'

'Click, click.'

Now he hovered over the beach and the edge of the neighbouring promontory. He was as low as he cared to go. Most of his effort went into keeping the kite steady at a point where she could line up the terraces down to the rolling breakers at sea level. But that cloud bothered him. It had bubbled up into a vast mountain: a dark ragged snout with boiling white above it; darkness in its upper levels and brilliant blue-green below. It was not good and it was coming too fast.

'Ros, we have to go. Are you finished?'

'Nearly. Just let me get this one.'

Click. Click. 'Ok'.

He pushed the bar out and then leaned left. If he was lucky he could use the front wave to push them over and out to the side of this monster. Somehow this unusual heat had created a freak storm that no one had predicted.

'Hold on!'

'To what?' she said.

She gripped the bar tighter and shut her eyes as the turbulence hit. The violence snapped her eyes open again. All around was dark cloud. They were in it and lightning flashes were all around them. They were a leaf spiralling skywards out of control.

Philip estimated that they were going up at around ten metres per second. Already it was cold. Soon they would be in danger of hypothermia and frost bite. It was all happening so quickly. Ice was beginning to form on the lead edge. Now it was harder to turn the sluggish bird. He had to get out of the vortex.

Ros had tried hard to maintain her disbelief but the mind set had broken with the ferocious swipes throwing them all over the sky. Swarms of golf ball hailstones pummelled her skin into bruises. Thank goodness for the helmets for protection. Lightning spears feet thick bounced around inside the mist and turned her vision red even when she had her eyes shut. The rain was like swimming in the ocean, so that she wanted to hold her breath to avoid drowning. She tried to fight it but she was terrified. Think woman, think, she yelled inside her head.

Philip knew her fear. He was pretty close to her thoughts inside his own skull. He leaned hard on the right side, her side, so that their combined weight would swing them into a spiral down and he hoped out of this maelstrom. But they were thrown back, again and again stuck in a lift and then reaching the floor with a thud before regaining some sort of forward motion again. Often he had to pull out when the kite was on the edge of flipping on to its back. If that happened they would fall like a rock out of the sky.

§

Mason had watched them use up their film. He ticked off the tasks as they did them. His will was with them as Ros worked to get that final shot that he had asked for. But then he saw that storm front roar in.

'Time to get out of there, kids' he said.

'Come on, guys, you've gotta move. Guys, it's not worth it. Get going. Yes, she's got it.'

He saw Philip gain height quickly and turn. But he was too late. They were sucked into it and disappeared.

This was not good. For all his bulk Mason was not a bad runner. At the front desk of the King's Hotel the desk clerk was surprised when he grabbed the phone.

'Excuse me, Sir!'

Mason's raised left palm silenced him.

'Police, please. Yes, I want to report a missing hang glider. Tintagel. Can you alert the Coastguard? They have been caught in a storm. Where do I think they will go? Good question. If they survive, with the prevailing winds, I would say they'd go south. Get your weather people to work it out. But I'd be looking on the south coast.'

§

Meredith heard the bulletin on her kitchen radio. 'Two people in a hang glider have been caught in freak weather at Tintagel today. Police hold grave concerns for their safety. Listeners should ring the police if they sight them.' Her hands stopped peeling and the spud splashed into the bowl of water.

'Jeremy. Jeremy.' She disrupted a Beethoven symphony as she shook his arm to break the news.

'Help them Elvan. They need you now,' Meredith said quietly.

'What are you mumbling about, woman?' Jeremy grumbled.

'Nothing.' She looked out of the window towards St Mawes, before returning to the kitchen.

§

This is not working, Philip thought. The spiral was more like duelling elevator stairs going up and then dropping like a stone. The fog was a chaos of blackness and illuminated shrieks of brilliance. Thunder was not sound just vast energy vibrating through every cell of his body, relentlessly. There were no reference points in the blanket of vapour. So far they had not been struck by the lightning but surely it was only a matter of time. He looked at Ros. Her eyes were shut tight and she was in pain, as he was. Think.

Then clarity of thought swept over Ros like a gentle hand stroking her brow. They could do this. Air and water, two of the four elements, and they were so alike. This was like a rip dragging them out into deep water, or in this case upwards and in towards that impossible core. If they could cross the rip to catch its partner; if they could enter a column that sucked down then they had a chance.

She shouted the plan over the helmet speaker. He knew what to do: a desperately risky procedure but what choice was there?

He held the bar with widely spaced hands and pulled in hard. They were still turning but there was forward motion. Just hold on to it. The creaking of the metal frame and the snapping of the fabric increased. If the kite didn't split the sail it would be a miracle. He held on and cursed the storm. Suddenly their bodies bounced upwards and their feet slapped the saturated fabric. Then the "leaf" was thrown towards the ground, wherever that was. Hold it, hold it, gently, gently, loose on the reins, go with it and wait. The air was heavier. He saw Ros suck in breath. The weight of the torrent of rain was pushing them down with its mass, like going over a waterfall. He had to time it right: too soon and the kite would be drawn back upwards into the storm's heart; too late and they'd be a messy statistic. There, a glimpse through breaking cloud. He pushed out hard towards what he hoped was the edge.

They were out: one moment there was black nothing, the next blue sky. Inside he had no idea of height. Now he could see the whole of Cornwall. It was beautiful.

'Ros. Ros. Open your eyes, Ros. You'll like this.'

He was surprised that the fear was not there. How could she do that? Now he watched her look around and ENJOY the view. Her smile was magical.

'Ros. We have to go down. We're too high. Are you ok?

'No problem.'

They had to be around twelve thousand feet. It was definitely still an effort to breathe. He didn't tell her that they were also close to commercial air space, seriously illegal and in danger of being hit by a plane. He spiralled down as rapidly as he could. Euphoria was there but the prevailing lower winds were pushing them towards the shipping lanes of the English Channel. With sheer determination he controlled the turns into the airstream, pulling the bar in to cut back towards the coast line.

Ros remained quiet and calm beside him. It was strange. No doubt she would tell him about it when they reached terra firma. The kite seemed airworthy still. The ice had gone from the leading edge so the device was more responsive again. With luck they would get down in one piece.

He began to look for a suitable landing site. There was no way he could fight the breeze and get back to Tintagel Island. The car could wait. Where was a good spot of dirt, in this land of creeks, cliffs and open water? Yes, that would fit the bill. He continued the corkscrew but let the winds take him across that big expanse of estuary, open water full of yachts and tankers coming up to dock.

'Ros. Are you ready?'

'Yes.'

He lost the last of the height and pushed out the bar.

'RUN.'

In fifteen steps they stopped. Philip unhooked both of them and collapsed the sail so the gusts did not drag it or them. They were in newly cropped pasture above St Mawes on Roseland. He proceeded to pack up the kite as well as he could without the cover that was still in the Woody at Tintagel car park.

'Are you ok, Ros?' One of her phrases, "like a stunned mullet", seemed to apply to her. But she was not hurt or visibly cold. It would be nice to see her a bit more communicative though.

'Yes, it's all good. How about we leave the kite here and walk down to the village?' She pointed towards a thatched stone two storey house towards the blue expanse of Carrick Roads.

'Alright.'

She was in one of those moods. Instead of questioning he held her hand as they walked down the rows of stubble. They smelt the sweet wood smoke rising from the chimney.

'Ee mus' be dem glider people ont' radio. Cummiz in, me 'ansomes.' The tall stooped man with wispy white hair combed across his head and National Health glasses led them into his kitchen. He put three spoons of tea into the pot, lifted the bubbling kettle from the wood Aga and poured.

'Sit eez down, me luvvas.' The well-used table and open backed chairs had been scrubbed for generations. After liberal quantities of white sugar and milk three cups made new rings on the wood.

'Thanks,' they said in unison.

It was not her choice of brew but it was nectar of the gods that they'd been too close to, as she sipped its life-giving properties.

'Would you mind if I made two telephone calls?' Philip asked. 'People will be worried.'

'Do'az ee likes, fella. Foniz 'ere.' Philip rotated the circular dial of the black Bakelite telephone for each number. He left a message with the King's Hotel to pass on to Mason.

'You're alive and not dead,' Meredith gushed over the crackly line. But then she politely thanked him for thinking of them. Philip tried to leave change to cover the calls but their host would have none of it.

'Sorry I didn't introduce us before. I'm Philip Trevasco and this is Rosalind Bernaud.' The handshake was firm for him and gentle for Ros.

'Isaac Bolitho.' His milky blue eyes smiled behind the thick lenses. 'Sit eez down ag'n n tellum 'bout things.'

Philip told him the story, with interruptions of 'Don' say?' and 'Gospel truth?' It was clear that the field they'd landed in was his. Philip was worried about Ros. She'd said nothing, just looked around the room and smiled when expected to.

'Can we leave the kite in your meadow until tomorrow?'

'Contrapshun's safe w' me.'

They walked out into his garden: there were potatoes and beans in careful rows in one section and half a dozen varieties of daffodils growing out of the lawn on the other side of the carefully-pointed, stone house. Leafless ancient trees sprouted from the stone hedgerow and the overgrown hill behind.

As they ambled down the lane they waved again to Isaac, who stood motionless supporting himself on the garden gate.

Ros led them into the village of St Just. In the lushly vegetated lane she was drawn to the Lych gate of its church. Once through they walked down the path through the hillside cemetery overlooking the picturesque tidal creek. Palms and elephant-leaved shrubs grew in profusion in this sub-tropical paradise. Inside the 13th century church vestibule Philip read the list of rectors going back to medieval times, and the un-named back to 550AD.

It felt right to light candles for Jeremy. Then Philip followed her outside to a seat overlooking the inlet. He sat beside Ros and waited for her to talk.

'It's so peaceful,' she said.

Half an hour later she was still sitting and he was looking at his watch. It was time to think of catching the ferry.

'We should move, Ros.' Her colour was better now. She appeared to have recovered her equilibrium.

'Do we have to?' She paused. 'Ok, let's go.'

They followed the public path out of the village into woods and on to grassy fields just above the water. They climbed up and over stiles between pasture separated by ancient stone walls lined with thorns and shrubbery. In the open meadows the sun was glorious, bright but with the chill of winter.

'Did you see the boy?' she said. They had passed Henry VIII's castle and were walking along the harbour front in sight of the pier.

'No.'

'He walked with us to the cottage and the church.' She looked at him earnestly. 'He was sitting beside us on the bench.'

'No. Sorry. What was he like?' This part of her character worried him.

'Oh, friendly. He's gone now.'

Almost like the shutter on one of her cameras her mood changed: click. 'No matter. Race you to the ferry.'

Sitting together on an outside seat on the boat he asked. 'Do you care to tell me what that was all about?'

She looked at him. 'Not yet. But it's all good.'

§

Back in the kitchen Meredith squeezed both of them "until the pips squeaked".

'Thanks Elvan,' she said inside her head.

The meal was cod and chips followed by tapioca pudding, 'frog spawn' as Philip remembered it as a child.

'Good to see you both,' Jeremy said. 'The quest shouldn't cost more lives; it's taken enough already over the centuries.'

He must be feeling a bit better, Philip thought. Was he thinking of Nazis or Arthur's knights?

It was an early night.

'You'll be snug as two bugs in a rug with these,' Meredith said as she handed them a hot water bottle each. The newsreader from the BBC's "Nine O'clock News" spoke loudly to Jeremy in the lounge.

'Thanks, lover,' Ros said to Philip with a kiss, before falling asleep instantly. He lay for a while before the day's energies subsided and he joined her. Both stirred for no reason. The lovemaking was gentle, quiet and slow before a deep sleep overcame them.

CHAPTER 6

Winds lashed the shuttered window spaces of the Great Hall at Camelot. On the ramparts guards studied the firelights of the villagers below. Looking into the distance their eyes searched the hills north-west towards the water and the Cymbrogi, south-east towards the Saxons. No beacon fires disturbed their watch. Inside the Great Hall I watched Arthur and Merlin move the ivory warriors to positions on the board. Arthur was moody and restless. Sometimes he startled and looked at others in the room, irritated by their laughter. Then it would take time for his mind to return to the game. He reminded me of a visit to Uther a long time ago. As before Merlin held back his skill and rested Arthur's mind as best he could.

Since Colgren and his men had been dispatched young warriors had flocked to him. Every Brythonic prince wanted a family member at his court. Yet the lords were still as disruptive and untrustworthy as ever, squabbling amongst themselves and resisting Arthur's requests for levies to maintain the fragile peace.

Next morning Arthur paced the battlements. Whenever he stopped he watched the younger knights practicing their weapons training. They had graduated from wooden swords against the pell, the wooden post painted as the enemy. Now they used real swords blunted at the point and sides against each other.

Amongst their number were Gawain, Agravain, Gaharis, Gareth and Mordred, sons of Arthur's sister Morgana and husband Lot, king of Gododdin in the north. Gawain and Gareth were strong and fearless, mighty additions to his teulu, but Mordred had something more, a spark of brilliance in his sword play that Arthur had never seen before. He walked again. Anguish was never far away. Arthur and Guinevere had conceived three more children but all had died within a week of birth. There was no son to carry his line, to give some permanence to his dream of a strong Brython land free from invaders.

'Well done, Mordred.' His opponent had been dispatched by a downward cut to the upper thigh. If not for the flat of the steel, death would have been the result, not a livid bruise that would take days to heal. Arthur studied the features of this dark-skinned youth, lean and strong, with eyes that absorbed more than the ordinary. Arthur donned the padded tunic, gloves and head garb to match his opponent.

Mordred bowed in respect. He imagined Arthur had looked like him, a bit taller and more muscular but essentially the same, before war and rule had aged him prematurely. The "Bear" was still a formidable opponent, as he watched him select a blade from the rack.

'Are you prepared, Sir Mordred?'

'Of course, my lord.'

Arthur stood and waited for the first blow. His sword rested in his right hand, point to the ground. First he watched the quandary in Mordred's eyes, the hesitation in his body language. To attack his leader, even in invited practice, was a barrier. But Arthur remained motionless: let Mordred work out his tactic. Then Arthur saw Mordred's demeanour change. It was a rare opponent who did not give a second's warning.

Mordred rushed forward raising his sword. Arthur lifted his to parry high, but then lowered it as Mordred turned the strike into a side blow to Arthur's left thigh. The metal sparked and Arthur took a step to his right to guide the force away from his limb.

Without giving a moment Arthur continued the spin and brought his sword down in an arc towards Mordred's back leg. But his opponent was ready and parried it by thrusting into the ground to block the blow. They now faced each other as before but on opposite sides.

'Again, well done.'

For the next minutes they lunged, parried and twisted to avoid each other's blows. Mordred was surprised that Arthur showed no signs of tiring. Then Arthur aimed an obvious blow, Mordred stepping forward to block, before Arthur advanced another step and tripped his adversary. Mordred was on the ground with Arthur's sword point resting on his heart.

'There are no rules on the battlefield, nephew,' Arthur said as Mordred stood to face him again.

For a second time Arthur watched the emotions: from anguish to resolve but with too much anger.

This time Mordred came like a whirlwind of cutting and slashing sweeps of his weapon. As Arthur avoided and obstructed, his circling opponent stepped in to feint a heel kick driven into Arthur's leg. Instead he slammed his shoulder in and Arthur cart-wheeled onto his back. But before Mordred's sword could connect Arthur scissored Mordred's legs from under him.

Both stood, breathing hard, eyes locked on the other's first move. Mordred struck out first, followed by a downward slice to the head and shoulders. It's a move he favours, Arthur thought, as he held the pommel and blade of his own sword and blocked, the sound echoing across the courtyard. Then he punched the pommel hard into Mordred's face. Blood trickled from the younger man's lips.

Arthur stepped back. 'Well fought, man. But channel that anger into strength not weakness.'

Mordred bowed. But Arthur glimpsed something deeper than rage in his eyes.

§

Guinevere sat enthralled by the music of the latest bard to grace Camelot. Her childhood with Cador was rich in such events. Arthur listened to the ballad of the brave knight facing impossible odds to rescue his lady. She had not noticed his entrance until some of the younger knights rose in respect. Then there was a cursory nod from her to acknowledge his disturbance.

He sat and watched faces. It seemed that many of them watched his wife more than the entertainment. Yes, Guinevere would try for another son for him before daybreak. Then he would head north against Caw, another northern chieftain who chafed at Arthur's leadership. Guinevere was always strong and independent, a princess of an ancient Brythonic line. Arthur might be her husband but he had no ownership of her heart.

§

Arthur and his knights slogged through intermittent rain along the familiar route, the Fosse Way. Roadside camps were rewarded with rowdy welcome from Gurgust in Lindum and others along Ermine Street to Eboracum. But then they crossed the Vallum Hadrianum into the wild forested land between the walls. Gurgust had told him that Caw and his renegades were beyond the Vallum Antoninum, travelling down the River Bassas to form up with Pictish tribes coming from the north. This whole countryside was seething against any form of collective resistance to the real enemies: the Angles, Irish, Jutes and most of all the Saxons. It seemed that the pillage and slaughter of one's neighbour was the only heroic, even honourable, way to live.

Arthur had moved quickly on the intelligence. Surprise, and his men's trust in his ability, would be powerful weapons. Arthur's scouts had watched Caw's progress down the river. In two days he would leave the narrow defiles and gorges of the waterway and enter rich farmland.

Caw came out of the forest. Ahead of him was Arthur with forty of his knights in a single line. Arthur stroked the head of Tsarati perched on his arm. His mind was inside the bird's, surveying the scene from a great detached height. Arthur had prepared everything possible and now accepted the will of the gods of battle.

Caw's rabble stopped to allow the stragglers to catch up. The leader and his companions were in discussion. Figures moved like ants as Tsarati and Arthur absorbed the landscape: the round hills to left and right, Gurgust's militia hidden in the valley to block any retreat. He and the bird waited. Surely Caw would form his men into something resembling a battle front? No, his arrogance knew no bounds. The air filled with gruesome yells and screams as Caw's army raced forward.

'Fly high, Tsarati,' Arthur said as he thrust the bird skywards. At this signal the line of horseman trotted forward in perfect rhythm. They were intensely alive in the face of imminent death. The hawk's flight was seen by the troops led by Gareth and Mordred, and by Gurgust's infantry.

Arthur remembered his training in Brittany, by the Sarmatian warriors who had served as Cataphracti, heavily-armoured cavalry, for Rome itself. Now the pace quickened and their twelve feet lances lowered in perfect unison. He hoped that Gareth and Mordred's men were just beginning the same. Their delay would mean that Arthur's impact hid their arrival until it was too late. Gareth was given the delicate task of leaving a narrow channel of escape, out into the open pasture where the slaughter would be easier than against men cornered and fighting to the death. Mordred would have to earn that trust.

The charge was clinical, incisive. Arthur's men speared men like chickens on sticks and broke through to the other side. At which point Gareth and Mordred appeared from left and right and did the same, so that the enemy were quartered. It was then that Gareth held back on his turn and made his way to block the valley behind. Mordred's men showed no inclination to stop the slaughter. Men released that maddened demon inside themselves. Their eyes gleamed with eagerness. Soon the escape became a rout as bleeding men littered the plain for the ravens to feast on. The sweet smell of death rose over the battlefield. Caw surrendered and grovelled for his life. He spent the rest of his days in Gwynedd, at Twrcelyn on an island of the Druids. Even in this faraway place our faith was triumphant as Caw helped Cadog in his Christian ministry.

That evening around the camp fires Arthur accepted the allegiance of the few brave survivors who were willing to fight for him. They would be tested soon enough. Merlin and I had saved so few casualties of the slaughter. It was as though in the minds of Caw's fighters defeat was death. What hope did we have of saving those who did not wish to live? Already the scavengers stepped lightly between the bodies robbing what they could. Their knives amputated ring fingers and levered teeth from rigid gums.

Inside the great circle of horses Arthur, his horsemen and Gurgust, sat and shared food. Caw had been surprisingly well supplied.

'Gurgust, it's your turn to draw blood.'

'Good. We are not happy spectators.' His lean, battle-hardened body looked down like a vulture on those around him. Arthur saw lusty delight in his eyes.

The Picts were moving through the Coed Celyddon, the "Caledonian Forest". Soon they would leave the mountain lands and enter the miles of marsh that fed the wide waters of the Werid Estuary, known to the Romans as the Boderia River, in the east of Gododdin lands. Forest and swamp were dangerous places for horses.

The first task of Caw's men was to act as guides along the narrow paths through the bog. Only as light was fading did they leave that treacherous place. But the tribal warriors were close. Arthur had to reach the cover of woodland before dawn. Men were near asleep and horses followed those in front. They progressed by sound in the darkness until a storm broke and filled the sky with brilliant light.

In a narrow pass through gently rising wooded slopes young and old Pictish warriors trotted in their continuous run that rivalled the native deer. Veterans were quiet as novices wasted breath on wild tales of what they had done and were about to do. The talk was of plunder that they would take home to wives and sweethearts to supplement the meagre offerings of their upland farms.

Then Mordred's troop screamed and their horns blared into the bitter cold of dawn. In the charge their lances picked off those at the front. Those behind them ran into their comrades' bodies and became the next. In seconds the veterans got off the path that had become a killing field. They fled in disorder in amongst the trees and up the slopes. But Gurgust's howl matched Mordred's as his men leaped down from high ground and ambushed individual men from behind trees. It was not a battle but hand to hand combat on a vast scale. Men screeched through bared teeth as they looked for that weakness in the man they must kill. Some warriors fled back up the path towards home but there they were met by Arthur' force. The butchery went on through the morning. Mordred delighted in it but many more than Arthur were sickened by the slaughter of these spirited poor men from the hills. He judged Mordred to be a brave warrior who knew no limits.

§

Guinevere looked resplendent in a blue Roman dress with golden belt and diadem. His battle colours never shone so brightly, she on Arthur's arm, as they welcomed the Cornish princes to Tintagel courtyard in the sunlight. Surely now, Arthur thought, these men would accept his leadership. Pictish loot adorned many in their courts. Arthur's peace swelled their coffers. It was months since Cerdric and his Saxon pirates had threatened their shores.

Only the day before I stood nearby as Arthur welcomed representatives from the tinners. They had been diligent in maintaining the beacon fire warning system that stretched across Cornubia and most of Dumnonia. It was they who had funded the refurbishment of Kelliwic for Arthur's private residence, but in truth it was to keep him closer to their mines that sourced their wealth.

Each of the nine princes from the lands of Cornubia, Defnas and Gwlad-yr-haf, which formed Dumnonia, were welcomed equally, however great or small was their entourage. In the Great Hall the round table grew to a circle of tables forming the whole. Arthur would give no one primacy or any excuse for squabbling. Against a common enemy all Brythonic lords were alike if they contributed to the peace. Amongst them was his old friend Tewdric, once a Visigoth admiral but now a substantial landowner around Heyl in western Cornubia. Older and more ample, his loyalty was least in question of all who were present. Only Arthur's uncle, Mark, King of Cornubia was not there. The bitterness of his childhood friend still rankled but it was beyond his help. Mark's brigandage was legendary. But as War Leader Arthur had no choice but to bow to Mark's superior title as King. This "Hound of the Sea" resisted sending any military aid to Arthur in keeping the peace; all except Tristan who Arthur respected as one of his bravest knights.

'Princes and lords of Dumnonia, our presence here show that unity is possible against a common enemy. You have seen the results of our labour. But our task is incomplete. Gododdin and Elmet in the north are still threatened by Jutes and Picts, as is Gwynedd and Powys by the

Irish. Greatest of the challenges we face are the Saxons. We have all been touched by the Saxon Terror.'

He waited for his words to work.

'As your War Leader I say that we must commit our hearts and our men whatever the cost. There is no easy solution. Beacons warn us of raiders.' He looked at representatives of the tinners. 'Tewdric's fleet encircles our coasts.' Tewdric raised a glass. 'My knights range Brythonic lands from south to north. With vigilance we will win.'

As Arthur sat down Merlin quietly joined him. The timing was perfect. Arthur rose again.

'My Lords, Cerdic's fleet of Saxon raiders has landed at Genvor Cove where land ends at Caer Guidn. Even now he is slaughtering the defenceless in the villages all around. Let us prove our united resolve against an implacable foe.'

Arthur's knights were first to be ready but the teulu of each lord present was close behind. Before they filed out over the causeway Arthur spoke to Tewdric.

'We have done this before, my friend. Let the sea meet the land.'

As two bears they clasped each other's shoulders.

'God speed,' they said to each other.

§

In two days the earth and ocean did meet. As small groups of pirates marched back to their ships with loot they were struck dumb by a cacophony of carnyx, each of the princes with a distinctive note. Soon they were run down by Arthur's lancers. The lords vied with each other in numbers of enemy killed, in the proof of loyalty in an easy task and for plunder. The enemy ships were beached in the secluded cove separated from a stretch of broad white sand by Trevedra cliff. Below it Tewdric's fleet appeared in the protected water to prevent escape. The survivors were trapped. With no escape they fought with bravery in what they knew to be their last fight. But steadily they were backed into the cliff. The ring of cavalry inexorably tightened the noose towards the void. Some were hacked down from horseback, others fared little better in hand to hand combat and many lost their footing off the cliff edge. They joined their ancestors with hideous cries in the air. The slaughter was near complete, but for Cerdic who escaped the impossible snare.

First those princes who were Christians gave thanks in the little stone chapel above Sennen beach. Arthur was among them. His battle standard of the red dragon had been aided by the Virgin Mary's image on his shield. Then there was feasting at the giants' stone of Lanyon Quoit. Arthur was vindicated in his resolve to gain peace in Brythonic lands. Maybe that was why he tried to change the rules of war. He ordered that the booty be returned to the villagers. He argued that these people were all Brythons like themselves. The lords only saw that their traditional right to plunder had been thwarted.

§

In what seemed weeks Tewdric asked for Arthur's help. Fingar, son of Irish king Clyto, was unwise enough to lead seven hundred warriors to attack Heyl, Tewdric's heartland. His Visigoth families had not fought for a generation but they had lost none of their ferocity. The Irish were not only driven back to their fleet but were chased across the Afon Hafren water, known as the Sabrina River in Roman times, to Demetia. There Tewdric placed his loyal ally, Aircol Longhand, on the throne.

But Fingar regrouped in Caerleon, once the city of Roman legions. Arthur's horses and riders were transported by the fleet across the water. Survivors of Fingar's sack of their city described the defences and where they were weak. This was no longer a fortress of impregnable Roman walls. It was a scatter of dwellings along the bow of the river beside a city of ruins.

Water and land ruled again. In the darkness Tewdric's four ships drifted gently under sail along the meandering river. It was difficult catching the delicate breezes at night, even with their guides' help. Silence was of the essence in the moonless gloom. One ship grounded on a sand bank. Its men paused for the others to anchor beside the docks on the river front. The stranded captain then slipped into the water and stood waist deep. They were close enough to wade through the shallows when the time came.

Arthur's knights waited a mile away in a forest glade. At his 'hoo, hoo' cry of a male Tawny Owl his men stepped their mounts forward, their hooves wrapped in coarse linen tied around the hocks. When he gave the short 'kewick' of reply from the female the troop stopped within smells of smouldering hearths and human waste. At the agreed time just before dawn's light Tewdric's men lit torches, gave their battle cries and raced into the city boundaries. Their guides made their routes easy. As the commotion reached its pitch Arthur's knights came down each street and lane from the land side in ones and twos and cut down Fingar and his men like wheat. By daylight the annihilation was complete.

Tewdric's forces stepped into the weakness that was Gwent. On his return Arthur gave Glywysing, the western portion of Gwent, to Tewdric. A strong ally across the water was vital in maintaining the defensive wall around Cornubia and Dumnonia.

§

On a rare, warm autumn day Arthur, Merlin and I sat in the upland meadows outside the twin ramparts of Kelliwic, his fortress on the road to Rhos, not so far from Tintagel. Despite its low altitude the views were broad: to the north over the wide estuary of Dowr Kammel, the "Crooked River"; to the south-west over the rolling grassland named after St Breoch; and to the east the far-reaching moor of Goon Brenn, from whence the Saxons might invade. It was unusual too because Arthur was not in the saddle. While the music from Guinevere's latest entertainment within drifted on the breeze Arthur was content to listen to our debate.

'The spiritual world is integrated with the real world,' I said.

'There we agree, Justin. There is no boundary between the world of magic and that of the mundane,' replied Merlin.

'My meaning was that God is in all that we see around us. It is here to test our worthiness for what comes after.'

'Well, there's a fault. Does your god create the catastrophes that befall innocents just to challenge their faith? If so he cannot be good or he cannot be all powerful.'

'Who are we to understand the ways of our Lord? I just trust, and give succour and comfort to those hurt by life's misfortunes, so many of which are created by people.'

'That is a weak argument. The ancient Greeks did not trust their gods because they acted like jealous children. At least disaster had a source: capricious deities. But yes, grasping princes and heartless warriors cause needless misery.'

'And suffering,' Merlin continued. 'What a strange idea is your death of Jesus. Why does a god need to die such a demeaning, poor man's death?'

'God's son died for our sins to show us the way to our salvation. His death and rebirth give hope to the least amongst us that they can reach heaven by living a good life.'

Arthur smiled and said nothing. Merlin was more skilled in debate than I was but he appeared to find some comfort in my words. Within the pause he drifted with the harsh screech of the Chough calling its mate amongst the rocks. Merlin had given him a great love for the land. As a Druid, a "treeknower", Merlin seemed to know all its secrets.

We observed the birds groom the feathers of their black coat with their curved orange beaks. Then they went back to extricating worms from the rocky soil. Merlin and I watched Arthur lose himself in these simple acts of Nature.

'Justin, I still find some of your beliefs strange, but you are a good man. Your faith will move mountains,' Arthur spoke from his distraction. At Caer Guidn he had carried the Virgin image on his shield. Maybe it was at this point that he was convinced that our way was the future for his people?

§

Merlin and I helped Arthur to fight the Warrior's Curse but I believe children aided in his diversion. When Gododdin was threatened Lot sent down his grandchildren for safety. Arthur led a happy band as he repeated his boyhood rambles through Cornubia, discovering birds, plants, and all that Nature taught. Merlin entertained them with slights of hand where doves and lizards disappeared and then returned.

Around the evening fire he recounted stories of ancient lore. But many times Arthur came with me to help the tinners. Just his presence seemed to give them the hope to get well. Children reminded him of much that he had never known in his boyhood. But there were occasions when a young life was lost to a simple infection or childish ailment. For one boy Merlin and I laboured for many hours, still without success.

'Nature is a barbarian,' Arthur said. In his eyes were memories of his own children, all stillborn. Merlin's eyes glistened. I struggled too.

§

In the late afternoon a familiar figure entered the courtyard. His massive form hid hard muscles under age and grey. Arthur greeted him as a brother. After food and ample wine for him and his retinue, the two walked outside again to catch the warm air on the intermittent, gentle breeze.

'You're always welcome, Tewdric, but I know that something brings you here.'

Merlin and I walked a distance behind, close enough for me to follow the language of their bodies, and Merlin with his powers to ascertain their minds. For Arthur's sanity was our ultimate task.

The admiral placed his goblet on the ground and carefully positioned his bulk on a rock. He read Arthur's face and laughed.

'Yes, I am weary and I am old. Every cut speaks to me now.'

Arthur sat opposite and leaned forward with his arms upon his knees. His own body had equal voices. Yet in the heat of battle he rarely felt any pain.

'How do you sleep, Artorius?' Tewdric's grey eyes held Arthur's gaze. He read him without any need of Merlin's gift.

'How do you close your eyes without seeing every face you cut down on the battlefield?' he asked more gently.

Arthur stayed silent: there was no need of reply. He thought back to his father, Uther, drunk as the dead each night to gain release. Then he studied the goblet of wine in his hand.

As we dozed, the two warriors recounted stories of great deeds. They laughed about how fortune played tricks with the best of their plans. Scars on arms and legs were badges of glory, and proof of how close they had come to the next existence.

'Did you ever wish for a different life, Tewdric?'

'I never did, until now. I am tired, my friend.'

Arthur looked at his feet. 'Like you I saw my task: the tinners and the ordinary people whom I could defend.' He looked up and into Tewdric's eyes. 'But there are times when I would escape my destiny, if I could.'

Tewdric had never heard Arthur show doubt. He was mortal like the rest of us. 'There is no other to take your place, Artorius.' He leaned forward and placed his misshapen hand on Arthur's arm. 'You cannot escape your destiny any more than your father could.'

Tewdric had had enough of war. He and I conversed many times after that day. Eventually his son Meurig took the kingdom and Tewdric joined our calling. For a time he was a hermit, content to explore the intricacies of faith. But then his son asked for help. Arthur felt grief and pride when he heard that Tewdric had died in battle, victorious against a Saxon war party.

§

On the first day of spring Arthur and his knights travelled north again at the request of Lot, King of Gododdon. The journey was familiar but hard: days of sleet, and rain that hissed in rivers down tree trunks and overflowed the stone drains of the old military roads; nights wrapped in cloaks that creaked in hoar frost by morning. Only the sounds of birds and shadowy comrades in the darkness gave comfort. After ten days they entered the Brythonic kingdom of Teyrnas Ystrad Clut. Emissaries of Beli, its king, escorted them into the fortified compound amidst rich farmland beside the River Clut itself. Out of the water rose the twin peaks of Dun Breatann, the "Fortress of the Brythons", their refuge against the Picts.

'Your name precedes you, Artorius, Dux Bellorum. You are welcome,' said King Beli. After lavish hospitality had been shown to his band Arthur explained his business in this northern kingdom.

'My brother-in-law, King Lot of Goddodin, has a hive of bandits, the Cynbin or "dog heads" led by Garwlwyd, "rough grey", on the western edge of his kingdom. They prey on travellers and villagers alike.'

'I know them. They have made an impregnable fortress at Tryfrwyd, the crossing at the Fords of Frew, in the labyrinthine marshes. They raid our territory too.'

'Lot's troops on the high crag of Striveling look over the serpentine twists of the Werid River. They are besieged more often than not. Trade with the high lands of the north is strangled,' said Arthur. The king was not surprised.

Next day Beli's men were willing guides along the pathways around the southern edges of the wet lands and to the mighty stone plug on which Striveling fortress was built.

In the courtyard King Lot greeted his sons Gawain, Agravain, Gaheris, Gareth, and Mordred. As Knights of the Round Table they had grown into independent, hard warriors, men he could be proud of. In the Great Hall of the stronghold Lot and his closest comrades explained the problem. Arthur studied a parchment map inscribed on cow-hide.

'Who knows the marshes and moss lands well?'

Alan, Caelan and Darragh were brought before him. Their ankle-length shirts of hempen linen tied at the waist said that they were poor men. But he was told that sheep and cattle grazing on the lush meadows gave them butter and cheese, and their tiny fields produced grains for themselves and their stock. The marshlands gave them peat for fuel. From their weathered complexion it was clear that they were fishermen and hunters. Their lives were richer than many, Arthur thought.

'Is it true that the moss lands are impassable?'

The three men looked at each other.

'Not to those who know, my lord,' said Alan.

'Could you and your companions guide horsemen through to Garwlwyd's camp?'

All three seemed petrified.

'Come, man, surely you want rid of the Cynbin?'

'We have no love of such company, 'said Darragh, the bravest of the three.

Arthur looked at Caelan. He recognised the set of his shoulders and down-turned eyes.

'You have lost family to them,' Arthur said to him. 'Look at me!'

Caelan looked directly into Arthur's eyes and held his gaze. This was a man who had loved. His empty soul had nothing to lose.

'Will you help us clean out these vermin, Caelan?'

'Aye, my lord.' He looked at his companions. 'You will have no shortage of willing guides.'

Arthur marvelled at the vast expanse of water and gently domed rounds of peat appearing through the early morning mist. Their guides were following tracks along the river banks where the moss grew least. Arthur's forces were split between himself and Lot's sons, each weaving a careful path through the wet pasturelands, bog and reedy mire. Arthur absorbed the swirling colours of the sphagnum moss and the lizards and snakes that darted across it. Despite his troop's silent progress marsh birds, Snipe and Stonechat, flew startled into the air. Then they slowly circled back to their nests once the men had parted. The horses were shod with sandals made of plaited straw tied around the ankles. Prepared thus their progress was made quieter and more secure on the squelching ground. Still the peat quaked beneath the horses' feet. On the myriad streams Caelan and his people pushed flat-bottomed punts filled with dry straw, moss and peat. The sun tried to cut through sodden cloud as Lot's infantry were led along other paths, so that all would meet at the small island of solid ground at the centre.

Arthur paused with his cornu in hand. His mind was with Tsarati, just for a moment. A strange peace filled his mind, a clear vision that this deed was good. He blew hard and long. The snap of bow strings and roar of fire arrows through the air was comforting as the plan rolled out in precise order. It had begun and there was no regret. In seconds he heard the crackle of fire and smelled the acrid fumes. As more smoke rolled in from the burning punts he waited like the rest, in a great ring encircling the "dogs" of Garwlwyd's encampment.

Soon groups of armed men rushed out of the mirk with their swords held high screeching bloody threats. Kay and Bedivere were the first of the knights to face them, for this was not battle between massed, ordered ranks of men. It was skirmish and slaughter on a personal scale; so that many knights earned glory on that day. But none slew so many as Kay, who hewed highways as he rode furiously through them. Those that Bedivere cut down were countless too so that it seemed hundreds, until he faced Garwlwyd himself. He was a short wiry man dressed in wolf skins. As Bedivere galloped at him Garwlwyd side stepped and received a glancing blow. The horseman cut and thrust but was always thwarted by his enemy's nimble avoidance at the last moment. So that Garwlwyd escaped into the smouldering huts and Bedivere was again drawn back into the conflict. By the end of the day the slaughter was near total. As so often happens, thought Arthur when he learnt of it, Garwlwyd was murdered by one of his henchmen, Diffydell mab Dysgyfdawd. A leader who could no longer provide plunder had no further use.

§

Amidst the celebrations in the Great Hall of Striveling a messenger entered. His clothes were saturated and coated in mud from his wild ride during this night of foul weather.

'My lord, Din Eidyn is besieged. Edlfled has landed with ships of Angle warriors on the southern shore of the river. His forces have slaughtered all before them so that they are now camped on the Hill of Agned.'

Arthur leaned towards his brother-in-law.

'It seems our services are still necessary, brother Lot.'

Leaving a skeleton strength in the fortress of Striveling, the main force marched and rode the forty miles east to Lot's fortress on the mighty crag of Din Eidyn. It was a long day through rich, rolling farmland enveloped in the mist and rain that rarely left this country. Arthur's cavalry settled into quarters late afternoon and the infantry arrived weary and footsore in the evening. Guards were set and the army rested for whatever the new day would bring.

In the early morning, as sea mist rolled in from the broad Werid Estuary, Arthur looked north from the battlement and wiped the dampness from his face. It was not hard to imagine what the inhabitants of Din Eidyn had seen and heard. Out of the north east the sails of the Angle fleet had cut through the floating cloud. As the alarm was raised guards had watched the landing at the port and the inevitable pillage, burning and distant screams. In a short time the pirate band's route would be marked by destruction and fire along the three miles to the castle walls.

But then the mayhem paused. What had stopped their rampage? The Angles and their leader, Edlfled, must have spied the vertical wall of rock that Arthur stood on. Better to make a safe camp on Agned Hill than face Din Eidyn without Garwlwyd's reinforcements. Arthur did not believe in coincidence in the realms of war.

As before Arthur and Lot studied the nature of the ground. Agned was a mighty mound a mile down the razorback ridge leading north from the sheer volcanic plug of Lot's fortress. Agned's western side was a high barrier of rocky crag, impenetrable to horse or man. But above it was a flat plain of coarse grassland with the pinnacle above on the eastern side. If the Angles could be dislodged from that mountain top then Arthur's horsemen could display their prowess.

Arthur called a meeting of his knights and Lot's best men. In the great forecourt just inside the gate warriors stood in a silent circle. They all knew that this was Arthur's way, that no man should show precedence over another, least of all Arthur himself. In the crowd Merlin and I stood behind Arthur. He did not say so but we knew he drew comfort from our presence. In the loneliness of command we were constant nurture to his soul.

Arthur sought plans to dislodge Edlfled from his soaring eyrie. A rush of men up that slope was too costly; a night attack was unlikely to surprise. The men of war slid into silence

'Caer Guidn!' I said to Merlin.

Arthur heard. 'Well, you two? What is your proposal?'

I stammered and looked to Merlin, who now stepped forward.

'Arthur defeated Cerdic and his Saxon raiders at Caer Guidn.'

I murmured agreement and Merlin looked at me. 'The cliff, but in reverse,' I said.

Merlin repeated my words slowly, frowning until he surmised my thoughts. Most in the crowd wondered how a priest could devise a war strategy. As did I when in a quiet time alone I realised that I had contributed to the deaths of men. Was this "Ius Bellum","Just War", that my father had spoken of? My soul was now entwined with Arthur's whatever my wishes.

§

Rested and confident Lot's troops marched down the ridge a way and then turned east up the lower slopes of Agned. Edlfled and his pirates watched them from the peak. The daily sacrifice of a Brythonic boy and girl was over. Their carcasses littered the ground below the crown along with the rest. By mid-morning the Angles saw the Brythonic militia formed on the grasslands leading gently upwards to the vertical drop of crag behind. Kay and Bedivere were masters of small forces of cavalry on the wings. Lot's sons stood with their father in the middle of his infantry.

§

'How do you judge, wife Beonwyn?' said Edlfled. His lofty perch encompassed a view north over the river and his moored craft, west and east over rolling rich grain fields that his men coveted for themselves, and south-east to the fortress of Din Eidyn. Below were the ranks of Lot's infantry and two paltry bands of cavalry.

Beonwyn was tall, more man than woman with her muscular arms and breasts flattened by a chest plate. As was Leofwen, their daughter, leaner and more lithe; both made more formidable with tattooed monsters on arms, face and near-shaved head.

'It is a trap, husband. They are bait to draw us.'

Her words did not please him. He looked at his closest companions, eager for the fight to begin.

'Wait a while, father. Test them,' Leofwen spoke.

Now he was being held back by womenfolk, even if his own. It was clear to Edlfled that there was no escape for the enemy when his mighty shieldwall marched against this puny Gododdin force. The carnyx blew a deep long note, as though cutting through fog, and the Angle infantry, men and equally fierce women, marched in confident formation down from their refuge to line up in front of Lot's men.

§

Before the din of battle cries and taunts flew across the divide between the two lines Arthur began the steady ride up the valley from the eastern side. His instructions were understood by all: stay silent and out of sight within the forested upland for as long as possible. Timing was everything. Edlfled would have left sentinels on the peak. As long as Arthur's horsemen stayed in the lee shadow of the hill they were invisible.

The pace was slow, unlaboured, to save the horses' wind for that final dash. The sturdy thirteen hand stallions carried fourteen stones or more of man and chainmail. Brythonic bred in well-watered grasslands the animals' strength and hardiness had been tested many times before. Arthur and Hoengroen's senses were acute to the nuances of sound above the valley.

The noise changed. The two battle lines were advancing and soon the crash of shields was clear. Arthur was well beyond half way up the valley. Now he must test the mettle of their steeds. He looked across at the stern, excited faces of his companions, their eyes fevered with exhilaration of the ultimate test to come. Horns warned from the peak but they were drowned out by the clash of steel below.

On the plain the two sides were one slashing, shouting maelstrom of iron and bleeding flesh. Kay and Bedivere harried from the edges, driving in and then retreating, causing most damage and alarm without being swamped by superior numbers. Their horsemanship was magnificent, lances impaling one then a second and even a third before wheeling away before a new attack.

Lot's men knew there was no retreat. Their elation at the annihilation of the Cynbin now turned to grim resolve to defend their king or die in the attempt. Their morale was high, their fighting superb but the Angles steadily pushed them back, closer and closer to that awful drop.

The ride for Arthur's troop was hard and the horses' breathing changed. Their mouths were wide open and their eyes stared. But stamina was what every sinew was trained for. As they cleared the rise and entered the plain they were in their second wind. Rider and mount were equally keen to butcher in defence of their comrades. The Angles' focus was on driving Lot's men up and over into the abyss. They heard nothing above the din until a disciplined line of lances hit their back in perfect formation. Horses bit and stomped the crumpled lines of infantry until their momentum slowed. Now each knight hacked and sliced into backs and then fronts of startled warriors. Men ran back in panic, singly and in small groups until the line split down the centre. Arthur and his men carved a path right through to Lot, who battled fiercely within the tight knot of men around him. The king and his teulu were just six horse lengths from the cliff.

Now Kay and Bedivere's troops cut in again from the sides, screaming fury unleashed on men who now saw the trap that had been sprung. Lot's infantry beat forward, away from the drop and reeled left and right, leaving the centre open for Edlfed's forces to be driven through by Arthur's lances and swords. The first Angle raider shrieked as he fell into the updraft of air. Soon his companions followed, the sexes fighting equally to the death with no quarter expected. Edlfled was flanked by his wife and daughter, slashing and cutting furiously at whatever was within arm's length. Now Lot's men were with the knights, driving from where the Angles had stood, pushing the raiders steadily backwards to their death. Mordred picked up two seaxes from the fallen and threw them at Edlfled and his family. Leofwen's bicep was cut through. Gawain and Gareth followed their brother and the blades met their marks. Leofwen fell and Beonwyn stood astride her body to shield her. But now their feet slid in the bloody mire and they heard the screams of those falling behind. Some, as their feet scraped and slithered on gravel at the edge, chose to turn and jump rather than feel the blade between their ribs. Now the Anglish leader stood on the edge, Beonwyn too, having dragged Leofwen's body with her retreating legs. For a moment his sword arm paused, as did Beonwyn's. They barely recognised their smiles beneath the bleeding pulp of their faces.

'It is a good death,' said Edlfled, as they held left hands behind their backs and swung once more with their right. Mordred's lance toppled the three bodies into the void.

CHAPTER 7

Philip left early to catch the bus along Dracaena Avenue to Falmouth Road. Winter weather had returned: wet, windy and grey. As he stood with his thumb out, looking at oncoming drivers, willing them to pick him up, he was surprisingly content. It was always a pleasure to remember the good things of the day before. They had achieved a step towards their goal and they were alive.

He was in a good spot near a layby. In ten minutes a lorry loaded with smoked Mackerel bound for restaurants in Chelsea pulled in. Philip shook off the rain, climbed in and introduced himself. For nearly an hour he learnt the intricacies of smoking fish using traditional methods and the evils of Russian trawlers vacuuming the sea just beyond the six mile limit.

Now he was at the familiar turnoff to the B3267 to St Teath and Tintagel. The sky filled with black clouds racing towards the sea. His anorak was being tested and his wet knees began to freeze. A green Minivan pulled up. An older lady wound down the window.

'Hello Philip. None the worse for your adventure?'

He recognised Avril and Vera by their matching scarves. Avril got out and tipped the bucket seat so he could climb into the empty back. He sat on the mound of the wheel hub, his feet on the bare metal covered in residue of hay and animal feed.

'Have you come for the Morris? Mason moved it into the hotel car park for safety,' Vera said, holding the steering wheel at six o'clock with one hand and leaning around to talk with the other hand on the back of Avril's seat.

'How did he manage that?'

Both laughed. 'He's a man of many talents is Mason,' said Avril. 'Twice this year he's rescued Vera's keys: he's a master with packing tape threaded over and down the driver's window to pull up the catch. The local tow mechanic did the rest.'

'It was lovely to watch your take off. Just like a seagull. But that storm. We were drenched in seconds and what was in the trenches flowed straight down the cliff in a mud slide. The only safe place was huddled against the castle entrance walls.'

Of course he described the flight, which silenced both in awe. 'Thanks, ladies,' he said at the car park. He accepted the motherly bear hugs from them both simultaneously.

It was well over two hours of slog driving in the rain and through road works in Wadebridge and St Columb Major along the A39 before the A3078 onto the bleak backbone of the Roseland Peninsula. Just above the village he pulled up and opened the gate into the sodden garden.

Isaac opened the door. 'Commiz ee' in. Tiz pizen dawn. Cup o' tay, fella'?'

'I wouldn't say no.' Philip wiped his feet on the porch mat and followed Isaac into the familiar kitchen. Inside the room he noticed the cream ceiling and walls darkened by the Aga smoke, and the ageing photographs on the dresser: unsmiling black and white wedding pictures of a strong man and a severe woman with her hair tied up in a bun. Beside them were smaller coloured snaps of a younger man and his family with the Sydney Opera House in the background. The steaming mug was placed in his cupped hands.

The old man's eyes noticed Philip's interest in the photo.

'Knaw 'Ostrelya th'n?'

'No, but Rosalind comes from north of Sydney, from Queensland.' He wished she were with him to answer the stream of questions. His son had emigrated fifteen years ago, loved the life there and had never been back. Isaac was too old to join him and his growing family.

In a break in the weather they walked at the old man's pace to the field. Philip removed the plastic and replaced it with the nylon cover. With the aid of Isaac's wheelbarrow they manoeuvred it across the boggy ground to the Morris. Philip propped one end on the roof and slid the rest into position before the skies upended again.

'You've been a real friend, Isaac. Thanks.'

'W'l don' go tearin' wi' rayn lashin', Phil'p,' before he hobbled quickly into his doorway.

§

That morning Ros heard Philip close the heavy porch door. Rivulets of rain lit by the orange street light tracked down the window. She didn't envy Philip's task. It was tempting to roll over in the warmth but that wasn't fair. After a shower she creaked down to the kitchen and made herself a mug of coffee. Research: a perfect day for it. Make a list like Philip's. What are the biggest gaps in our knowledge? Make it Jeremy's type of facts and leave out her "feelings" for the moment.

Well, there was the Grail. The search for it broke the knightly bonds that kept the Round Table and Camelot alive. This led her immediately to Arthur's grave, the first task. Jeremy believed that it was in Cornwall, which made her think of Camlann, the final battle between Arthur and Mordred. Would the grave be close to the battle site? How had the Grail and the grave been hidden successfully for so long? She came back to Guinevere, the person buried under Christian misinterpretation, and her homeland, Lyonesse.

Ros' steps were compelled towards Jeremy's library. Surely given the task he would not object to her entering his domain alone? It smelled of books, some dampness of carpet and wallpaper near the window, and his studded red-leather chair. She put down her coffee cup on the window ledge and let her hands graze the titles in the bookshelf. Each text she removed was meticulously put back in its correct position. Jeremy would have no reason to grumble. Translations of Geoffrey of Monmouth's "History of the Kings of Britain" and Chretien de Troyes' studies, both originating in the 12th Century, butted against dissertations on Malory's poem "Le Morte d'Arthur". Works by 19th and 20th century historians were heavily annotated with Jeremy's pencil markings. His own judgements in numbered school jotters were out of bounds, in respect for his privacy and the need to look at the material with new eyes. By the time her brain overloaded her coffee was cold.

Back in the kitchen she made another and then visited Meredith's studio. Maybe inspiration, or even a "feeling", would come to her there. In the limp daylight through open curtains Ros lifted canvases out, propped them in the light and stood back. Again she admired Meredith's ability both to record and to catch the mood of this land. Beyond the promontory fortresses there were details that appeared again and again: storms and wrecks, hints of a Roman presence, megalithic dolmens alongside the early acceptance of Christianity, and ruins of the tin industry. Whether by research or feeling Ros decided that the Lizard was at the centre and another flight was necessary.

Back in Jeremy's library Ros found several books on tin mining, another of their black holes of ignorance that needed to be plugged. Then she followed a hunch. She combed the book spines for their titles. Despite all the examples of Romance literature, in all forms of text, there were no books of actual poetry. Novels were the domain of Meredith not Jeremy. In his LP record collection in the lounge there were no choral pieces or simple songs. But there was a definite preponderance of pieces by Mozart, Bach and Schumann, all of whom used mathematical formulae in their compositions.

Before Jeremy settled into his armchair with Mozart's "Magic Flute", she asked him why.

'Why would I read romantic frippery and speculation? My passion has always been to cut through the flummery to the truth. There is no need to obfuscate facts with poetic flights of fancy.'

Descriptive and terse but he's in less pain, she thought. His tone was kinder and he was actually speaking to her without Philip present.

'We've never been down a mine, Jeremy. Have you?' There was a trace of irritation as he put the record stylus back in its cradle. I've just hit my limit, she thought.

'When I was younger but not recently.' There was a pause. 'I can organise a visit if you'd like.' The stylus went into the groove. The audience was over.

Meredith appeared with more coffee and toast dripping with yellow butter.

'You don't need to take the film to the chemist. Jeremy built a dark room years ago. Come on.'

By late morning Jeremy was enthusing over his copies of Tintagel from the air.

'Such detail. I doubt if any archaeological site has received such treatment.'

'So Rosalind is not just a pretty face, then?' Meredith waited for his reaction.

Jeremy returned a smile that combined a frown, which Ros took as agreement.

When Philip walked in she showed him their copies of the photographs and the batch to give to Mason. In her lap was an imprint of William Blake's "Jerusalem" from the preface of "Milton: a Poem", that Meredith had loaned her.

'"And did those feet in ancient time

Walk upon England's mountains green:

And was the holy Lamb of God,

On England's pleasant pastures seen!

And did the Countenance Divine,

Shine forth upon our clouded hills?

And was Jerusalem builded here,

Among these dark Satanic Mills?"'

'Inspiring words,' Philip said.

'When Blake visited Glastonbury he was told of the legendary visit of Christ and Joseph of Arimathea: that the cup used by Christ in the Last

Supper was buried under the Tor; and the resultant spring flowed to Chalice Well,' said Ros.

'As I told you, monkish propaganda, which just muddies the waters,' Jeremy interrupted, before closing his eyes into the music.

Meredith beckoned Ros and Philip; shut the door to the lounge and the three ensconced themselves at the kitchen table. 'Cranky pants,' she said.

'What's the weather going to be like tomorrow, Meredith?' Ros asked.

'Let's find out.' Meredith turned on the wireless and rotated the dial to find the coast guard report.

'Outlook for the following 24 hours: Fal Estuary and the Lizard. Weather fine with possible light rain late afternoon. Sea state moderate to good. Wind west to south west. Visibility good.'

'Philip, do you feel like flying over the Lizard tomorrow?' Ros said.

'Ok. What are we looking for?'

'Lyonesse.'

'Can we come? It would do Jeremy a bit of good to get out,' Meredith said.

'Of course, it's your car. Are you thinking Porthleven, Meredith?' Philip guessed.

'I've seen young people at the cliffs near the Atlantic View Hotel. We can have a wander and pick you up when you land.'

'That's a plan then,' said Ros.

That evening, as the rain and wind pummelled the front garden and drove the street yobs into the pubs, all four sat reading in the lounge. The coal fire gave a steady heat, topped up with the occasional lump that Meredith lifted out of the coal scuttle. Philip sat on the floor reading a translation from the French of the story of Tristan and Isolde. On the poofee at Jeremy's feet Meredith was engrossed in another Jean Plaidy. Settled deep in his chair Jeremy studied an article in the Cornish Archaeology Journal on the Drustanus Stone from Castle Dore. Its two lines of Latin inscription were reputed to read "Drustan (or Tristan) lies here, the son of Cunomorus (or King Mark of Cornwall)". Rosalind was curled up on the lounge like a cat reading Tennyson's "Idylls of the King". Her smile was decidedly Cheshire.

§

Next morning Ros walked into the kitchen as Meredith was tidying the collar of her dress.

'You look good, Meredith.'

'Thank you. It's all about how you wrap the package.'

'A bit of bling doesn't do you any harm, does it?' Ros said.

Meredith turned away from the mirror. 'Jeremy might notice.' They laughed together.

§

The girls were in the back, Philip driving and Jeremy navigating in the front.

'Now, lad, are you sure you know where you're going?'

'I'm sure you'll help me if I miss a turn, Jeremy.'

Along the terrace a man sat on his front step lighting up a smoke from a packet of Capstan. His wife with another cigarette glued to her lip read the paper; beside her two young children played mud pies in the empty garden bed.

'Dole bludgers,' said Jeremy. 'My taxes have kept that lot for years.'

Meredith whispered to Rosalind. 'Jeremy's definitely taking it back now with all the government help he's getting.'

Ros could feel the tension in the front seat building. Philip got the hint when she tapped his shoulder.

'Turn right into Woodlane, then right again at the roundabout. You know Dracaena Avenue, don't you?' continued Jeremy.

Philip did as he was told and thought of the flight. He was determined to enjoy it. Jeremy spotted a vicarage and the carefully built stone wall surrounding its garden.

'I have always admired the Victorians,' he said. 'They built things to last: railway viaducts, the Albert Hall, Porthleven harbour. Not like today where a house is expected to last twenty years before it's knocked down.' They sat at traffic lights for more roadworks. 'Oh for Roman roads,' he moaned.

Just before Penryn Philip turned left at the polytechnic onto the A394 and asked Jeremy how many had searched for the Holy Grail.

'Arthur's knights if one accepts a modicum of truth beneath the legends. But it does not exist if Chretien de Troyes invented it in his tale "The Conte del Graal", "The Story of the Grail", around 1180AD. Probably most famous of the Sangreal hunters, meaning "Holy Grail" or "Royal Blood" according to your preference, were the Nazis. Before and during the war Himmler employed Otto Raum and later Otto Scorzani to search for it. Raum believed it was hidden by the Cathar sect at Montegur Castle in the Pyrenees. When they were besieged by the Pope as heretics, knowledge of its whereabouts was lost when the Castle fell in 1244. Montserrat Abbey was mentioned in a Catalan folksong as its home but again the Nazis gained no result. Himmler finally committed suicide.'

'However, they were all missing the point. If the legends of Joseph of Aramathea coming to Britain with Christ, and returning here with the Grail after the crucifixion, are true, then they predate Troyes' creation by a thousand years.'

'Why didn't the knights find it?' asked Ros.

'That's an excellent question, Rosalind. Maybe the church led them in the wrong direction? Did they ignore the stories of the peasantry? Was it deliberately hidden from them? We have no answer.'

Philip trickled the Morris down the narrow lane into the centre of Porthleven and parked back from the stone harbour. Inside the formidable Victorian bastion against the south westerly winter gales a dozen fishing boats in the inner harbour bounced at anchor. Periodically spray slapped above the stone walls and swept across the road. Beyond the mighty stone bar the sea churned from a storm three days before. Cars parked near the breakwater had been swept off and lost, and hundred foot breakers had broken high over the rooves of the Institute clock tower. All along the Lizard coast around to St Michael's Mount waves had thrashed the tops of cliffs, and beaches had disappeared in the tumult. But today was a good day: fine and warm out of the behaving wind.

Philip helped Jeremy from the car and retrieved his two walking sticks. While the girls found their jackets and Philip locked up, Jeremy strode aggressively ahead along Harbour Road.

'I can manage,' he said as Philip reached to support him onto the quayside seat. Philip sat down beside him and enjoyed the sun and wind in his face.

'Ros, you help me get the pasties,' Meredith said, beating a strategic retreat.

Inside the shop she picked out four on the counter still warm from the oven.

'Tha' be 64p, please.'

'Thank you.' Meredith put away her purse in her handbag while Ros picked up the four paper bags.

'Spectacles, testicles, wallet and watch,' Meredith recited as she patted herself down to make sure she had not forgotten anything.

Ten minutes later they silently devoured the hot meat, potato, turnip and onion wrapped in a lard pastry liberally seasoned with pepper and salt. They blew steam between each mouthful, their hands cradled around the paper bag. Philip's head was partially in the flight. Ros was building her Suspension of Disbelief mental armour. Jeremy steadily munched and Meredith brushed away pastry crumbs from his knees until he snarled.

Philip drove the Morris along the harbour edge and parked beside the seat. Again he hovered as Jeremy lowered himself into the front passenger seat, and put the sticks in the back. Out of season the town was quiet enough for Philip to turn left up the narrow lane of Salt Cellar Hill and negotiate a tight right hand turn on the slope into Peverel Terrace. He pulled up outside the Atlantic View. He stood outside to absorb the terrain, the wind and where there was open field above the beach. Ros enjoyed the elevated view of shimmering water. Meredith drifted in memories. Back inside Philip started the car and turned right into Cliff Road, then a left onto Loe Bar Road and dawdled in second gear until he found the place.

In the layby overlooking the water Jeremy dangled his legs through the open door. While Philip assembled the kite Jeremy asked questions that Philip had no intention of answering. When he was ready Ros crouched and he hooked her in and tested that the carabiner clip was locked. Headset check: 'Ready?' he said.

'Definitely.'

He looked at Meredith who held up the stick with a pink ribbon into the wind.

Ros looked ahead towards the vast expanse of azure ocean and the two tankers far into the distance. Not as high as Tintagel, this was a gentle grass slope almost down to Porthleven Beach. To her right were the Clock Tower and the harbour entrance, to the left the stretch of pebble and sand to Mullion and the cliffs above Kynance Cove.

'Nearly,' Philip said, as the breaker of air approached.

'NOW.'

Adrenalin pumped energy into their opening step, the second was a sluggish stride, the third drove them forward, the fourth was light footed and the fifth pointless motion as the air carried them over the water. This time it was easier. What could be worse than last time? She pushed that thought away. Her feet fed into the cocoon without a hitch. The roar of air seemed gentle as Philip crossed left and then right along the land's edge to gain height. Motion was restrained, slow and floating from the great wing above their heads. She was looking out over Mount's Bay, the rocky outcrop of St Michael's Mount clearly visible to the north-west. Inky, rock shelves beyond the pale orange sand below her led into the deep. Her eyes searched the seabed for remnants of ancient forest despite reason telling her proof of Lyonesse would not be so easy to find.

Now they were two thousand feet up and following the beach south. The gently humped shingle and fine gravel below was Loe Bar, with the kidney-shaped Lake held behind. Steep wooded edges contained the grey steel water. Emerald green fields bounded by Hawthorne hedgerows rolled across the landscape towards Helston and Penryn. For the first time she relaxed, her stomach muscles sinking soft into the harness, her shoulders loosely supported by her hands on the aluminium bar.

"'Come forth into the light of things,

Let Nature be your teacher,'" she said.

She couldn't help it. Wordsworth felt so right. She saw Philip's sideways smile. Yes, she was more in control. What did she feel? The quest was never far away. The lake below held memories: farming and fishing lives going back generation upon generation, until she knew that the presences she'd felt at Roseland had been here too; mixed emotions of greatness and sadness, suffering and peace.

'We know Dozmary Pool near the Jamaica Inn on Bodmin Moor is the usual choice for Arthur's Ladies of the Lake and Excalibur,' she said to Philip but more to herself. 'But Alfred Lord Tennyson didn't believe that.'

"'There likewise I beheld Excalibur

Before him at his crowning borne, the sword

That rose from out the bosom of the lake," she quoted from the "Coming of Arthur".

'It has a presence,' Philip said looking down at its two mile circumference, 'but can we prove it to Jeremy?'

'Maybe, but then we might not have to. It's not part of our job description.'

Philip looked inland up the green valley of the Cober River scarred by the tin industry. Helston was the centre of the tinners' ways crossing the poorer high country before leading down to Gweek and the Helford River. Other ways traversed to the north-east to Penryn and

Falmouth Harbour. Again his eyes followed the Cober Valley back to Loe Lake and Mount's Bay.

'In 1725 Daniel Defoe described Helston as a passable port for the tin trade. What happens if he was right?'

Both looked down at the natural dam wall. Could it be transitory, he thought, built up or taken away by the sweep of currents along the shoreline?

'Can you see the shadow of what looks like a river bed outside the Bar?'

'It goes well out,' she said. Could there have been Oak trees lining its banks before the lush valley to a lake anchorage that once served Cornubia and Lyonesse?

He made another turn south towards Gunwalloe and Church Cove, named for the Parish Church of St Winwaloe. Above its solid stone bulk he said, 'It's a similar date to St Just in Roseland, the five hundreds or earlier.'

This whole land was steeped in memories, she thought. Here was no different. A little way on she spotted the double rock formation of Gull Rock, with Asparagus Island behind, protecting Kynance Cove. Soon they were sweeping over red and green Serpentine crags spiking through white sandy beaches. The water was turquoise, revealing an undisturbed sea bed.

'Can we go lower, Philip?'

'Of course, the sea breeze is good.'

She spotted them again: dark shapes in regular formation between Asparagus Island and Gull Rock. The tide was high but if it was low they could negotiate those rock stacks to get very close.

'Worth a second visit, Philip, when the tide's out?'

'Ok.'

Her mind rambled as Philip made the next sweep before heading back. It was not fair on Meredith and Jeremy to stay up longer.

§

Outside a dress shop on the harbour front Jeremy sat on the bench watching Meredith trawl the racks. In one she found arm length gloves in golden lame. As he looked up she waved a gold pinky at him, then smiled and lifted her middle digit instead. She laughed at his "can't take you anywhere" scowl.

'Watch the gears,' Jeremy said as Meredith nibbled the teeth of reverse on the way to fourth, because he was watching her.

'How can I do that? I'm driving,' she replied.

She took the B3304 Porthleven Road out of the village and negotiated her way across to the A3083. Their vision from this height easily took in the blue dot of the kite over the sparkling ocean. She parked for a while to watch their manoeuvres. Rosalind must have brought this glorious weather with her, Meredith thought.

'A priest could die with a view like that, 'she said. Jeremy gave her a sideways glance but said nothing.

'But then religious people usually don't want to die, do they?' she continued.

Not too many people do, Jeremy thought.

Meredith looked at her Timex wrist watch: nearly 3 'o'clock. The sapphire speck was on its way back. She started the engine, pushed Jeremy out of her mind, and made a perfect pull off. She indicated right into Meaver Road and travelled along until she found a parking spot close to a field between the road and the cliff. On the car aerial she tied the pink ribbon, which held steady in the breeze from the sea.

§

Ros pointed to the Morris and Philip nodded. He did not have to lose so much height since they were not landing on the beach. He felt the clear direction of air to land into. But he still gauged the distance from the cliff edge and left a good margin.

Meredith left Jeremy sitting in the car with his door open. 'How wonderful!' she said as Philip pushed the bar out for a perfect landing. 'I would have loved to have done that when I was young,' she bubbled.

Ros thought of her own trepidation and smiled. 'You could take her up some time, couldn't you, Philip?'

'We can do that, Meredith? Are you ok with heights?'

'I'm better than Jeremy. I think so, but I'm too old.'

'Nonsense,' said Ros. 'You're as young as you choose to be.'

'Well people my age do act so much older than me.'

Back in the car, all loaded up, Philip gently pulled away for the drive back.

'Don't be daft. You'll break your neck, woman,' Jeremy barked when Meredith enthused about a future flight. Ros felt Meredith's crushing descent into silence.

'Such a nasty Pasty,' Meredith said very quietly to herself.

Philip broke the silence when a Sea King rescue helicopter flew overhead on its way back to RAF Culdrose.

'Was the Lizard important in the war, Jeremy?'

'Decidedly so. In 1940 Radar installations were set up to spot enemy aircraft crossing the Channel to bomb Falmouth and the South East. The first was at Dry Tree on Goonhilly Downs and there was a later one at Lizard Head. Another site at Treleaver helped our fighters bring down German bombers at night. The success rate of the 604 squadron made the authorities invent the myth that eating carrots helped the pilots see at night, just to stop the enemy learning about Radar.'

'Aunt Doreen was with the Wrens,' said Meredith. 'They reported on E boats shadowing convoys and planes laying mines in the Channel. It was so cold in winter that men on guard duty would swap an armful of firewood for a hot cup of tea.'

Meredith "warmed" to her subject. 'Sea mists rolled in so thick they held hands at night to go between buildings. And how Doreen slept through that fog horn: Boom-wah, boom-wah every few minutes, goodness knows.'

'Radar was vital in the defence of Britain.' Jeremy took over again.' It was all top secret, of course. Accuracy was such that a Walrus air-rescue plane was once guided to within a mile of a pilot bailing out off the coast of France. By the time he hit the water the crew were there.'

'What about D-Day, Jeremy?' Philip asked.

'By 1944 the Germans had radar but for months before June bombers jammed all signals to hide the fleet build up. Pretend convoys were sent out, with planes dropping "window", silver foil strips, to make them look real. One month before Mandrel transmitters created a curtain of "white noise" around the English coast and gradually across the whole Channel. When the landings happened the German technicians in Normandy were taken completely by surprise.'

'Arthur might have preferred radar to fiery beacons on hill tops.' Meredith ignored the withering look as she opened the doors of the garage.

§

Philip filled the coal bucket and carried it in from the garage, across the causeway to the back door and plopped it beside the fire in the lounge. In the middle of the kitchen table Ros laid out the warmed plates and bowls of cooked veg, salad or "rabbit food" as Jeremy called it, chips and sliced corned beef. She had noticed Meredith lugging in the coal now that Jeremy was too weak to do it.

'She's wearing herself out, Philip. It's good we stepped in.'

That evening Ros and Philip researched tin mining, tunnels and caves. With an industry that existed for thousands of years there had to be a connection to Arthur. And what about smuggling, another ancient art in this part of the world, which used holes in cliffs and coves?

Jeremy was restrained and helpful. In his library he found the texts they needed and shared his notes. Their extent showed that he believed there was a link too. Ros could feel his rising desperation to finish the quest before his own exit.

At one point she noticed Meredith smiling at Jeremy's enjoyment. Unintentionally she picked up Meredith's butterfly mind.

'Soldiers who returned to Australia after that war often came back to their wives as different people,' Ros said what she was thinking. She remembered friends of her father who took to the drink and bashed their wives and kids. Then she regretted opening her mouth as Meredith had moved on with her.

'Some came back to Porthleven from the Far East like that,' Meredith said dreamily.

POWS from Japanese camps, Ros thought. Meredith was too close.

'Every soldier comes back with Soldier's Heart, whatever you want to call it,' Jeremy said. 'My father would never talk about what happened on the Western Front. He just worked hard and looked after his family.'

'Most men just faced it quietly,' Meredith.

'It's what they have always done throughout the ages,' said Jeremy dismissively.

§

'Good night you two,' said Meredith. 'I hope you find what you're looking for tomorrow.'

She put away the dishes and tidied up while Jeremy took forever in the bathroom. Meredith had taken to putting a spare toothbrush in the kitchen. Thank goodness for the extra loo downstairs. She was in bed with her book when he slowly got under the covers and turned out his light. Meredith looked across. It had been a good day with the trip to Porthleven and recollecting stories from war-time. Having young people in the house lifted her mood. During the night she dreamt of their young life together. The poverty she pushed away but there were parts that she missed.

As muted light and the seagulls woke her from a mother's light sleep she looked across at Jeremy. How many more mornings would she be able to do that? His face was relaxed, younger. Ever so quietly she got out of bed, dug around in her bedside drawer, took off her nightie and slid under the covers with Jeremy. She lay there for a time warming up again. Then she let her hands stray over his chest, parting his shirt and then sliding down, undoing the draw string and stroking him gently. In the semi darkness she felt him surface but not object. As she put the tube of jelly outside the sheets and squeezed some on to her hand it squirted out in a loud dollop. He jumped and his eyes opened.

'It's a while since this tube has been used,' she said laughing. Then she raised herself up and sat on his thighs, steadily applying the lubricant before sliding over him.

A single bed was a bit cramped, she thought, gently moving up and down. She listened to his pleasure and enjoyed hers more because of it. As they rose together she thought of their wedding night: more of a bit of fumble in the dark, really, but nice. Later it got better, quite spectacular even. As she felt their combined flow it occurred to her that this was nice but not spectacular. Then she noticed tears running down his cheeks.

'Why?' she asked.

'Because you are beautiful,' he said. 'I never …'

'It's all right, Jeremy.' She paused for a long time. 'You meant well. I know that.'

§

In the morning Ros creaked open the attic door and nearly tripped over a carrier bag on the landing. Meredith had left sandwiches wrapped in grease proof paper, some tea and coffee, and a Thermos flask of boiling hot water. The Morris started first go with plenty of choke. Ros shut the much-patched garage doors, climbed in and they were on their way. Once through the familiar streets of Falmouth they drove down towards Lizard Point, through Helston still lit by street lights, past the well-lit twenty four hour activity of Culdrose air base and then turned right after Kynance garage. As the sun threatened to appear over the wine dark sea they pulled up at wooden posts in the deserted car park.

With their rucksacks bouncing they walked steadily along the track to the ocean and then down the steps to white sand shadowed by the cliffs behind them. Red and green serpentine stacks of the Steeple and Bishop Rock glowed in the lukewarm light. Asparagus Island and Gull Rock rose in variegated shimmering pink and jade in front of them. It was 6.09am, five minutes past a low tide of 0.86 metres.

Philip led the way across the connecting ridge of sand between the mainland and Asparagus Rock. In the ebbing waves from north and south he automatically scanned for anything different, as on a dig survey. He saw lots of different pebbles that lapidaries would delight in but nothing archaeological. He picked a route up through a fissure scoured by tides over millennia. The rock was multi-coloured up through the seaweed line to mosses, lichens and the wild Asparagus that named the island. The stone was crumbly and he guessed treacherous on the seaward side.

Ros was content to follow. She had been the guide over the past few days, with the flight over the Lizard and now following up what she had seen in the water. The weather was mild and the wind had not stiffened yet. Maybe the prediction of moderate breezes with a chance of light rain might hold true. On top the gusts were more substantial so they were glad of a corresponding crevice and connecting ledges that led down to the platform of harder rock on the northern edge of the island. Now they were as close as possible to what she had seen from the air, short of swimming.

The black shadows, a metre or so below water, were man-made, something wrapped in dark tarpaulin and each marked with a buoy that bobbed in the gentle swell. She sat down on the rock bench disappointed. Surely there was more to it than this. Last night she'd filled her head with stories of wreckers' lanterns in storms guiding unwary ships to their doom. Jeremy had dismissed her questions as unproven fiction, just tales to beguile the tourists. But he did not doubt the evidence for the smugglers who thrived for centuries until modern customs officers broke their trade. Was this what she was looking at? She doubted it was tins of pilchards.

Philip had come to similar conclusions but could not stop his search. This coast had hundreds of ships wrecked along it. The sweep of sand carried by currents that drifted up and down the shore was caught here, in this unusual formation called a Tombolo. Between the Island and the mainland two currents, north and south, created waves that crashed against each other. The result was a sand bridge piled up in the quiet water between the two. Surely something archaeological might be trapped and then surface here. While he scanned the depths Ros scrambled among the fractured rocks. His was the first call, almost simultaneous with hers.

'You first,' he said.

'There's a cave here just above the high tide mark. What have you got?'

'Just south of the sunken bags I can see some pottery shards and something else. They look promising.'

She scrambled down and followed his finger. 'Looks like yours first and then I can warm up again clambering around the cave.'

'Does it look safe to you?' he asked as she sat in her swimming "togs" while getting courage for the cold water.

'It's shallow; with some sort of rip that doesn't drag those buoy lines too much. I think it's ok.'

'How about a rope, just in case?' That was a statement not a request, as he pulled out the coil of climbing cable from his rucksack.

Fair comment, she thought, since he can't swim. Now she looked again at the water, with cord around her waist and the loops beside Philip on the closest part of the shelf.

'See ya.' She slid into the water quickly but the icy chill stole her breath. Blasphemy was in her head but the words wouldn't come out. She was not going to hang around in this. Get to the spot, grab the stuff and get out of here. Her eyes and toes located the cracked curve of orange pottery.

'Catch!'

He caught it and laid it beside the coil. Several more pieces flew through the air and were snatched successfully.

'You might play for Australia yet,' she managed to squeeze out of her lips. Humour always helped her in adversity. She'd have a fit of the giggles if she didn't finish up soon.

Her toes spiked on something sharp. She'd have to go under to get it. The current pushed her shoulders but she dug with her hands and closed on three small items. That's enough: time to quit while we're winning.

He helped her out and buffed her shoulders hard with the towel while she put the bits with the others. Then Ros put on her shoes and climbed to the cave. Philip followed with the rucksacks and the rest. Out of the wind she dried and changed but continued to rub her hair.

'These are bits of wine amphora, I think. There's a buckle or clasp, a bit too degraded to see without laboratory work. And this.' He held out a silver disc with lettering barely discernible after centuries of being tumbled in abrasive sand.

Ros rubbed it with the wet towel. There was no real difference. She held it in the shaft of light and both tried to work out letters. Inevitably Philip had a small notebook and pencil.

'I-PCAR—, then three chunks clipped out of it, then AV—G. Something of a crown over a smooth blob of profile face.'

Ros deciphered the obverse side. '-EG then I—I, with a skinny four legged creature facing right. It probably gives us enough to look up a coin book when we get back.'

Philip wrapped the finds in a cloth handkerchief and put them in his bag. 'What have you got in here?' he said, looking at his watch.

'Lots of shattered driftwood as you would expect along this coast. These two have hand-made nails in them.'

'Worth keeping, I suppose,' as he put them in the top of the bag. Then he retrieved something.

'Why am I not surprised that you have a torch in there?' She laughed.

They found more planks, opaque plastic bottles, broken rubber sandals and some polystyrene. But right at the back, around a protected bend, were boxes stacked three high. They looked at each other and said, simultaneously, 'We shouldn't be doing this.'

But then curiosity, and that they had come this far, made them look closer. One crate had been opened and hastily tapped shut again. It was an easy task to look and put it back as they found it. The question was whether they should.

'If we don't look then we can say we don't know what's in them,' he said unconvincingly. He saw Ros' "Yeah, right!" look. Then he said, '"Scientia est Potestas".'

'"Knowledge is power,"' she replied. It was her school motto.

With his penknife Philip carefully pried off the lid. Inside were individual bars of a silvery white metal. Each of three columns contained a different type. Without metallurgical knowledge he could only guess at silver but two were too soft to the fingernail for that.

Ros picked up from the fourth stack. It was obviously gold. If the other ingots were of similar value then these piles represented considerable wealth, she thought. She reckoned they might be in a spot of bother but did not say anything.

'Time to go,' she said.

He replaced the lid near perfectly and they both climbed out into the bracing air. As they reached the top she looked at his watch.

'Oops, I think,' said Ros. It was after 7.30am. She kept up with Philip as he moved quickly over the top and then down the rift in the rock. The beach was now mostly between ankle and knee deep water, depending on the flow in or out. The two lines of breakers crashed into each other before scouring back into deep water. The nearby blow holes roared and screeched like Transylvanian church organ pipes.

Philip started to take off his clothes and push them into the sack.

'Wait,' she said and sat down, silently watching the water.

He put on his swimming trunks and did the same. This was her element.

'When's high tide again?' she asked.

'A bit after 12.'

'Over five hours between: so next low tide is around 5 this afternoon. Let me try the water first. We just might do this.'

She was back in her bikini and the rope that Philip insisted on. Just after the impact of waves she jumped in. The beach was not quicksand. There was rock beneath it, at least in the centre. She stepped back on to the ledge and looked at her watch. Again as the waves hit she jumped in but this time ran fifteen metres out and back again before the next wallop. For a second or two there was nearly dry sand. After two more goes she knew, but it was dicey.

'Get yourself ready, Philip. I want the rope on you this time and a few metres between us.' She watched the wave interval, a pattern of seven.

He tied the loop but threw most of it over his shoulder. 'Give me your hand.'

'Ok.' She watched. 'Ready?'

'Yes.'

'GO.'

She led as he pumped her hand into extra forward motion. The first step was almost a stumble with the drag of water. The second footstep was more forward as the sand was nearly dry, the third was longer; the fourth was pushing to win. They were striding like sprinters, barely touching the sand, lifting spray out and above their heads. He just hoped they could keep up this coordination, like some crazy three legged race. There was no thought of breath, just mad power to skirt the sloppy shingle around that rock and beat the incoming sweep of the southern wave. It was gaining but they ran harder. They synchronised leaps over two streams with treacherous soft gravel. We can do this, was their telepathic thought. As the wave hit they were on the gentle rise out of the cove. It swept into their ankles, slapped up to their knees but they were upright. A dozen long paces and it had receded again. For the sheer thrill of it they ran the last twenty metres to the high tide mark.

§

Meredith stood at the lounge window. Jeremy looked up, saw she was bothered about something, and went back to his music. Her hands came together, 'Are they ok, Elvan?'

Jeremy looked up again. 'It looks like they've been waylaid somewhere,' he said with little point.

'Let's hope the operative word is "laid" rather than "way",' she said.

'Stop it, woman.'

§

'Good fun,' Ros said. Her laughter was infectious. After they'd dried themselves off and put on warm clothes, Ros looked up. In the tufted grass high on the cliff face a bird with red legs and beak looked down and screeched at her. The Chough's wings were a mass of black feathers spread like fingers.

'It's Arthur's bird. He's checking on us.'

Was she joking? Philip didn't know.

CHAPTER 8

For months Ælle, Bretwalda of all the Saxons in Britain, had gathered fighters from across his lands. Saxon and Angle chieftains who owed him allegiance gathered their hirthmen, those chosen men who shared their hearth and food and would die rather than betray their lord. They arrived in the South Saxon lands. They numbered many hundreds of the finest combatants ever gathered, not least Ælle's own Gesith, three hundred of the best. Ceorls, Saxon free men who farmed his lands, would join his number. Octha, of "the blood knife", son of the great Hengist of the Saxon Terror, led his men from Cantaware, south of Londinium. Cheldric, Balduph and each day a great many other famous warriors arrived for the great foray into "Welsh", the "Foreigners" lands. And from beyond the sea came Frisians, Danes, Franks, Norsemen and Geats attracted by Ælle's name as a lavish "gift giver". All assembled to plunder but most of all receive from their Bretwalda the gift of land, once all of Britain became Saxon.

Arthur watched the gathering storm. Brythonic princes and lords from Gododdin to Dumnonia felt the danger but resisted sending levies until they knew who was threatened.

'Excuses, Arthur, as always,' said Merlin. 'They will bleat and shy away from action until the horde knocks on their door not their neighbours.'

'Precious thanks for all that you have done for them,' said Bors.

Arthur rested his elbows on the great table and leaned his head into his hands. Waiting was the hardest task for him. He shut his eyes and tried to enter Tsarati's domain. The air was clearer from this height. Tewdric's fleet was still formidable but without his old friend's guidance. Tinners' funds kept the beacons ready. His knights were blooded and prepared, with more young men clamouring to join their ranks. But until he knew Ælle's mind he could do nothing more.

A familiar face entered the room.

'Ah, Bedivere, most faithful of knights, what news, Sir?' Arthur said.

'The Saxon horde moves, Sire, south to Londinium and then west along the Devil's Causeway.'

Arthur looked at the hide map of Brythonic and Saxon lands with the old military roads in red.

'If I surmise rightly he comes for us, here in Dumnonia; or if not here at Camelot then maybe somewhere along the road itself. He plans to tear our kingdoms asunder, cutting off north from south. Once we are thus divided he sees us as easy pickings.'

'Cador, will you help me?'

Guinevere's father was an aged man now but still retained the sparkling eyes and keen mind of his younger days. He had no regrets that he had given his daughter to Arthur at Merlin's request.

'When we muster up our force and head east to face our enemy will you and Guinevere raise another assembly to join us? Ælle has a plan but I do not grasp the full import of it.'

Riders were sent north to Gwynedd, Elmet and Reghed. Surely now they would come with levies of troops. In the days of preparation the Saxon force laid waste Calleva, Spinae and Cunetio. Next would be Aqua Sulis, the "waters of the Sulis", a town of hot springs known as Badon in the Saxon tongue.

On the way east word came to Arthur's force that the Visigothic fleet were hard pressed to contain Cerdic and his Saxon raiders. Their pillaging was a strategy to pin down the Dumnonian lords so that Arthur would be alone.

Arthur's knights made camp in rolling woodland a few miles from Badon town. Ælle's host encircled the walled city. The meagre defences would not hold for long. Arthur joined his scouts to reconnoitre the land. Among the hills, defiles and open farmland one choice of position became clear. Mons Badonicus was a flat-topped mount four miles north east of the city. From its height of six hundred and twenty five feet he could see all of Badon and Ælle's encampment to the west, and the Afon River a mile to the south, with a distant escarpment as its backdrop. Its three sides were steep with near impenetrable forest clinging to its slopes, except for one opening. Here was an exposed, almost gentle slope facing Badon itself. A single defensive ditch and stone capped rampart surrounded the horizontal elevated triangle of grassland. Arthur and his knights made ready on top of the knoll and waited for the enemy to make a move.

'Whatever his plan, if I was Ælle I could not stomach us here,' Bors said. 'He can't attack the city for fear we will attack from the rear or cut off his supplies. He has to face us.'

'Sound strategy,' said Arthur absently, watching the horses graze the lush meadow. With their supplies and this at least they would not starve for a few days.

Just before dusk of the second day watchmen spied an army coming from the south west. Younger eyes than Arthur's picked out Dumnonian pennants. Cador's army was a day away.

'Now the Saxons will move,' Arthur said. 'Be ready for tomorrow.'

Hours before dawn Arthur heard the sound of marching feet and clanking weapons. Merlin and I watched with him as the sun rose on an amazing sight: rank upon rank of Saxon, Angle and all their comrades' shields faced us at the base of the one grassed access to the stronghold. The Saxon lords had come to Arthur. All he had to do was rest his troop, knowing that time was on his side. Every hour brought Cador's men closer. Ælle would not face a combined army. Rather would he take this desperate gamble.

Arthur waited. Merlin and I stepped back. He and Tsarati were closer now. Looking down on the world was not just a feat of imagination. We both knew his need for solitude at this moment.

The Saxon ranks began to move. Precise horizontal lines of men climbed the undulating grassy ridges of the slope. Arthur's knights and horses stood still on the verdant hilltop, in wedge formation, with

Arthur, Kay and Bedivere at the apex. His thousand knights knew their advantage but against such odds, maybe ten to one, there was no surety of success. This would be a desperate day. Each man knew it could be his last. Arthur's shield with the Virgin Mary emblazoned on it shone in the sunlight glinting through cloud. His lance with the Red Dragon pennant was lowered, as were the rest.

The knights watched the lines climb and waited for Arthur's signal. Steadily the Saxon numbers strode forward and upward. Some now paused for breath. Gradually the Brythons saw men tire and the rows become ragged. Carrying two throwing axes, heavy throwing spears, a light stabbing spear and in armour across chest and head, fit men were tested. Arthur remained motionless. Ælle and his sons, Cissa, Cymen and Wlencing, were at the centre. They helped their aged father climb with the rest. Still Arthur held back for that moment when his chance of success was stretched to its greatest.

Arthur raised his lance to vertical and a thousand others did the same. In the stillness horses whinnied; they knew and were ready. Now many of the foe leaned on their spears and rested on the slope. They had climbed four hundred feet. Arthur's breath steadied, his time slowed, he was of the moment. It was as if Tsarati was on his arm speaking guidance to one hunter from another. They knew the precise instant. His lance dropped and in a roar of thundering hooves and wild cries the wedge hurtled down the incline. Arthur's lance pointed directly at Ælle flanked by his three sons.

Saxons, Angles, Jutes and Frisians looked upwards. Some froze. Others hastily formed a semblance of shieldwall on unfavourable ground. Brave men flinched and wondered if service to their Bretwalda was worth the price.

The impact of mighty beast and man in full charge was weight multiplied and unstoppable. The point crashed through the first and second and third lines and still carried momentum. Lances stabbed and pierced left and right and centre, so that soldiers barely had chance to lift their spears to parry. Axes thrown were few and fell short against their fast moving targets. Reins slipped through enemy fingers as Brythonic swords struck home. But some horses were pierced, gave a shudder, and carried on. For minutes they supported their rider and crumpled their adversaries with crushing hooves before their blood was spent and they slumped in death. Arthur, Kay and Bedivere thrust their lances through Ælle's sons before Arthur pulled his lance out and skewered the struggling old man himself. All along the slope the precise excision of leaders was clinical. Without their chieftains the bond of allegiance was broken. The Saxon shieldwall shattered and each man ran to save his life.

But that was no easy task as the Saxons were far from home and without ships to slip away. Most never escaped those four hundred feet of terror as they tumbled and fell and tried to see their opponent before their demise. More were butchered along the Afon River in the open grassland contained in a bow of its banks. The flat terrain was perfect for Arthur's knights to display their skills with wanton release. Cador's army arrived next morning in time to clean up fleeing bands of men and share in the plunder. There was no quarter given to descendants of those who'd executed the Saxon Terror. The murder of grandfathers and Brythonic lost pride were assuaged in this single conflict. So that the Saxon head was cut off and the body would not regrow for generations.

§

In the days and weeks that followed I watched Arthur. All around him celebrated this greatest of Arthur's twelve battles. Lords from South and East and West Saxon kingdoms sent emissaries to Camelot to sue for peace. Guinevere was Queen of a court equal to her dreams. Poets and minstrels entertained night after glittering night with tales of her husband's exploits. To be a knight at the Round Table was the pinnacle of a warrior's life. But Arthur was lost.

Like Tewdric he was tired of war. When his companions spoke of driving the Saxons into the sea or restoring Brythonic lands to include all of Roman Britannia Arthur said no.

'We have fought long and hard for a secure peace. Now that we have it why tempt the gods of our past and the God of our future with renewed war?'

Each Saturn's day I gave a sermon in the chapel of whichever court Arthur and Guinevere chose. In the morning we would travel again to Arthur's favourite, the upland fortress of Kelliwic. But this time was at Tintagel.

I reminded the small gathering that the Sabbath was the day Christ was in the tomb, before the Sunday of his resurrection. At this time of Christ's preparation it seemed apt to study the Sermon on the Mount. Here He had explained four of the Ten Commandments and one of his own. Arthur stood unnoticed at the back in the shadows.

'Christ told each of us to give honour and respect to our parents. They brought us into this world, nurtured us and gave us the strength to go out and achieve greatness.'

I knew that Arthur was not the only person to doubt: so many in the room saw little to admire in the souls of their fathers.

'Do not bear false witness against thy neighbour, He said. The truth of your word, the trust that others place in what you say, is the measure of your worth as a man.' In my own mind it was easy to see how so many lied and cheated their way into power and the keeping of it. How much more for my congregation?

'Adultery is betrayal: a friend's wife, the loss of honour that you give to your own. It becomes a cancer that eats into a man's heart.' My words made men glance downwards. Guilt showed in many of those knights of Arthur's inner sanctum of the Round Table.

'Christ told the crowd not to kill. I am sure his intention was the subject of murder but for those in this room this is an especially hard commandment to keep.' I was sure I heard "impossible" and "it is our destiny to kill". 'My interpretation, for your help, is that the taking of life must be justified. I have wrestled with this dilemma for most of my years. I still have no complete answer. I know you, as Christian warriors, have taken many lives. But if you fight for good, for a better world than you came into, then I believe Christ will forgive you.' Listening to the murmurs and doubts I hoped that these men would respect my honesty.

'Christ's own commandment I have chosen to keep as my guiding principle. All other instructions are subservient to this. "Love thy neighbour as thyself".' Did I lose them in the silence?

Merlin and I watched as warriors began to leave Arthur's court to return to Reghed, Gwynedd, Gododdin and Dumnonia. Each was now wealthy enough to support his own teulu. Arthur gave his blessing to all of them.

'They have promised to return if I call them,' Arthur said.

'How do you know that these men will not use what you have taught them to turn on you?' asked Merlin.

'I don't know their hearts. But I do know that those skills, taught to new generations of warriors, are enough for the Brythonic kingdoms to protect themselves when I am gone,' said Arthur. 'I hope, and I know, that it is better to spread knowledge freely rather than it be lost.'

One knight stood to one side, almost within earshot.

'And you, Mordred? You are restless. Will you return with your brothers to Gododdin?' Arthur said.

'For a time, my lord, but I would welcome another chance to serve under the Red Dragon banner so that my weapons and skills do not rust through lack of use.'

Arthur could see ambition in his eyes. If he, Arthur, could not find that task then Mordred would find his own.

§

As a young man Arthur had faced the need for a navy to support his campaign on land. Tewdric was the solution. Now he faced the collapse of the dream of Camelot, that peace maintained by knights who supported Christian ideals. What were warriors to do if there were no wars to fight? As usual he sought our opinion. Merlin and I were seated on granite rocks under the shade of an oak tree at Kelliwic. He joined us.

'Tell me again about the Otherworld, Merlin,' Arthur said.

'It is a place of beauty and joy just beyond the misty edges of this one. The Cymbrogi know it as Annwn but we call it Avalon. It is a world like this where the eternal soul learns before it comes back: over many lifetimes the spirit finally reaches the Source from whose flames all things are created, even the gods themselves.'

'And Heaven, Justin?' he asked.

'Heaven is a place of everlasting peace and happiness, a reward for those judged by God to have lived a good and honourable life. There our souls rest for eternity, away from all the troubles of this world.'

'What is a good life, Merlin?' he asked.

'It is when a man seeks justice, honour, and the care of all things. It is no accident that many of our number are judges and peacemakers. Honour is shown in many ways: keeping truth, being loyal to family and friends, showing courage in difficult situations where others shy away, and most of all hurting no one if it is possible.'

'And you, Justin?' Arthur said.

'As you heard in the chapel: the commandments guide us, the greatest being: "Love thy neighbour as thyself".'

'Would you disagree with those Christian commandments as good instruction, Merlin?' Arthur said.

'I might qualify some. For instance there are times when it is right to kill if justice is to prevail. You know this from your own life. As a Druid I would add some teaching but these are valuable rules to live by.'

Arthur sat for a time. We waited for his thoughts to unfold.

'It seems to me that Druid ways are for Druids, the few who can attain the Source, whereas Christian ways are for the many, where Heaven is reached in one lifetime. You and I, Merlin, delight in the beauty of the Natural world but so many cannot see beyond bloodshed and barbarism. Will Brython be killing Brython a thousand years hence? I want a better way of living. You strive for peace, Merlin, but how can we soften these people? Instead of the eternal cycle of life and death, where so few learn, can we harness the power that all men, rich and poor, no longer fear death? Can we make them see that peace at home with family is good? The tinners have wished this for generations. Can we make war a rare thing, something necessary only to maintain peace?'

He paused again. 'Otherwise I am no better than Uther or even Aelle. Already I know Uther's pain.' He looked at us and our faces could only agree. 'He protected Britain with constant effort. I wish my suffering to produce a greater result, a new beginning where men value and strive for peace.'

Arthur looked at his mentor and friend. I believe Merlin knew his words before they left his lips. 'Justin's way offers the better chance of winning the battle for good,' he said quietly.

Merlin's eyes never left Arthur's face. He knew this day would come. On so many subjects our views matched. He was a good man and a courageous one.

'You are right,' Merlin said without malice.

'Can we make all of these knights Christians who fight for good and the ideals I have strived to share at the Round Table?' Arthur said.

The three of us listened to the wind in the leaves above us. Through Merlin I also had a deeper appreciation of all things natural. I looked up and waving sunlight speckled brilliance into my eyes. The glow remained when my eyelids were shut.

'Do you remember the shield you raised at Guinnion Fort? At the sight of the Virgin Mary all the lords of Dumnonia raised a roar that took out the hearts of the enemy,' I said.

'Your lance with the Red Dragon pennant was also powerful,' Merlin said. 'These are superstitious people who search for a talisman to make them invincible. Our stories around the camp fires are full of sacred cups and cauldrons with miraculous powers that are fought over by the gods.'

'Like Excalibur?' I said.

Merlin smiled. 'But of the Christian variety?'

'Justin, often your sermons deal with the lives of Christian martyrs,' said Arthur.

'They show men how to live a Christian life,' I said.

'In our court Guinevere is frequently presented with pieces of these men and women. She often keeps a bony finger or toe for supernatural protection even though her thoughts remain in the old ways.'

'Maybe you should give more sermons about these martyrs, Justin, and where to find their remains?' Merlin said with a little mischief.

Arthur's smile was my bidding. Over the next weeks fewer knights left. Their imagination had been stirred, as Arthur found out whenever the members of the Round Table met.

Merlin delighted in a new plan. 'Surely relics of worthy souls who have died by Roman hands are good. But what of items once held by the Apostles or even Christ himself?'

'By all means let our knights find Christian relics. They help men to fight on the battlefield and scare our enemies to maintain the peace,' said Arthur.

When warriors were idle Arthur encouraged bouts of knightly contest. Since the times of the Romans soldiers had fought tournaments between each other to maintain their fitness and battle skills. But now Guinevere was persuaded that tournaments were also feats of splendour that her poets and troubadours might find worthy subjects. Many knights returned with relics that seemed to give them power over their opponent. God appeared to be more on their side. Guinevere was entertained and the knights vied to please her. Arthur did not object.

'What of Joseph of Arimathea?' I was often asked. 'Did he not come to Brythonic lands years ago? Did he not share in the life of Christ himself? Where did he go? What did he bring after the Crucifixion that we might find for ourselves?'

I did not enjoy speaking with everyone that asked me. But Arthur and Merlin's plan had put new life into Camelot. Wherever the court travelled men praised him and the peace he had brought. Maybe I had been with Merlin too long for I found myself accepting baser ways as a means of achieving greater ends.

Whenever Merlin left for a time, if he was not with Nimue and the other maidens of Avalon, knights returned with pieces of the true cross or the lance that pierced Christ's side in his final agonies. I spoke of my concerns to him but he dismissed them as anxious fantasies.

Arthur, at Merlin's request, summoned his remaining knights to a meeting of the Round Table. Chief amongst those present with Arthur, since there were many more than would fill the original twelve seats, were: Lancelot, Percival, Bedivere, Kay, Galahad, Bors, Gawain, Tristan, and Garath. Mordred was absent. Arthur knew that he was now attached to King Mark's court at Castle Dore and it saddened him. Galahad, Lancelot's son by Elaine of Corbenic, was new to the table. Galahad was a brilliant knight with simple Christian virtue and yet with the heart of a lion. One feat of his was to climb to the Seat of Danger high on Grey Rock. St Michael the Archangel had reputedly been seen on the very chair. Many had tried and fallen but Galahad attained his goal, no doubt with the Archangel's blessing. His seat at the table was opposite to Arthur and all named it the Perilous Seat after Galahad's ability to face danger with impunity.

Arthur studied his warriors, those who had travelled as his companions since youth and those who had proved their worth in those eleven terrible battles that brought peace. Amid the battle scars, of mind and body, was a new zeal to prove worthy as Christian knights. There was healing in their goal. Talk was of travelling the land in search of Joseph's communities and the relics that would aid Arthur's peace. Each recounted deeds that matched Arthur's ideals: aiding the weak against the strong and giving leadership to villagers fighting rapacious war bands. Christian zeal had replaced the joy of killing their neighbour. It was a reason to celebrate.

'To the Christian knights of the Round Table,' said Merlin as he raised his goblet, 'and their just leader, Arthur Pendragon.'

At the moment of the toast a bright light appeared to fill the room. Each man felt its brilliance as though only for him. From a shimmering cup of glass there flowed food and wine and wisdom. We were all mesmerised by what we could not explain. But there was no doubt: this was the cup of Christ. Each knight's task was just penance for all the blood he had spilled in war. The quest had truly begun.

As his companions prepared for their individual journeys Arthur confided his concerns. How many would return? Was it irony that the Christian ideals he had inspired might bring about the destruction of Camelot?

My concern was one I carried alone. What would men do with the simple earthenware cup that Christ had used at the Last Supper, the cup that held his blood at the Crucifixion, and that Joseph had brought to Britain for safekeeping? Arthur was right that this madness would not end well. Over days and weeks I retreated more often to my cell, for the burden of silence was mine alone.

Knights set off for all corners of these islands: west to the Cymbrogi kingdoms, north to Gododdin and the high lands beyond. Every strange story was investigated. Many seemed to involve a Corbyn or Crow or one of its relatives, the Ravens and Arthur's beloved Choughs. Merlin was consulted for his knowledge of Nature to explain the creatures' behaviours. I scoured the texts for references to these strange black birds. From the Ark Noah sent out a raven which "flew here and there until the water was dried up from the earth". Luke's lesson in trust was delight for some of the more devout. "Consider the ravens: for they neither sow nor reap; which neither have storehouse nor barn; and God feedeth them: how much more are ye better than the birds?" "For life is more than food, and the body more than clothes". The quest for the divine was palpable and unstoppable.

Months passed and Arthur's fears were realised: many came back injured with stories of dead comrades. A year passed and Bors, Percival and Galahad had not returned. When Bors arrived alone, gaunt and changed, he told a strange story. His speech was halting, distracted and not of the man we had known.

'We rode west through the land of the Cymbrogi and then north into the mountains of Powys. Percival was told of a place of Crows, a barren place where only they would find food. Days and days of harsh weather and cold nights brought us to a wasted land with a mighty fortress called Castle Corbyn, or Corbenic, which is the castle of the Crows.

As we approached the gate it was opened and we were brought before Pelles, an aged and infirm king seated on a dilapidated throne. He welcomed us as comrades of Lancelot, but most especially Galahad. For Pelles' daughter Elaine had conceived a son by Lancelot: he was Galahad. As a child Galahad had been raised by nuns under the guidance of Pelles. Now he had returned to fulfil his destiny.

At the celebration feast, mostly of fish since the king had been maimed by a battle lance and was too infirm to do anything but wield a rod, this Fisher King brought in a cup and a lance. Percival and I did not recognise them for what they were.

Galahad's eyes brightened and he asked, "Is this the cup Christ held at His Last Supper? Is this the lance that pierced Christ's side?" Pelles gave Galahad the cup.

"I am the last of the Fisher Kings who have guarded the Grail. You have freed me and this land. Now you must decide the Cup's fate," said Pelles.

Galahad gazed in a trance upon the goblet for a long time.

"Camelot is not worthy of the Grail. We must travel along the route taken by Joseph and his followers and return it to the island of Sarras."

'Who were we to gainsay one who spoke as a Christian prophet? So we took ship and sailed south and then east towards Jerusalem until we came to the island. There we stayed for a year while Galahad converted the pagans. At the end of this time we experienced a wonder: a precious light shone from heaven. It took up the Grail and Galahad. Percival and I were awestruck, so much so that Percival became a hermit there. It was left to me to return to tell our story.'

I tried to question the detail of Bors' account because I could not believe what he saw was true. Merlin did the same. But we were unsuccessful. Bors no longer wished to be a knight of the Round Table. For the remaining months of his life he was cared for in my parish so that he could find peace.

§

One Tintagel afternoon on the eve of winter Arthur was eating pieces of roasted chicken beside the fluttering fire. He shunned the company of the Great Hall, being content with our company and that of Samson, the giant brown shepherds' dog I had given him as a present from the tinners. Samson's large grey eyes followed Arthur's every move, his head tilted in question of "What about me?" and the drool from his mouth stretched in a line to the floor. Arthur's mind was immersed on the battlefield: the instant between life and death; the lightness of the hawk before he swooped for the kill; the instinctive joy of each living moment. Arthur had escaped into a place of Nature, battle or sky that Merlin had taught him so long ago. He seemed to slip into these thoughts more often lately.

'Death is not the problem,' he said again, 'or even the pain of leaving; it is not having enough time to do my allotted task.'

Then I reminded him of his achievements, not just on the battlefield but for the ordinary people now able to enjoy peace.

'You have given them choice, Arthur. They can be honest because they don't have to do whatever it takes to survive. Maybe they will become Christian. That is your achievement, Arthur. You have bought time for the Christian word to change society for the better.'

Merlin frowned but could only agree with the benefits of no war.

'Is that what you will write about me, Justin?' Arthur said. Samson caught the bone in mid-air between his teeth and settled closer to the fire.

'If you wish, and a lot more,' I said.

'And you, Merlin? Will you tell my story too?'

'Of course, our tales will be from different minds but truth nonetheless.'

Merlin and I kept our promises. His treatise was kept by the Cymbrogi peoples and I have heard that it was much sought after by scholars of many persuasions. Mine I have kept closer to my heart. The madness of the Grail quest with its conflicting tales and promises made me wary of

166

sharing the truth. Arthur's name would be great in history. Many would distort veracity for their own ends.

Arthur ambled towards his chamber. Minstrels told their tales in the Great Hall and many knights drank deeply. He thought of Guinevere, the early days of eagerness before the long absences of war separated them in so many ways. Her life was at court: one of poetry and courtly love set to music. After so many failed attempts at children she now chose the solace of her own chamber. Yet he knew that Guinevere still wanted to produce his heir. Her role as Arthur's wife was incomplete.

A short while ago he had chanced upon her in the walled garden, an arbour of shade against the wind, a trap for the sun in a paradise of fruit trees espaliered against the stone walls, and a verdant haven of herbs and flowers. A chess board filled a small table to one side of the group. Knights sat around her in a semi-circle. They were attentive, cultivated in the topics of their speech, virile and their eyes drank of Guinevere. Music played and her laughter was like a tinkling brook.

Later he criticised her familiarity with them. She laughed.

'Do you doubt my honour, husband? A queen may be a queen.'

'Guinevere?' he said as she made to walk away.

'Yes, my lord?'

He studied the nuances of her body, the quicksilver youth within her eyes. There was still something of him inside her mind. He smiled and left her to her diversions.

In the late afternoon he left his chamber to walk along a section of wall available only to him. From it he could see Guinevere alone with just two dress maids in attendance. The weak, end-of-day sun was gently warming when protected from the wind. His thoughts were drawn to the flat sculptures of apple trees trained so well by Nimue's maidens.

For an hour he walked aloof, detached, in his own world before returning to the same place. He heard rhythmic breaths and delicate groans that he knew too well. Arthur looked down again into her garden. The chess pieces were fewer, a strategic victory of sorts he judged. Her maids were outside the locked door. Within the garden was Guinevere. Her robes were open and lifted so that her long legs and firm breasts were exposed to the dying sun. Half-eaten apples lay on a bench with a carafe of wine and two goblets. Beside them was Guinevere being pleasured by Lancelot.

Arthur felt shock, and yet he had wondered before. For a moment he watched. No, this was not pillage it was her choice. Arthur looked to his feet and Cavall who sat beside them. His shaggy companion was the latest gift from the miners when Samson left too soon.

'This was my fault for not sharing more of my life with her. Who was I to cage her spirit?' He turned away more alone than ever.

'Tell me about Lancelot,' he said to her when they were alone.

'In what way, my lord?'

'Do you love him?'

Guinevere was motionless as Arthur's anger enveloped her. He had seen them at last, she thought. Maybe that was for the good.

'No. I married you alone.'

'Then why do you share your body with him?'

'Your kingdom needs an heir. I chose Lancelot from the greatest warriors of your court. He can father a strong son so that all your achievements will not be lost in one generation.'

'Do we share you and the kingdom?'

'No. He will be eliminated as soon as a pregnancy is clear. The boy will have Arthur's name. There will be no pretender to the throne.'

He sat beside her now in her garden and listened to her thoughts.

'When you rode off to battle did you think of me? If you were lost how would I survive against the powerful lords? I have cultivated your knights as a teulu of my own. Using my position and my sex I decided a long time ago that I would survive. So would Arthur's son if I could bear him, by whatever means. If the gods wish it you will have an heir.'

'I am not worthy of you,' he said. In the silence he thought of how a woman was stronger than a man; that she appeared to give in but took control for a purpose. Like a tree she was not sturdy by her bulk or girth but by her flexibility in a storm; her ability to sacrifice limbs for the whole to survive. To Guinevere her body was expendable, a tool for purpose and not of her soul.

But in the quiet Guinevere studied Arthur. She had hurt him to the core of his being and could not take his torment away.

'You knew, Merlin,' he said as the four of us shared the warmth of his fire. Cavall was now his constant companion.

Merlin said nothing.

'Of course you did.'

'Your realm must last beyond one man's lifetime,' Merlin said.

'Those are the old ways of thought.'

'Then you are too good for this world, Arthur.'

'I try to do what is right.'

'So do I.'

'Let God decide, Merlin.'

'Which one?'

We left Arthur brooding by the fire, Cavall at his feet.

CHAPTER 9

Down in the kitchen Ros stood beside two cups on the kitchen bench, her coffee and Philip's tea, waiting for the kettle to boil.

'Stand up, Jeremy,' she heard from along the corridor. Nurse Jennifer stripped the wet bed sheets. 'Now we might give you a little wash before we change into dry things,' she said as if to a child. Ros pictured Jeremy standing obediently as the nurse sponged him down and dressed him for the day.

Ros poured the steaming hot water and softly climbed up the attic stairs.

'You don't need a doctor, Jeremy, you need a plumber,' said Meredith in exasperation, just as Ros returned the empty cups to the kitchen bench. Meredith turned on the clothes dryer and set up the washing machine for the next load.

§

'Remind me why we're doing this, Philip.'

A fair request, he thought. If he could explain it then there was a valid reason.

'Cornish tin mining is older than Arthur, older than Christ. If we accept that Cornwall was the heart of Arthur's support then tinners were probably among them. On a different note there are the legends about Joseph of Aramathea bringing the young Jesus here. They met the miners.'

Philip drove the thirty five miles to the Geevor Mine on the north coast. Between Helston and Penzance the road skirted Mounts Bay. St Michael's Mount, perched on a volcanic extrusion, was in clear view for much of the hour's journey. Ros reflected on its silhouette, which was almost a caricature of a fairy-tale castle. Philip pondered its role in the tin trade and early Christianity.

At the site office Oscar Penhaligan, a fit thirty four year old in orange dungarees, miner's hat and welly boots, shook their hands.

'Thee be Mr Pasty's friends, then.'

'How do you know him, Oscar?' Philip asked as they were being kitted out in the locker room with overalls, waterproof jackets, hard hats and boots.

'E be mi' teacher a' school.' He shut the lift cage door. 'No 'a gud studen were I,' he said laughing as he pressed the button. They dropped like a rattling stone, around twenty five feet per second.

'Be'er th'n ladders thi 'ad in ol' days.' He had noticed them swallowing to pop their ears.

In the next hour he explained how the tin was drilled and blasted from the granite, a process which left huge caverns that supported themselves without pit props. Small electric trains pulled the wagons of ore to the surface. Massive pumps removed the fresh water and in turn stopped the sea water from flooding in. Level fifteen, where they were, was fifteen hundred feet down. Once mined it became a hundred foot cavern for eternity. Pay was far better than the building sites that Philip knew so well. And a hard day's work was comparatively safe with modern methods.

But if you took away the technology, went back only a hundred and fifty years, this became a brutish, dangerous existence that shortened men's, women's and children's lives. Without pumps the mines were as shallow as the water table. Miners waded up to their knees in mud and rainwater. Hearing was sacrificed to the repeated boom of sledgehammers on steel drill bits. After months and years of headaches the pain subsided into permanent deafness. Heat increased the deeper the adit went in. In 100% humidity workers wore little and tipped out pints of sweat from their boots at the break. Every swing of the pick added to the impenetrable dust that filled lungs with silica. Arsenic, a valuable by-product, slowly poisoned everyone. Yet workers were only paid for what they produced, not the hours spent each day on ladders getting to their stope. And the only safety was their comrades.

No wonder these were strong people used to sacrifice and hard times. In Arthur's era they appeared to live in villages, unprotected by city militia or a lord of the manor. They traded with the world but Philip wondered how they survived? Meredith's line, "Wherever in the world there's a hole in the ground there's a Cornishman at the bottom" rang true but only because these people did what they had to do to live. When the work dried up they emigrated. Theirs was an underground life. The tunnels were a labyrinth that only they could navigate. But many tunnels exited in cliffs and coves. Was that "hole in the ground" their hiding place against the Saxon raiders? As traders were they also smugglers in times of need?

Ros stood beside the processing plant. After the ore was crushed to fine sand she marvelled at the numerous stages needed to produce the ingots of silvery tin. She tried to picture the division of labour in the past. In Victoria's England kids were still sent down chimneys, and slavery produced the wealth of London, Bristol and Liverpool until William Wilberforce came along. In a world with no rules she guessed the miners and their families worked together according to their abilities. Nothing in modern sensibilities could really relate to their perilous existence.

Inevitably her thoughts came back to religion, despite her deep disbelief in a benign, guiding deity. John Wesley was well received in 18th century Cornwall. His Methodist brand of intense personal faith still dominated. If Jesus himself came to this place what effect would his visit have had? He was young but surely inspiring. The promise of heaven, a better life for the poor but pure of heart, must have fed willing minds. The support structure of the early church would have mirrored that of their community. But was there really any truth beneath the legends? Jeremy would probably say no and she had insufficient proof to disagree with him.

§

When they dropped back at mid-day Meredith already had Jeremy's lunch on his side table in the lounge: bacon with the rind on, well crisped egg and two slices of fried bread to soak up the juices. It was his usual; all recorded on the seven day menu discussed each Sunday night for the week to come.

'Would you two like anything?' Meredith asked.

'Just a cuppa, thanks,' said Philip. They sat with Meredith at the kitchen tabletop.

'Jeremy wants to buy a bigger tv,' Meredith grumbled. 'What's the point if what's on is all rubbish? A bigger tv just makes it bigger!'

'You live such interesting lives,' she said after they described the morning at Kynance, minus the smugglers' cave. 'But then the grass is always greener on the other side of the stable door.'

In the lounge Meredith removed the dishes and reset the side table for Jeremy to explain his research on what they had found.

'Four items remarkably preserved considering seawater and sand.' He held up the two pottery pieces now glued into the clear curve of an amphora. Jeremy opened a volume dealing with marine archaeology in the Mediterranean at the marked page. 'This was a transport amphora from the Ist century AD. This profile,' pointing to the curve and the beginnings of the base, 'is of a two-handled jar traditionally sealed with a cork and cement which held seven gallons of wine. It matches this one found at Adria in Italy.'

Moments later he picked up the clasp, shaped like an ornamentally curved door hinge, now cleaned brass or bronze. 'This held the front to the back section of the Lorica Segmentata, the segmented cuirass or chest plate issued to Roman legionaries from the Ist century BC to the late third century AD. Here it is depicted on the Arch of Constantine erected in 315.'

As before Jeremy expected no disagreement. Philip did not give him any. Jeremy seemed to be spot on with his judgement.

'The javelin point is too rusted to place accurately with the Romans, Arthur or even later Anglo-Saxons. But the coin is another matter.' Meredith handed him the numismatic compendium at the right page. 'Carausius usurped control of Roman Britain between 287 and 293AD.

The coin came from the London mint and was clipped three times for its silver content. 'IMPCARAUSIUS AVGGG, with his crowned head, and on the obverse LEG III FL ML. The emaciated creature with long legs, Rosalind, is a stylized lion.'

'Why would a late Romano-British coin turn up here?' Philip thought aloud.

'Very few coins were minted in Roman Britain after this date,' answered Jeremy. 'There were no hoards in Cornwall that I know of.'

'Could it have been kept, a souvenir or a remembrance of a better time?' Ros said.

Philip nodded. 'Maybe. Still, we have dates for what looks like two events: wine from the 1st century AD and the coin and warrior accoutrements from the 4th century or a bit later,' Philip said.

'Not a bad day's fossicking,' said Ros.

§

On Tintagel Island Mason appeared to appreciate the update. They had provided a new perspective on his work and had definitely earned his trust. By four the paltry sun was battling large black clouds coming in from the west. The colour and turbulence of the waves below suggested another storm was on its way from the Atlantic. It was time to go. As Philip and Rosalind drove up Dracaena Avenue the fading winter light disappeared into hissing rain. The wipers swished like eyelashes through the dripping murk. At Clarence Terrace Philip closed the garage door and raced down the garden and across the causeway just as Ros unlocked the back door. Inside they took off wet shoes and enjoyed the towels Meredith had left on the clothes' hooks.

'Well, lad, are you any closer?' asked Jeremy.

'Of course, a lot,' parried Philip. He looked at Ros sitting opposite Jeremy. Her suntan was rosier with the help of Tintagel's weather. Meredith dozed on the poofee at Jeremy's feet. He rubbed her back and stared at the Bush twenty inch television set on steel legs in the corner. His movements suggested that he was about to ask Meredith to get up to turn down the volume button. Philip suddenly thought, did he really feel like a Jeremy discussion, one-sided and merciless? It had been a good day. Why spoil it? He nodded to Ros, who shrugged her shoulders as if to say 'whatever you think'.

'We might head down to the Orient for an hour. It would be nice to wind down from a full day,' he said.

Meredith opened her eyes and picked up their mood. 'I'll leave tea in the oven. Have fun.'

It was only a short walk along the Terrace to the deserted garden of wooden tables and benches. Inside the warmth, smells and conversation welcomed. Ros bagsed the window seat left of the door, her hands sliding along the table edge as she clambered to the far end. Philip's head was immersed in Jeremy as he returned with a half pint of Newquay Steam made by Devenish and a glass of Mateus Rose.

'For someone who's not scared of too much you must face up to him some time, Philip.'

'True. As soon as he says 'lad' I react just like always.' He took another sip. 'He's not much better with you.'

'Yes but I push it away. He's sick, Philip. Give him some space. He doesn't know what he's saying.'

'Yes he does, precisely so.' He looked around the room for the first time: half a dozen propped against the bar, two older couples seated at tables at the other end, two blokes at the dart board nearby with cigarettes off their lips, squinting through the smoke to add up the score. He and Ros watched people until their glasses were empty.

'Another?' he said.

'Yes, please.'

He ambled to the middle of the bar, beside the sodden drink mat next to the taps. The genial barman pulled a half pint of Greene King's Abbot Ale, steady and slow. He placed it beside the Mateus.

'That'll be 15p, sir.' Philip fished through the new decimal coins to give him the right change. As he reached for the glasses there was a cry. He knew the voice.

§

What's this fellow up to, Ros thought. Philip was on his way to the bar as the solidly built man with ruddy face and calloused hands got up from the stool and made a beeline for her. His suit was soiled and the off-white shirt opened at the neck showed too much grey-haired chest.

'This seat's taken,' she said.

'Yes, by me, darling.' He sat too close and looked into her face. She felt the leer and heard the ready reckoner beneath his coarse face sizing her up. The smell of Scrumpy would put her off the stuff for life. But he was not just a drunk who fancied her. His manner was business, a task to complete. Her neck felt the shivers.

'What were you two doing at Kynance?'

'None of your business, fella!' she said. His accent was Cornish but not local. She tried to pick it, northern Cornwall maybe, and it idly crossed her mind that she might need to remember some of Philip's tricks.

'Ah.' Her cry was involuntary after he slapped her across her left cheek.

'Better attitude, luv! What were you doing?'

§

Philip turned, saw, slopped the drinks as they wobbled on the mat, and took four steps to reach the thug's throat. His right hand grabbed shirt, stubble and suit and lifted him vertically over the table, before he hurled him across the floor towards the dart board. The players scattered to the edges as the man scrambled up fast.

Ros half rose behind the table. Philip stood in front of her facing the lout.

'Gud a' 'itting girls, eh? E' bladder o' lard!'

Where did that come from, she thought? Philip's back and spread thighs were taut like bow strings. The tiny shiver of muscles betrayed his anger.

As the man rushed at him with bent arms protecting his face, Philip skipped forward and booted him hard in the sternum. The roughneck's forward motion was lifted off the ground and he spreadeagled a metre backwards. He wheezed in rage as he got up slowly. There was a doubt in his mind, she thought.

'Stop that there glumpin. E' all mouth and trouser,' Philip taunted.

The bull roared forward again. Philip slid his left foot in front and kneed him hard in the gut with his right, before rabbit punching him in his right ear. In a second Philip had bounced back to his spot in front of Ros.

This isn't right, she thought. Philip has his measure. I- we, are safe. She was worried. Philip seemed to be playing with him, like pulling legs off a beetle. This was beyond the need of the moment and verging on cruel. That slap had triggered something.

The bruiser got up. In his mind he had no choice but come on again. Philip stood lightly on the balls of his feet.

'E' couldn't fight e' way out o' a paaper bag.'

Philip's hands dropped loose by his sides. He reminded her of a cat, alert, waiting, building up.

He's a strange mixture, Ros thought, sort of dancing but deadly. At other times he would speak of sufficient force to deal with the problem. In Iran it was wonderful that he was on her side; civilised values over primitivism. Otherwise why bother with civilised values? Here she saw the thin veneer of civilisation that hid the barbarism. Is this what Arthur was trying to change when he talked to Justin, she rambled? She could hear Justin's argument for thinking peace not war; that the price of life should be costly not cheap. What was the value of this goon in Philip's eyes? Not much. The Old World produces Philip and the New World me. Yes, this fool is a ratbag but I am the one thinking give him a second chance.

'Cummiz on!'

As she observed the victim, because that was what he was now, Philip turned side on with the barest lift of his left foot. As the man rushed in to try to get inside Philip's range, Philip lifted the front foot slightly and spun clockwise into the jump. The sole of his back foot, the right, rose above the protective fists and slapped into the man's right cheek.

It's still a game to him, Ros thought in the fraction of a second.

As his right foot came down and he was in the same stance again Philip milked the momentum and spun vertically again. This time was no play. With pent up force and fury his heel rose high and cracked down like an axe into the side of the dupe's head. It was enough to smash the thickest skull and the bloke went down hard on his back. Miraculously, slowly, the gorilla surfaced. As he opened his eyes Philip's right foot was poised three inches above his nose.

Philip was side on to her, perfectly still apart from the steady rise and fall of his chest. Even though she had never seen it she knew his mood. It was uncontrolled rage, blind and lethal. But there was something else. The Hammurabi code of an eye for an eye had defeated all the legal codes of Justinian and Napoleon and the rest without a blink. There was never a whisker of doubt in his mind as to what was right and what was wrong in what he would do next.

As his breath slowed his muscles built up in preparation.

'PHILIP!' she said loudly, to break the spell.

In his mind he had failed her. It took seconds for the cloud to lift from the antediluvian depths of his brain. But then he gradually turned and observed her. She saw that look: steel, cold; something deep within him that had no limit. It was that primeval instinct to protect his woman. She was awfully glad that he was on her side.

'Philip,' she said quietly, that special tone that spoke everything that he wanted to hear. He was coming out of the trance. Now he was back to a purpose not incandescent vengeance.

He smiled at her and his eyes inspected the bruise rising on her cheek. The dope beneath stared motionless at the sole of Philip's shoe. Then she saw Philip absorb the people in the room. At the counter a forty-year-old man, fit and with brains, passed eye signals to three locals.

She saw the barman close to the telephone but holding back. There was silent stare from everyone else, except one. Both recognised him. The lean male used to hard work walked through the frozen statues to what must be the boss.

'They be Pasty's mates,' said Oscar.

The man stood down his men with a low pat beside his waist. He nodded respect to Philip.

Philip smiled. He was in control again. His foot dropped gently on to the nose and rested there. He kept his eyes on the boss. In a fragment of time he twisted. Everyone in the room heard the crack. Then he gently lifted his right leg and stood facing the leader.

'Let's talk,' Philip said. He pointed to their table in the window alcove. Philip waited for him to take a chair before he sat opposite him, beside Ros.

'Peter,' as he stretched out his hand.

'Philip,' as he returned a firm handshake, 'and Rosalind.'

'I'm sorry about Brian. He's a friend's brother, from Camborne. I had to take him on. You know how it is. There are better methods of finding out information than that.' His manner was matter of fact about ways to reach a goal.

'Why try to frighten us with ruffians? If he'd asked me nicely,' she said.

'With me present,' Philip cut in.

Ros gave him her 'yes we got that' look.

'What were you doing at Asparagus Rock?' Peter was not a man to dwell on apologies. Once was enough.

Philip looked at Ros and then explained.

'What are you looking for Arthur for?'

Ros described their quest for Jeremy. Peter nodded. She knew he would check all that was said with his network.

'People around here think highly of Arthur. Some like Brian might think you plan to take him away with you.'

Strange that they think of him in the present tense, thought Ros.

'We saw you in the glider thing. Was that Arthur too?'

'Yes.' Ros told him about Lyonesse, which he knew despite a card player face.

'And Asparagus Rock?' he continued.

'We saw bags in the water but didn't touch them,' said Philip. He then described the finds and how they might relate to the search.

'And the cave?'

They both knew that this was the sixty four dollar question. Peter's eyes searched their expressions as they looked at each other for agreement.

'Yes we looked inside the cave,' said Philip.

'I found it,' said Ros.

'Curiosity can get you hurt, Miss Rosalind.'

'Maybe,' said Philip. Brian's near demise was just beneath the surface.

'We saw boxes, one of which was open,' she said. 'There were metal ingots, some gold and others a type of silver. What are you smuggling, Peter?'

'Why did you go down Geevor mine with Oscar?'

'Arthur, of course. Philip has a theory that the tinners and Arthur were connected in some way.' Despite her surface dislike of Peter she opened her thoughts about how hard it must have been for the miners in ancient times.

Peter raised his hand to pause and stood at the bar with Oscar for a time. Had she said too much? What she'd spoken seemed innocuous enough to her.

Oscar pulled over another chair and they sat down. 'Oscar seems to believe that we can trust you,' Peter said. 'Can we?' He cracked his knuckles and studied their reactions.

'Our goal is to help Jeremy and nothing more,' Philip said. 'We are quite close to winning.'

Ros nodded.

There was that something extra again, thought Philip. 'When we learn we will publish most but not all. There will be no stealing of Arthur.'

'What do you know of the Tinners' Mite?' said Peter

'Nothing,' they said together.

'Is it like the Widow's Mite?' asked Philip.

Peter nodded.

'A poor widow puts two small coins in the temple collection plate but wealthy people put in much more. Jesus tells his disciples that her gift is greater because it is so much bigger in relation to what she has,' explained Philip.

'N' a small gift go's long way,' said Oscar. 'What's e's price, Philip?' he paused, 'n' Rosalind?'

'We don't have one,' he shrugged.

'W't 'bout them things you find? Don't e' get somethin' for 'em?'

'No. They go into a museum. If we're lucky we get basic pay.'

Peter and Oscar laughed. 'E' be mad buggars,' said Oscar. 'Naw share lik' wi' gentry then?'

'So you want knowledge of Arthur?' said Peter.

'And the Grail. That's the other task Jeremy gave us,' said Ros.

'That be Jesus and ol' Joseph of Ar'mtea then? Me granda' speak o' 'im.'

'And what about Justin, Oscar? Did your grandad ever speak about him?' asked Ros.

Peter's poker face slipped.

Oscar studied Peter. 'Maybe.'

Philip heard but knew enough to wait for the next instalment. There was silence at their table and only safe whispers in the rest of the pub. If he was a regular would he want it known that he had heard?

'If we help ...' the pause was definite. 'In return you say nothing of what you've seen.' said Peter.

Philip and Ros looked at each other. Neither man was laughing at their quest.

'Nobody tells,' said Philip. It was the ancient code of the smuggler. He held out his hand to Peter, then Oscar. They shook and Philip waited. Ros' right hand lay uncurled on the table.

'Well?' Philip said, looking at Peter and then at Ros' fingers just left of his vision? 'She has a brain too.'

'Ee, Phil n' Justin, then,' said Oscar. He held out his hand first and she took it.

Peter smiled and did the same. 'What about the days when a man spoke for his woman' was clearly written across his forehead? The deal was done.

'Now can you tell me what those silver-looking ingots were made of?' asked Ros.

'People would kill to know that, Rosalind. You need to watch that inquisitiveness.'

'But we were searching for Arthur, not contraband.'

Peter held his face immobile with difficulty. A deal was a deal.

'Contraband? Yes and no. Yes it's sold on the open market. No because it's the cream off the top of tinning used for a good cause.'

'A good end justifies some slightly dodgy means to get the cash?' Philip said.

'A fair summation, Philip.'

'By the end you mean helping the miners?' Ros said.

'Their wives and kids. The state does a bit and National Health too but we look after our own in times of trouble.'

'Most tinners be dead b' forty. Som'uns got t' 'elp poor buggars left behin',' said Oscar.

A good cause she thought but she didn't want to remind them that that argument had been used by Robespierre and Hitler, and probably Genghis Khan too. 'And the silvery stuff?' she reminded Peter.

'Indium, Tantalum and Palladium. Indium is used in cars, tvs and the military. Tantalum, rarer than gold, is used in electronics, alloys and surgical instruments. One use for Palladium is in white gold wedding rings,' Peter said, pointedly looking at Ros' empty finger.

Ros smiled and said nothing: none of his business. A contract doesn't mean we're best buddies. But she did like the use the cash was put to. 'How do you help the kids?'

'Education. We help kids stay out of the mines with learning. It's too late for Oscar and me but I'll be damned if we let another generation be killed off.'

It was the first passion Ros had seen in Peter.

'How is Mr Pasty, Mr Pascoe, involved?' she asked.

'E' be me chemistry teacher a' skul,' said Oscar.

Peter explained that Jeremy's classes gave Oscar and the rest the skills to understand the refining process. They took the scum off at the end and turned it into their "cream on the top". The mine owners turned a blind eye, giving back for how hard they were in the old days. Not every owner was good but those who ran Geevor, Wheal Jane and South Crofty all helped.

'Jeremy knew all this?' said Philip.

'Course. E' b'n gibben money fir years, ever since 'is boys go t' boardin' skul. Giv' loc'l cheldern a chance too. Mr Pasty were always g'd to tinners.'

'He constantly put aside money for poor families. When a Dad was injured or dying from silicosis in his lungs, or the slow sweetness of arsenic, he always gave.'

'Ow 's Mr P?'

'Not good, Oscar. He hasn't got long,' Ros said.

Philip stood up and the men stepped aside from the table. Ros felt strange as Peter held her jacket so she could slide her arm into the sleeve. Yet again she had been part of a manly game. As they turned towards the door she noticed that Brian was gone and the blood was now a clean wet patch on the carpet. People acted the same as when they had walked in, almost.

Outside the gang lined the pavement beside the low wall of the pub garden.

Not again, Philip thought, as he tucked Ros a pace behind his back. He cracked his knuckles and sucked in a long calming breath. His patience was very thin.

Philip recognised him as he stepped into the light of the doorway. His deputy and the rest of the gang sat down on the damp wall. The leader was lean like Philip, similar height but his drink-red cheeks and seafaring tattooed arms spoke of another life. Silver studs punctured his right ear, nose and bottom lip. His gap-toothed smile showed nicotine stained teeth. He was king of the street through rat cunning and the brutal crushing of all opposition. He stood in Philip's way and his milky blue eyes stared into his. This was power play and entertainment for the boys.

'Narley Man,' he said as he hooked his arm out for a sideways handshake.

'Philip.' He returned the handshake and waited.

Ros read his back again. The build-up was taking place.

'Did ee kil'm?' The laugh was a higher pitch than he expected. 'Naw. B't Brian's scritchin' like a pig.' The gang laughed with him.

Philip guessed what happened in the Orient had been telegraphed. This was pecking order. If Narley Man harmed Philip or his girl then Peter would kick him and his gang from here to breakfast time.

'Yer stand' by yer standin' xackley way we us'd te do it. Yer a firm gurt fella,' Narley said and he took off his hood. His minions did the same.

'Thanks,' Philip said as he walked the gauntlet past them with Ros in tow. At the house he kept going towards Jacob's Ladder, but then turned left around the corner into the back lane. In a shadow but close to an open patch of way lit by the street light he waited, still holding Ros' hand. After ten minutes Ros walked to the garden gate and unlatched it. No one followed her. Philip caught up at the back door.

'You're a primitive really,' she said to him as they climbed into bed.

'Mm. Maybe. I just look after my own.'

'Careful.'

'Ok. I didn't mean quite that. I look after you. And I know that I don't own you.'

'Not that I don't appreciate it,' she said as she kissed him goodnight. As she straightened the pillow, 'Maybe you're more suited to Arthur's time. In the Saxon Terror I doubt if I'd have batted an eyelid however you rescued me, as long as you got there in time.'

In the darkness her thoughts wound down, only punctuated by the lights from the dock cranes through the steamy window. Peter and his mates were smugglers but not of grog or ciggies or even people these days. Somehow the consignment hidden in boxes of pilchards picked up by the fishing fleet off Britanny, and the cause it served, made it into a good. Could they trust them? Philip thought so. Why was Jeremy so harsh with Meredith, she puzzled? He was so good with tinners' kids and yet sent his own away to boarding school.

Philip cradled her head into his shoulder. He enjoyed the gentle change of her breath into sleep. His intellect followed the mining tunnels again. You could hide anything in those vast caverns beneath Cornwall. The earth had its secrets.

CHAPTER 10

The journey back to Ynys Wydryn seemed longer than before. News of our presence in Powys along the Eastern border with the Saxon kingdoms had scattered the incursion before we even arrived. No battle and no plunder left our party in a poor mood, except for Merlin and me whose healing skills had not been required. It continued as we rode in file along the wooden tracks floating on this sodden landscape, the rain steady and merciless. Now we camped on the lower slopes of the Tor itself as our mounts grazed the lush green near the well. Our guard beside the covered bonfire on the hill above could barely see a mile in any direction through the mist. Only if the warning beacons had been lit on the hills north-west and south-east of us would we have known where the boundary between Dumnonia and the Saxon settlements was.

'What were we there for, Arthur?' I said as I handed him the bowl of watery stew provided by our surly hosts. The sudden arrival of a teulu of eighty knights had strained their resources however great the name of Arthur.

Merlin gestured to leave him with his thoughts. We guessed he was soaring high over sunny vales or in that sublime moment before his lance dropped into the charge. He might even have been with Guinevere at Kelliwic, the fortress he had favoured more often of late, where we would be in a day's time.

'Powys had more to fear from cattle reivers from Gwynedd than Saxon raiders,' Merlin said cynically. He looked at Arthur's downcast eyes and felt the presence of Tewdric, now long gone. 'We were there to solve the problems of others, as usual. But our prompt arrival showed Arthur's vigilance still maintains the peace.'

I studied Merlin as his raised voice crackled. His arthritic hands wrapped around the bowl quivered as they absorbed the heat. The staff propped beside him was less symbolic of Druidic status than a crutch to support his crumbling knees. He was venerable when I first met him. Once he was the boy who had outwitted Vortigern; the man who had advised Ambrosius and Uther; and the mentor who raised Arthur to greatness. Now he was an old man who could no longer ignore his years. Rarely did he put so many words together now, in the belief that silence might hide his forgetfulness. Notes written in Ogham script hidden in his sleeves were reminders.

Around the camp fires were faces younger than ours. As with other sorties among the Brythonic provinces and into the Anglish lands there were few familiar comrades. Kay, Bedivere and the rest were constantly called away to their own strongholds or on another quest for a Christian relic. Caer Guidn, Agned and Badonicus were names of revered battles that these young warriors had never known. The men were untested and only the presence of Arthur kept away the wolves. Merlin was right: Arthur was always in the saddle to maintain the fragile peace. In the surreptitious glances of these fledglings towards the brooding Arthur was veneration as towards a god.

§

At first light we rode out over the marsh tracks, past the grass tufts and the pools of water lying after the overnight rain. On the lower slopes of uplands were the purple and grey patches of leafless trees within days of budding green. During the morning I saw Arthur absorb the gloomy quiet along the coast and the mudflats of the estuaries. Flights of birds circled and landed to feed in the retreating tide, among the ribs of rocks, the kelp and the bubbles of brown seaweed. Our horses' hooves broke the quiet as they clattered over the wooden beams bridging the Tamar River into Cornubia. I noticed the small craft spaced along the muddy reaches, part of Arthur's warning defence. But soon a familiar sound surfaced over the distance across the open moorland: shouts and the clash of shield and steel. But the cheers were louder. A shaft of sunlight cut through the mist as Arthur led us through the outer defence of Kelliwic.

Inside the inner ring of wall and ditch were the Great Hall and the outbuildings of stables, kitchens and servants quarters. In the space of green in front was a melee of armed men and horses as if in a ragged battle. To one side was a rough framework of timber lashed together to form elevated seating for the notables of court: knights recently returned, wives and ladies in waiting and guests from afar. At the centre of the group was Guinevere with Lancelot on her right and Mordred on her left. The gathering was her latest choice of entertainment, a tourney.

Arthur disbanded the troop and servants took horses and baggage. Soon the younger knights joined friends as seconds to the competitors or became part of the milling throng of spectators. Originally for training with use of sword, spear and arrow: they whiled away the boredom between serious conflicts. But this was a pageant. Arthur nodded to his queen who bowed momentarily before her eyes returned to the spectacle. Stools appeared and we three watched the proceedings with the rest.

Furthest from the people were circles of coiled reed set in stands of heavy timber. At marked distances of twenty, thirty and fifty paces were men with bows and others with spears. Stewards led each group of five men forward. After the projectiles flew they measured their accuracy on the distant targets. Over the afternoon the best were found and pitted against each other.

Within wicker squares fought pairs of knights with shield and sword. Many were evenly matched for weight and strength but others relied on wits and courage to bring down the bigger opponent. In the centre before Guinevere was a rectangle one hundred paces long divided by a single rope. At either end was a knight on horseback, spear in one hand and shield in the other. They waited for the raised pennant to fall before they drove their steeds at each other, left and right of the divide.

Merlin and I were glad of two things. Of all his wife's amusements this pleased Arthur most. His mind was in the moment, his hands twitched with each blow, his eyes danced at the clash of steel or the penetration of spear into wood and hide. I hoped that her timing of the event at his return was not accidental. The other was Arthur's command that swords and spears be blunted. He had need of well- trained knights but not of those maimed in their preparation. Merlin and I were still called to ply unguents to bruising and wrap linen to stop bleeding. But we were not overwhelmed as in the slaughter of battle.

Guinevere watched the progress through the contestants of Tristan, her younger step brother who she had grown up with in the court of Lyonesse. All his skills were significant but the years on campaign with Arthur had trained him in sword and spear to be a formidable champion. Matched against him was Arthur's nephew, Hoel from Britanny, that part of Roman Armorica settled by Brythons fleeing the Saxon Terror. His record at the Hill of Agned and Mount Badonicus was no less worthy than Tristan's. Arthur loved both men as younger brothers. Tristan's service at the court of his rival, King Mark, was not something Arthur held against such a worthy knight.

Now Tristan and Hoel faced each other in the lists. Their horses snorted in defiance, keenly aware of the clash of arms that was about to take place. Unlike the battlefield there were no taunts or malice between two comrades who were pitted against each other. I could see Arthur was with them in spirit, feeling that glorious tension and the moment of release as they drove their mounts hard down the corridor of picket and cable. Guinevere gripped her palms together and sat motionless as the momentum of their speed grew. At the moment of impact the blunted spears gauged paths across the shield hides as each knight skilfully repelled the main force of the blow. But as the horses' shoulders collided each man gripped reins tighter and twisted to keep his balance. Guinevere leaned forward and several in the crowd groaned. But the combatants remained upright and returned to face each other.

In the moments given to the horses to regain their breath I saw Tristan rotate his shoulders and rearrange his feet in the stirrups. Hoel was winded but sat in the saddle more determined than ever, waiting for the nod from the steward. When it came there was no one whose eyes were not absorbed in the hooves driving clods of earth skyward or the grim faces of the warriors as they raced towards each other. As the spears struck neither man deflected, so determined were they to unhorse the other. Tristan's lance impaled Hoel's shield and drove a gash along the outside of his left arm. But Hoel's pike shuddered and snapped so that the flying broken end caught Tristan's padded shoulder and helmet glancing blows. Both horses reared and neither warrior retained his seat. Man and beast fell backwards. But under the flailing limbs and vast weight of the horses' trunks each knight rolled, as they had done instinctively in battle, and avoided being crushed.

As they stood breathing hard their chosen compatriot handed them a sword and a new shield as the rope barrier was removed. Guinevere looked towards Arthur for the first time. Was she asking for the contest to stop? Arthur chose not to understand and gave the sign to begin again.

Each waited for the other's first move, which did not come. Energy had to be conserved for the fury of a sword fight would burn up their hearts in few minutes. They watched and focused, before Hoel made the first strike to the neck, which was parried by Tristan's raised sword, so that Hoel's blade slid away. But Tristan made the same move, was blocked and his energy was dissipated; each fighter struck with his right hand so that blows became a circular dance. Tristan broke the spell by blocking with the shield in his left hand and swinging backwards with his right. But Hoel parried and copied so the combatants turned around each other in the opposite way. Hoel jumped aside and Tristan did the same, building up their lungs for whatever came next. The audience cheered as Hoel nodded approval for his opponent's prowess.

Then Tristan removed his helmet, dropped his shield and saw Hoel do the same. What they lost in protection they now gained in vision. Lancelot shifted position and nodded. Mordred's eyes showed that he would not have weakened himself thus. Guinevere drew in her breath and Arthur's gaze become more intense. These were brave men.

Tristan drove his weapon straight to the chest of Hoel, who parried with his blade in his right but then gripped it with his left and brought the handle down towards Tristan's head like an axe. The crowd gasped. Tristan lifted his blade so it held Hoel's blade in mid-air for just a moment, before Hoel pulled the steel down to loosen Tristan's grip and drive his pommel up towards Tristan's chin. Merlin and I groaned. But Tristan let go and suddenly the advantage was his. He drove his blade towards Hoel's stomach. But the latter knew the move and side-stepped and struck his opponent's blade upwards so that Tristan was barely able to keep hold of it. We all cheered.

Each man stepped back and bowed. When they smiled we all laughed.

Arthur could see that they were evenly matched. Their bravery was equal to their chivalry. No one wanted a loser. He raised his hand and the contestants paused.

'I value such warriors. Let us test their skills with the longbow.'

Tristan and Hoel might have had other thoughts but they accepted the Pendragon's judgement. They walked over to the targets and the assembly followed them. While each man inspected the bows cut from Yew wood and tested the linen strings chairs were found for Guinevere and the rest. When all were ready the steward led Hoel and Tristan to the fifty paces mark. Each man studied the distance and the air before loosing their bolts. As expected the goose-feather flights guided each arrow true to the centre of the mark. At one hundred paces dark clouds changed the light and the breeze increased. One of Hoel's friends was sent to throw grass into the air for the contestants to gauge the wind.

Hoel stood on the line. His gaze was on the cascading green slivers for moments before he raised the bow and fired. The arrow arced through the air and struck the target a little left of centre. The steward then gestured to Tristan since the wind was a factor to reckon with. A single arrow would suffice until a man faltered. Tristan watched the grass fall and then fired. The arrow sped to the target and struck just a knuckle bone from the other.

'One hundred and fifty paces,' Arthur commanded.

Tristan studied the sky and then looked down to place the shaft on the bow string. He paused momentarily, before lifting the bow and letting loose the string, as if carelessly. The wood seemed to fight the air yet hit the target at its centre. Hoel stood beside him and swiftly matched the feat.

'Two hundred and fifty paces,' said Arthur. 'Three arrows to each man.'

The audience inhaled. The target was lifted to the inner wall. It could go no further and stay within the defences. As before each man fired alternately in the gusts that heralded a rain squall. Hoel's first arrow whispered to the left of the round and struck the turf. Tristan repeated the action but leaned a smidgin more into the wind. The bolt sped in a high curve before descending towards the mark. The barb cut deep into the reed.

Hoel nodded approval and took his turn at the line. As the rain began to fall and the audience squirmed his concentration was intense. This time his angle into the wind, despite the rain drops, proved true and the projectile dug deep beside Tristan's.

I studied Tristan's black hair as the water dripped in points and began rivulets on his back. The arrow was loaded. Would the bowstring stretch with the damp and spoil his aim? He was ready. Through the same veil of water that mired my vision he fired. The shaft went wide of the mark, this time to the right as the wind became fractious.

Hoel lay his hand upon Tristan's shoulder before taking his place. Arrow secure he studied the target for what seemed like a long time. There was no need to throw sodden grass to guess the wind's strength. Slowly he pulled back the bending wood and used his great strength to hold it steady. His blonde hair caked flat to his skull and the rain steamed off his glistening skin. We waited and held our breath with him. At last the dart flew through the raging elements and submerged itself in the heart of its goal. The audience erupted.

Tristan stepped forward and clapped Hoel's shoulder hard. Both men laughed as friends. Then Tristan placed the shaft against the string. He studied the distant orb through the sheeting rain. He raised his bow and held it steady as Hoel had done. Could he really equal such a magnificent shot? The arrow sliced the shimmering grey light and inclined towards its mark. It struck close to Hoel's and we roared. But it was brief. As we watched the shaft it lowered and lowered, until it dropped to the ground. Hoel's arrow stayed true.

That evening Arthur sat with Guinevere at the high table. The hearth crackled with wet logs as the weather closed into night. Tristan and

Hoel stood before them in bright dry tunics. The Great Hall was full but none made a sound.

'Come forward Hoël Mawr ap Emyr Llydaw, Prince of Britanny,' said Arthur. 'You have done well, nephew.' Guinevere smiled and presented a casket containing a gold ring inset with rubies in the shape of an arrow point.

'And you brother Tristan, Prince of Lyonesse. Your prowess is no less.' He received the second casket with a silver ring set with sapphires in the V shape of an arrow. Both men bowed and clasped hands in friendship.

'These knights have shown bravery, skill and, no less worthy, chivalry,' Arthur said to everyone present. 'They are worthy incumbents of the Round Table.'

Later Hoel approached and Arthur spoke to him. 'I wish your father well at this time, Hoel. He is a good man. I hope for a speedy recovery from what ails him.'

'Thank you, my lord.'

'Give my love to your mother. Sister Anna and I were good friends growing up in difficult times.'

'I will return as soon as I can.'

Arthur clasped him close. 'We have need of warriors such as you, Hoel. God speed.'

A short time later Tristan approached Guinevere.

'I envy your stay in Lyonesse, brother. Give my love to our parents.' Her embrace was warm and long.

Arthur now observed Mordred and Lancelot, so popular among the others, as they immersed themselves in the celebrations. The evening was for songs, dances and telling of tales about the day's events, glorifying victors and their feats of prowess with lance, sword and bow. Guinevere sat beside him and held his hand. He had not pulled away. She could still draw a longing in his loins. That night in the warm darkness she asked.

'I have a liking to return to The Lake and Avalon. Will you take me, husband?'

'Yes, with pleasure.'

§

Our party was a collection of friends rather than a war-like teulu. As we travelled along the spine of Cornubia, on the ancient tin ways that gave glimpsing views to the oceans north and south, Merlin led the way. As I rode beside him he was quiet with what I guessed were thoughts of Nimue and her minions. How many more times would he make this journey?

The people of Hellys were generous hosts to Arthur and his guests; for they were tinners who had much to thank him for. Peace meant trade and time without fear for their families. I was welcomed back to their hearths, where I returned for a time to my old ways of healing the sick and giving communion to those who asked for it. This was a Christian community long before other Brythons chose our ways.

In the morning Arthur stood beside his queen ready to help her up to the saddle. The four guards were discreet shadows in the background of the simple keep that was the only defence in the town. Merlin was agitated, enough that I followed him to Arthur's side.

'Return before nightfall, Arthur.'

Arthur turned to his voice and studied him. It was unusual lately for Merlin to say much at all to him, never mind give him a command. His eyes took in his mentor and reflected my sadness at Merlin's decline.

'You must return. You must promise me, my lord.' Merlin was adamant.

'Yes, Merlin, I will take your advice.' Arthur was curt but said no more, for memories of better times.

While I spent the day with miner's families their conversation was spiced with Arthur and Guinevere's rambles down the river, through the apple orchards of Avalon, to the great Lake and its open mouth to the sea. Several small craft were anchored out of the wind under the steep sides of the northern shore. For the tinners always knew of events, and had always known, for knowledge was power to protect their own.

The sunlight flecked the wind rifts of the lake and down the river through the Oak forests to the distant silver breakers beyond the river mouth. Amongst the apple trees Guinevere retraced her marriage steps through the avenue. The trees were laden with ripe fruit, protected from the south westerly winds by the great forests at the edge of Lyonesse.

'Can I tempt you, husband?' she jested playfully as she put an apple in his hand.

Did she know the Christian story? Arthur thought. Of course she did, and why should it worry him.

'Why not, "Fair One"?'

He bit into the apple and gave it back to Guinevere to finish. In the warmth of the afternoon he slept with his head in Guinevere's lap. Through fitful dreams she stroked his brow.

'Another battle, my lord?' she said as he surfaced.

'Not this time. Uther had such nightmares and I believe they were terrible. Mine are just rooms of scheming princes. The moderation of good men goes unheeded. In my dreams the strong become weak.'

'But they are just imaginings. You must not regard them.'

'Greatness carries such a terrible price,' he rambled. 'Princes and lords will always talk you out of humanity. They look to the worst and then find it. Why can they not search for good?'

Arthur studied the now cloudy sky as Merlin had taught him to. The wind was changing and thunderous black clouds had bubbled up from the distant sea. Within a short time they would be glad of cover from icy rain.

'Come, wife. Merlin might still have the gift.'

The guards beyond the trees saddled up and all were just in time to enter the courtyard and find the sanctuary of a warm hearth against the breaking storm. I had no need of Merlin's instruction to know that unseasonal heat created wild weather. He was at an upper window of the stone keep looking towards The Lake and beyond. When I entered the room the agitation had not left him. His eyes were haunted and soon the ghosts within controlled him. He was impervious to my words or the grip of my hand as I sat him down.

Distant thunder approached from the ocean. Within a short time it was overhead and it was barely possible to open my eyes in the flashing blue and white. As one loud crack made others in the building cry out involuntarily I felt a strange shaking at my feet.

'It has begun,' Merlin shouted.

The quaking ground continued for minutes and the storm's noise and fury continued unabated. Then there was a brief gap in the blackness. From the south west came another sound, a colliding and a swallowing mixed with breakers crashing.

'What has begun, Merlin?'

He was deathly still. Barely audible, he said, 'The destruction of Lyonesse.'

We looked together from the window and a tumbling wall of trees and vegetation approached us with crashing foam behind it. Inexorably it came and came, until it swallowed The Lake and the trees of Avalon. And still it came, a black swirling tide of debris and destruction, until it engulfed the lower floors of the fortress. And then we looked out of the opposite window as the flowing obliteration continued, swallowing miners' cottages, churches and all manner of structures as it continued its appalling path. Well into the darkness we heard the lowing of cattle and bleating of sheep as they helplessly floated by. Surely this was God's wrath, or so many of us thought. During that terrible night the cries of people running before the deluge was replaced by the moans and despair of the living.

In the morning I left Merlin in a deep sleep from one of his potions that I had found in the room. I joined others as we cut our way out of doors and windows and clambered over mountains of wreckage: shattered trees and Nature entangled with rotting corpses of animals and people.

Arthur was holding Guinevere's shoulders, her whole body convulsing with sobs. His face showed that he had been little better when the waves rolled in. He must have fought his boyhood memory throughout the night. Now we looked down over what was left of The Lake. All around it was bare of anything but sticks. The water itself was piled high with ruin. Beyond it, between the cliffs either side of the waterway, was a great barrier of rock and sand piled high with Oak. Outside it was open, brown ocean where forest had once been. Hellys, the river and The Lake were cut off from the sea by this mile-long bar. Guinevere knew. Her home of Lyonesse was gone for ever. But what of her father, mother and her brother Tristan?

On the second day Arthur led a small troop of warriors north from Hellys. His instructions to Kay and Bedivere would begin the reconstruction. Guinevere was dressed in sombre clothes with black predominant. By whatever intuition she perceived that Merlin knew of the event beforehand and had not given her time to warn her family to go to higher ground. She never forgave him.

'Why did you not tell her, Merlin?' I asked him on the journey. His gift of prophecy was alien to my belief but I respected the man.

'Years ago I described to you a cataclysmic event, the destruction of Lyonesse, that came to me from the earth we stood upon. The gods showed me what would happen but not when.' Merlin paused. This was difficult for him as it felt like failure. 'On the day I warned Arthur I felt he was in danger but not why. When it began I knew but it was too late.'

In his silence I thought of his criticism that God could not be good if he let terrible events happen. His gods had not told him enough. Like Merlin I had no answer.

It took a day to reach Pennsans. The devastation we had witnessed at Hellys was repeated all along the coast, to Karrek Loos yn Koos and inland for miles. The wealth of Lyonesse was spread across southern Cornubia. The next day we reached Penn an Wlas, a high point where once we had seen green pasture gently sloping down eighteen miles to the distant capital, the City of Lions. This day we were where land ended and sea began. Other than fragments crashing in the coves and rocks below us there was no proof that Lyonesse had ever been. The City was just a swirling reef to trap unwary mariners. With the death of her father Guinevere was now Lady of Lyonesse, a kingdom that had been swallowed by the waves. With no hope of aiding her countrymen we turned back.

For weeks I was called to help the tinners and their families. The death and injury toll was enormous: some were extinguished in their sleep, others crushed and drowned when they tried to flee before it, others died in the flooded pits without any hope of exit from the water. With Merlin by my side as on the battlefield we saved many. Arthur's troop had fared better since they had been more in the north of Cornubia. But this was now a starving land: crops and livestock were gone; ships were smashed all along the coast, even in the protected waters of Carrick Roads. There was no trade for the tinners or anyone else as the disaster had struck the old Roman provinces of Armorica, Hispania and Lusitania, some said much worse than in Cornubia.

Arthur knew that the Saxons, who had suffered little, would look to pillage in this time of weakness. Arthur's men were ruthless in their search for sustenance for so many. Princes were given no excuse but to help the defenceless that they had so little care for. Arthur waged the campaign tirelessly.

As I looked out over this new bay I knew that much could not be repaired. Merlin saw it too. Without that Oak forest the vale of Avalon had no protection from the mighty south westerly storms. Not even Nimue and the wisdom of Druid lore could change that fact of Nature.

But Merlin had to try. As I continued to help the tinners he helped Nimue and the other Ladies of the Lake to repair the vale of apples. Shattered trees were healed with honey and pruned for the years to come. Uprooted trunks were stacked and burnt and new seedlings from Ynys Wydryn took their place. What mental and physical energy Merlin had left was expended in the restoration of Avalon.

Most knights drew favours from their kingdoms: Reghed, Elmet, Gododdin and the rest. Help came from many directions, but always less than Arthur's generosity would have been. When Tewdric's son placed a protective ring of ships around the coasts of Cornubia Arthur was visibly moved.

'My old friend's spirit still aids us from the dead.'

§

But there were exceptions. Mordred did not return with his brothers to Gododdin. Instead he went to King Mark's fortress at Castle Dore near the "Beech Trees" of Fowydh on the southern coast.

Inside the twin-walled fortress King Mark sat in the Great Hall. Mordred judged those who surrounded him to be cut-throats and wild men. He could not help comparing the cynical leader, his face aged into lines that spelled out his bitterness, with Arthur and the Knights of the Round Table. Out buildings were piled high with loot from piracy, what he called the flotsam that he garnered from the sea. The Hound of the Seas was in his lair. His teulu was to be reckoned with, always waiting for a weakened Arthur to take what he saw as rightfully his.

'Why should I help Arthur, the usurper who casts eyes on my throne? What reason have I to help his beloved tinners? He can rot in whatever Hell he now believes in before that will happen.'

But King Mark had been lucky, thought Mordred. Through a trick of Fate, Fowydh's position further east around the coast, with four major peninsulas blocking the worst of the waves, the damage to Mark's kingdom was light. Mordred tried to explain that help now could translate into influence and power later. Arthur was old and tired. Mark should seize the opportunity that was in front of him. With Mordred's help other fighters of like mind would follow the king's lead. Too many younger knights despaired of Arthur's new-found Christian virtues. His ideas of chivalry, helping the weak and protecting the defenceless, made men feeble. Mordred described how he and Mark were of like mind in wishing to bring back the Brythonic warrior code, the glories of strength shown in war.

'When Arthur is removed will you be ready?'

Mordred saw the greed in Mark's face and his fear of Arthur's prowess in war. But he was not averse to seizing an opportunity if a ship of Fate should happen to pass by.

§

When Mordred returned to Camelot he shared stories of Tristan that I found offensive. Although a fearsome warrior Tristan had been a Christian with the virtues of a chivalrous life.

'Tristan was given the task of bringing back King Mark's bride from Ireland, Iseult the fair. Our chaste young knight seduced her on the way back to Cornubia. And worse, the affair continued under Mark's nose until he could stand no more. If Tristan had not run to Lyonesse he would surely have been hanged for his crimes.'

'How do you know this to be true, Sir Mordred? You blacken the name of a good knight,' I said.

Mordred and his listeners laughed.

'What would you know of such things, Justin? It is through your Christian ways that Arthur is made weak. Are you worried that the real Tristan was not good enough for you?'

If I was a violent man I would have replied. Instead I walked away from their taunts and lies.

'My sources say that it is true, Justin,' said Merlin. 'Arthur is deeply saddened.'

'Was it a Druid's love potion that swayed a good man's heart?' I said, and instantly regretted it.

'Or a mercy since Tristan knew Mark too well? Do you believe in simple, unconditional love, Justin?' Merlin replied.

He was right to rebuke me. Love of family and friends, love of my God, I understood. Total dedication to a woman I would never know.

Soon word came from the tinners that Christian missionaries were being harassed and killed in the south of Cornubia. Some said that the old gods were angry so they had punished Lyonesse and Cornubia for deserting the ancient faith. Mark's thugs delighted in their creativity: martyrs, men and women, were crucified beside the tinners' ways.

But the tinners' fortunes recovered: with family labour the mines were drained; through enterprise fresh ships arrived at a new port, Gwig, a village in the forest three miles south of Hellys. Its river, the Mahonyer once known as the Cerrion River, flowed into open water outside Rock Anchorage. When the miners' prosperity recovered funds flowed again to Arthur for his knights to defend the peace.

§

Arthur prowled the walls of Tintagel. Often he would pause and study the portents of the sky or the murmurings of the sea. His mind was harder to reach even for Merlin. Guinevere had stayed in her chamber for weeks.

'She stares blankly at the wall, Justin,' he said. His tone was bleak. Through the troubled years he had maintained a love that was infinitely greater than forgiveness.

'Guinevere does not sleep,' he said to Merlin. His potions worked for a time until she realised their source. But it did not heal the grief of her mind. Guinevere's lands, her people, her family were all gone. Like the old ways, gone to Christian "chivalry and platitudes" she would say. In desperation Arthur asked Lancelot for his help. Through his remorse the knight agreed. But he failed as we did for being Christian. The great arbiter of ancient lore was never spoken to or pardoned. Merlin was a dead man to her. Only one could gain her ear.

Mordred knocked and was let in by a maidservant. Guinevere stared at the embers in the fireplace.

'I have brought you flowers, my lady,' said Mordred. He placed the yellow and white daffodils on the table beside her.

Her eyes lifted and for a moment there was recognition and a smile. 'What news, Sir Mordred?'

At which he would recount what was spoken at gatherings of knights and meetings of Druids. Always it was the growing strength of resistance to the words of Christian missionaries from Ireland. Arthur's knights were indulgent of pleasure or vainly pursuing some ridiculous relic: the pickled ear of St Peter or another splinter of the True Cross .Often Arthur's name was linked to age or failure. But King Mark was the new, strong saviour from the south. In her weakened state of mind

Guinevere listened and eventually believed. To Arthur her door remained closed.

But the rest of the Brythonic world continued to call on him. Merlin said that his name was of a god. I would prefer that his fame as a powerful and just leader spread because there was no one like him. Emissaries came from all the Brythonic kingdoms but also from across the water. Britanny was like a second home for us with so many families related to ours. Hoel had returned in time to nurse his father in his final days. When Hoel was crowned king of Britanny a civil war broke out. But his past prowess with Arthur at Caer Guidn and Badon Hill came to the fore and he quickly dealt with the revolt.

The flow of reports described a kingdom ruled with a wisdom and justice that pleased Arthur. But the much larger Frankish and Visigoth kingdoms, which bordered to the north and south east, were restless. Britanny was peaceful, prosperous and a prize. King Hoel mobilized cavalry units in the manner of Arthur. Tewdric's extended tribe marshalled a fleet based in the many coves and inlets like Cornubia. Together Hoel was ready by land and by sea. But his enemies were numerous and determined. Arthur watched as attacks became more frequent. He was waiting when the call came.

'It's time to do what I do best,' Arthur said as we sat near the cairn on the slope above the chapel, in the shade of the Yew Tree. Our eyes were drawn to the incoming tide filling up the wooded inlet in front of us. Arthur's concentration left me and joined a sea hawk hovering over its prey in the gently lapping water.

'You have made a good place, Justin. My mind always finds peace here.'

As war leader Arthur had prepared well. He had amassed an army of young knights and some old comrades, which would be embarked on ships at Heyl. Once out to sea they would join King Hoel's navy; a reunion of cousins and brothers that Tewdric would have delighted in.

'God protect you, old friend,' I said.

He smiled. 'And you, Justin.' His guard was waiting for him in the lane way above. The hooves were sluggish to my hearing; as though Arthur paused to savour just a little more of this place before his mind was ready for the onslaught to come.

§

Guinevere was sitting in the Great Hall of Tintagel when I returned. Her eyes saw me but gave no courtesy of recognition or welcome. Mordred stood by her side and smiled in mockery. Merlin was nowhere to be seen. That night and those to follow I spent in the service of the tinners. They told me that Merlin remained with Nimue and her maidens. We were outcasts and in danger. The tinners' sources told me that the war in Britanny was bitter and protracted. Arthur's presence had not magically dispelled his enemies as at Powys. His military prowess was being tested as it had not been since Badon and the Saxons.

The tinners protected me by changing our whereabouts constantly in their network of refuges underground. Others who preached the Christian faith were not so lucky: cliffs became killing grounds. Merlin would have fared little better. In Avalon he was grudgingly protected but to most Druids he was a traitor because of his friendship with me. Without our wayward influence Arthur would have been the king who restored all of Britannia to Brythonic rule.

Guinevere soon tired of Mordred and his followers' raucous behaviour. Most of the knights of Arthur's Round Table were fighting alongside Arthur or had returned to their own kingdoms. She hankered for the delicate music and courtly pursuits that she had grown up with in Lyonesse. When she retired to Kelliwic with retinue and guard she found them for a little while.

§

'Open the gate,' commanded Mordred at the head of a column of knights. The morning was fine with a cold wind and distant thunder.

The guards looked at each other and then the lord. What choice did they have? The heavy wooden doors were opened and the horsemen poured into the courtyard. The guards were quickly dispatched with spear and sword, as were others near the Great Hall and in the stables. Soon the smell of acrid smoke rose above the uplands.

'What gives you the right, Mordred?' shouted Guinevere seated on her chair in the Great Hall.

'The right of war, my lady.' His men seized tapestries, silver and gold vessels, anything of value before the building was torched.

'And what of me, knight?' Her tone was imperious and thick with sudden realisation.

'You are my spoils of combat,' Mordred said quietly.

'You would not dare. I am Lady of Lyonesse and Arthur's Queen.'

Mordred laughed. 'One no longer exists and the other is no longer true. You are my queen now, the key to Cornubia.' He dragged her from the throne and across the floor. 'I suggest you do not test my patience further.' After he let go and looked down at her prostrate form Guinevere slowly rose and followed him.

Her horse was led by one of Mordred's knights across the courtyard. Scattered through the field of tourney were bodies of servants, grooms, her handmaidens, all pillaged and gutted by these rampaging barbarians. As she looked back through tears the flames curled into the rushing clouds of the coming storm. Through the hours of her journey, uncomfortable, wet and cold, Guinevere had time to think. She had always thought she was in control of her own destiny. But it was clear now that Arthur or Lancelot had always protected her. At this moment she was a pawn in a dynastic chess game, nothing more. What have I done, Arthur? I did not listen to an honourable man.

She recognised the lakes amongst lush green fields and orchards. Mordred's men at arms crossed an oak-planked track near Ynys Wydryn but rode on. She could see their destination across the marshland, less than a day's ride from Camelot. The force arrived just before darkness. His wooden bastion on a peak, ringed with log palisades and surrounded by water, reminded her of Tintagel, a fortress with no womanly graces. She listened to the wind build into breakers that crashed against the denuded hill and its lonely citadel of power. It was not hard to imagine the seas booming into the cliffs of that forbidding place. It would be a wild night; better to be indoors and safe from the tumult. Soon the men set to carousing and wenching in the warmth of the Great Hall. For a long time Mordred sat and drank. He studied his bedraggled prize.

'You were loose with your charms, woman, with Lancelot and the others. Why not me?'

'I chose carefully and definitely not loosely,' Guinevere replied. Her liaisons were none of his business.

'But you were Arthur's woman.'

'I was faithful to my vows,' she said.

Mordred laughed. 'Old whore. How can philandering be faithful?'

'My reasons are between my husband and me.' She saw one of the girls being struck for resistance. She, Guinevere, would find a way to survive. Arthur, I am sorry for all the pain that I am responsible for. That night she submitted to Mordred's rough lovemaking but not before she had buried him with every curse she had ever known. In the morning she awoke to leathery hands and painful thrusting. Would the darkness never end?

§

I looked down the valley towards Deveryon and Rock Anchorage beyond. It was a long time ago that Merlin and I had watched Arthur's men annihilate the Frankish raiders. Trees thrashed and cracked around me as the tinners' wives and children took shelter in the tunnels. Within the inlet swollen waves heaved and in the open waters crests were whipped into white horses galloping across the void to Rhos. Tewdric's navy, led by one of his grandsons now, would have taken shelter. No enemy fleet would raid in such weather. 'Look after Arthur and his men, Lord. And Merlin, who needs your protection,' I said as I turned to join my hosts in the warmth.

§

Along the southern coast east of Rhos King Mark studied the prevailing winds driving into the Fowydh estuary.

'Light the beacons west of the harbour. There are sprats to be caught tonight.'

The cavalry troop rode south from the fortress. Fires in braziers guttered madly in the contrary blasts. Down in the rocky cove huddled a ragtag army. For most of the night they all waited, fishermen waiting for a tug on the line. An hour before dawn the horsemen saw the shadow of a barque making for the harbour bar. It listed badly in the cross wind and was low in the water.

'Strike up the lanterns,' King Mark commanded.

Slowly, steadily he reeled it in, towards the cove, just short of the safety of the harbour. On board the sails went up. The captain had seen the trap and taken the only desperate measure he could to avoid the granite teeth below the lights. As the wood splintered and the rock spikes held the ship in their grip King Mark heard the familiar cries of desperate men.

The army of rags needed no instruction. Down the scree, sodden grass and slimy rock the glistening bodies clambered. Their silent concentration was met with gasps of drowning men and the dull slap of bodies driven onto the rocks with each new surge. Some of those above lost their footing and their cadavers joined the other flotsam. But soon boxes and sacks were swept on to the sand. The people of Fowydh, men, women and children, fought like brutes over the cargo. The few survivors of the wreck who had managed to climb through the weed and up to dry ground were clubbed and pushed back into the maelstrom. In the frenzy bags were stuffed and leather skins filled. Old mining tunnels, caves and cellars all through the town were packed tight with loot. During the night bloated bodies were weighted with rocks and sunk. By daylight there was only drift wood from the storm and no witnesses.

§

When Lancelot heard of Guinevere's capture he returned from his homeland of Eriu over the Western Sea. With his own knights he searched until he found her among the lakes near Ynys Wydryn. But Mordred had chosen his citadel well, protected by water and lofty hill as well as a mighty force of young blood baying for Arthur's companions of the Round Table. They laughed at the "Adulterer" as they paraded his "Strumpet" Guinevere along the wooden ramparts.

Sortie after sortie against the high fastness left Lancelot's men bloody and disheartened, none more so than Lancelot. Entreaties to other knights came to nothing: they would fight for Arthur's wife but not Lancelot's concubine.

Merlin and I sent regular reports of the state of Cornubia to Arthur. As once promised we told different stories but always the truth. Hoel's forces had held back the jealous hordes of Franks and Visigoths and now the weather had begun to close in. Fighting men went home to their hearths for the cold months of winter. With skilful sailing and brief clement weather Arthur's battle-hardened men returned to the chaos of Cornubia. Christians were in hiding or slaughtered. Mordred's men gave free licence to plunder at will. The knights of old had returned to defend their homelands. Only one man had the name to bring them back.

Cavall lay at Arthur's feet in the Great Hall of Tintagel. The prodigious, dishevelled beast soaked up the heat from the log fire. He opened an eye as Merlin and I returned. His master did not acknowledge our presence. Arthur was deep in a melancholic place of his mind: his Queen was being pillaged like those of Trelivel. The lines of his cheeks and his thinning hair reminded me of Uther. We sat with him and waited.

'He weeps inside my skull,' Merlin murmured. His anguish was inconsolable: the boy he had guided to greatness was beyond his help.

Next day Merlin drew Arthur out to the cliffs. Together they flew with their hawks, bringing down pigeons and coursing rabbits in the long grass blasted by sea spray. Arthur's mind was high in a better place. Over days knights came from many western kingdoms, the last from Gododdin. Only Gareth came with twenty knights. His brothers, Gawain, Agravain, and Gaharis stayed, unwilling to fight their brother Mordred whatever his crime.

Arthur no longer debated Christian ethics with me or Merlin. Beneath the quiet exterior was a boiling cauldron of rage that would not be assuaged without blood. The mercy of the commandments had lost their power over the vengeful warrior. His host, adequate only because Arthur was at their head, was small compared with the numbers at Caer

Guidn or Agned. As always the kingdoms spoke of crises at home or losses in Britanny and gave as little as they could.

§

As we camped in the marshes beneath the hill our situation reminded me of Badon. But we were below, where the Saxons had been. Mordred and his supporters knew better than to face us on the plain. As before Arthur sought advice from the men in the circle around stuttering fires.

'A frontal charge up to the entrance is suicide,' one young knight began.

'Starving them out would take months,' added another.

'Trickery is difficult but possible,' Merlin said.

'Mordred has fought long enough with us to know all of our tricks,' an older knight grumbled.

'Can you use the weather to your advantage?' I asked.

'Trickery and inclement weather,' Arthur said with a smile. 'Merlin, that sounds like your domain.'

Arthur listened to more suggestions but then chose to complete the plan by himself. Gareth, for all his loyalty, was one who might be tempted to reveal enough to his brother.

'Every man should rest until nightfall. Be ready for instruction then.'

At midnight Merlin and I watched men gather in groups around their tutor. At two Arthur and twenty knights walked ahead of their muffled steeds. Their progress through the thick mist up the hill was slow. Soon after two groups of men with mud-splattered shields picked their way carefully on foot up to left and right. Their mounts were held by the newest knights in thickets nearby, ready to be led up when the signal was given. We followed much later, prepared to apply our healing skills when the need came.

§

Guinevere listened to Mordred breathing heavily in sleep. How she cursed him and her circumstance. What supreme irony would it be for her to conceive with Mordred? The thought repulsed her but she knew that an Ergot potion would terminate the pregnancy if required. Women were powerful in their own way as there was always a means to abort the unwanted and allow those advantageous. Arthur did not want that male heir. Now her instinct and knowledge of Arthur made her listen more intently. There was no sound but she knew he was there. Her few possessions were close at hand. If given the opportunity she knew her skill with knife and sword was equal to most.

§

At dawn Merlin and I looked down on the rippling cloud below us formed like waves across the valley. The weak sun crept across the peaks of the breakers and then over the hollows and came towards us; until it engulfed the breaking surge of mist and everyone with brilliant light. In front of the wooden gate were Arthur and his knights astride their mounts. To the guards on the walls nothing else moved in the mud and grass at the top of the slope. Mordred was called to see for himself. He pondered. This was one of Arthur's trickeries. His force was too small to storm the gate. He could not bring mounted reinforcements up that slope quickly without exhausting the horses. What was the strategy?

'Every knight must mount up in readiness,' Mordred told his followers. 'Archers and infantrymen line the walls and come to our aid when I give the signal.' Guinevere was left in her room with two guards and forgotten.

Mordred sat high in the saddle at the head of his band of knights. Along the wall the line of carnyx sounded above the golden sea of vapour. He nodded to the keepers and the heavy wooden gates swung open. He dropped his spear as in a tourney and led the charge through.

Arthur waited until Mordred's horsemen were both outside and inside before he moved forward to block. I saw Arthur in the thickest part of the melee, driving his spear into man and beast, slashing at anything on the route to Mordred. Arthur was fury in the flesh. In seconds muddy shields rose up from the grassy edge and rushed forward to cut into horses' girths and thrust into the legs of men. Shortly after Arthur's men entered the courtyard and brought down knights to gain their steeds. The shields men mounted and joined the troop. Mordred saw the trap unfold and did what Arthur might have done in his position.

He blew the horn to charge forward. As each knight left the struggle he rode headlong down the slope to safety. Arthur did not have enough mounted men to follow. Mordred was free.

'Not quite,' said Merlin. 'But then who dares to take a hilltop fortress with cavalry?'

Now Arthur's men scoured the buildings for men and loot. Guinevere's guards wisely bolted the door and called for Arthur. In return for their lives his Queen would be safe. Arthur agreed.

'Take them, brand my name on their foreheads, and set them free. For the rest do as you will.'

'Arthur, you should not,' I pleaded.

Merlin just looked into his eyes and said nothing. This vengeance was beyond Druid healing.

At mid-day our party rode out of the smouldering ruin, its scattered dead already drawing the crows. The two witnesses to this atrocity shouted obscenities in their maddened pain.

On the journey Arthur rode beside Guinevere but said nothing to her. Several times she tried to say sorry in some way but I believe that inwardly she knew that what they had known was gone. The next day Arthur left Guinevere in the courtyard of Tintagel. Lancelot stood beside her. The men studied each other and their eyes said too much. Arthur turned his mount and rode out. He had no intention of disbanding the troop. Only the complete annihilation of those who had rebelled against him, and Mordred's head, would suffice.

The path of destruction was easy to follow. Mordred's men took what they needed without mercy. At first his goal appeared to be south towards Fowydh. But clearly Mark had sent cavalrymen to warn him away. The King had no intention of facing Arthur, however weakened. Mordred could fend for himself. The trail now turned north-west, away from the rivers and inlets feeding Rock Anchorage. The tinners told Arthur that Mordred was aiming for Hellys and its fortress. But after one night Mordred moved on. He was headed down the river towards Avalon and The Lake. None of us could escape the irony of his choice.

'Will Nimue and her maidens give them sanctuary?' I asked Merlin.

'Will Arthur be stopped if she did?' Merlin replied.

Mordred's men supported the old ways but no Druid could condone the slaughter he had written across Cornubia. When Arthur arrived at The Lake Mordred's men were camped on the far side on the bar of sand which bottled it like a cork. Beyond was the sea which had once been Lyonesse.

We were all tired from the constant chase. But now Arthur could see his enemy just across a small stretch of water, however magical. He prowled the camp as the dampness closed in. The wind dropped and the mist flowed from the sea. Soon we could barely see The Lake. In moments it was gone. Arthur's energy growled inside his mind.

'You must rest, Arthur. In daylight he will be easy prey,' said Merlin.

'With sleep you will find the answer,' I said. 'Enough blood has been spilled.'

At midnight he called a meeting. As always men old and young stood in a circle and listened. Arthur's words were short.

'The enemy is here right beside us. Now we have surprise on our side. Who will follow me?'

There was murmuring and disagreement. Many said that Merlin and I had spoken truth. But Arthur would have no rebuke.

'All my life I have been trained for war. I have found good cause for my skills. Mordred's rebellion has threatened everything I have strived for. Now I must finish the tourney. If you will not come with me then I will go alone.'

As he buckled up his sword and shield each man in the group looked at each other and then did the same. Arthur disappeared into the swirling ether towards the western side of The Lake. Every knight followed in his footsteps.

'This is madness,' Merlin said. 'Arthur, you cannot,' he shouted many times. Soon his voice, subdued by the fog, was drowned by the shouts and cries of battle. Without horses this was a morass of single combats scattered across a mile of beach, a slender space between land and water.

'He is shouting inside my head,' Merlin said.

'Arthur, you cannot,' Merlin wailed.

As he and I tripped and fell towards the awful clamour the haze became thicker. We stumbled into bushes and into ruts so that we were coated like tinners by the time we reached the sand. There the murk was impossible. How could men see each other let alone fight? Who was friend and who was foe?

Merlin yelled more. 'Arthur. Stop. You cannot. This is madness.' So many times he shouted the words over the din. And then he came across the first corpse and then the second and fifth: men locked together in death struggles from which neither escaped. Knightly blood spilled into the shingle and rock, the best of warriors who had once sat at the great Round Table.

But now the tumult was subsiding. As I staggered closer to the heart of the noise I found more and more; few alive and none within our skill to save. Merlin was somewhere in the nebulous vapour yelling like a deranged man.

Then I came upon Arthur and Mordred. Each was bloodied and exhausted. Arthur had found the stamina to keep sway with the younger man.

'Stop. Arthur. Mordred. Enough.'

'Yes,' Arthur gasped. 'It is enough.'

But my words seemed to give them strength. I saw Mordred raise his sword high above his head. But Arthur was equal to the move and drove his spear through Mordred's chest. As the lance came out of his back Mordred's eyes registered that this was his death cut. Then, in a final scream, he used his legs to push his body forward along the shaft to get close to his enemy, as Arthur had once taught him. With all his remaining strength Mordred brought his sword down upon Arthur's skull. The blade met its target. Through the gash on Arthur's helmet oozed livid blood. He and Mordred fell together and lay still.

I dropped stunned to my knees beside Arthur and called for Merlin, who was still sobbing far into the clouds. I turned to a presence beside me. It was not Merlin but Bedivere, much damaged but alive. He and I removed Arthur's helmet and saw how deep the cut was across his temple and cheek. When Merlin lurched into Bedivere it was clear that his healing knowledge had been strangled by grief. Who else might have the curative understanding equal to this terrible wound?

As a gentle breeze blew in from the sea and dispersed the fog we saw the senseless butchery all around us. Merlin's cries became louder and more pitiful. Then Bedivere and I carried Arthur's body to the great stone by the avenue of apples and there Nimue and her maidens did what they could. Bedivere left for a time but returned from the battlefield with Arthur's sword, Excalibur.

Arthur opened his eyes and saw his faithful knight. He motioned for him to come close.

'It is done,' Arthur whispered. 'Excalibur must return to the waters.' Nimue nodded. Merlin briefly stopped whimpering and shook his head up and down in agreement. For it was the Druid way. I watched Bedivere do what he had been asked to do. Miraculously he found strength to make a mighty throw so that the sword sank near the centre of the Lake. Then we let go of our grief as we watched Arthur gently slip away into the other world.

I stood for an age, and then sagged against a tree, and could not believe it. For a while my faith was damaged. How could this death be a good thing, some part of the Divine Plan? I thought of our friendship, all of the events that mattered to us and so many more. It was all gone.

But out of despair something better came. What could I do for my friend? The Brythonic kings and princes would fight over his body. There were some who would desecrate his bones as well as his name. Where was a safe place of rest? Of course, I knew when that thought came to me. I had been given an answer. It was within my power to give him peace and to spread his fame amongst future generations.

Soon the tinners stood and grieved with us. They were content to help Bedivere and me with the plan. Two parties of men and animals left

Avalon. My journey took me south. Bedivere's took him north and east to Ynys Wydryn. The body of Mordred, wrapped tightly in a thick shroud of white linen, was interred by Bedivere without ceremony one night three days hence. When asked by the priestly custodian of the ground who it was, Bedivere said that this was the body of the great king Arthur.

King Mark strode into the void that was Cornubia but never attained sufficient stature to stand in Arthur's shoes. Without his leadership I doubted that the princes could halt the Saxon tide as it swept west.

Only I and the tinners knew Arthur's final resting place, a haven of peace that we both knew well. Our secret stayed with us as I wrote my account for the tinners to keep safe. For a time I nursed Merlin through his madness but to no avail. In one lucid moment he asked me to take him back to the land of the Cymbrogi where his life began. My choice was Ynys Enlli, an island inhabited by many of my faith. I knew they would look after him.

One day the tinners told a strange story. Arthur's queen and her lover did not remain long at Tintagel. Both struggled with what they had done. The miners said that Guinevere was seen at Ynys Wydryn crying over "Arthur's" grave. One remembered her words. 'I gave you pain but not a son. I was your queen but failed in my duty. In the afterworld, of whatever belief, will your heart forgive me?' Soon after this she entered a cloister of Christian women.

Within days Lancelot stood at the grave.

'Hic iacet Arthurus, rex quondam, rexque futurus ,"Here lies Arthur, king once, and king to be,"' he was heard to say before he took cause with a cell of Christian men. I doubted if either would ever leave their chosen places of seclusion.

§

My role as his guardian is now fulfilled. What is left for me? It is my intent to carry out my other task: to serve the tinners of Cornubia as best as may be; until it is my time to join Arthur, in that place of peace.

CHAPTER 11

Philip was alone when he awoke at 8. The rubbish men clattered bins in the street and the seagulls complained that their food supply was being taken. From the bathroom he heard Meredith talking to Jeremy.

'You'll have to stop peeing and pooing everywhere, Jeremy. Nappies on back to front so they leak? What about pointing Percy? It's getting decidedly messy. Now put your other leg in so I can pull them up and put on your clean trousers.'

Philip found Ros in Jeremy's study, a spent coffee on the floor beside her and four opened books on the table in front.

'Hi,' as he kissed her on the forehead. 'What are you up to?'

'Just fossicking in these geology books. Oops, apologies to Meredith. It must be catching.'

'What have you found?'

'An explanation for that bag of broken beach glass that we saw in the box. "Pipe-like extrusions of volcanic rock through the granite often contain amethyst and sapphires and are a likely source of diamonds."'

'Peter didn't mention those,' Philip said.

'And neither did we. It's quite exciting to think that diamonds exist in Cornwall isn't it, most likely in the Lizard?'

'They fit Peter's need for a small, high-value package easy to translate into cash,' he said.

§

Jeremy was reading the paper when they joined him in the lounge.

'A person in Camborne tried to hang himself but didn't succeed,' he said without lifting his head.

'Oh, I'm sure he'd get the hang of it eventually,' Meredith replied.

'Don't get hung up on that, Jeremy,' Ros said. She couldn't resist.

Philip pulled up a side table for Meredith to place the teapot. Ros rearranged the cushions on the sofa opposite.

'Hello, Jeremy. Would you like a summary of our findings so far?'

For a moment he did not seem to hear her. Then he put away his paper. Meredith put a cup of tea in his hand. Philip sat with Ros, his tea and her coffee by their feet.

'We've learnt a lot, Jeremy, but we seem to have hit a plateau with our research. Maybe you can help us.' Philip smiled at her diplomacy as Ros covered their time at the fortresses of Tintagel and South Cadbury and religious sites on the Lizard.

'What about St Michael's Mount?' Jeremy said slowly. 'It's sacred, definitely trading and probably military.'

He seems a bit better today, Meredith thought.

'Our research,' said Philip, 'told us Karrek Loos yn Koos, 'the Grey Rock in the Wood', was a candidate for the tin trading city of Ictis, mentioned by Diodorus Siculus in the 1st Century BC. Bronze and Iron Age relics have largely been destroyed by later work on the castle. Ros was interested in it because it was once six miles from the sea until the great flood that destroyed Lyonesse, supposedly on 11th November 1099. The St Michael bit, as you know, comes from Archangel Michael appearing to local fishermen in the 5th Century AD. But there is nothing to suggest Arthur or the Grail.'

'But there is a link with its sister island of St George off Looe,' Jeremy parried. 'Joseph of Aramathea and the young Christ were supposed to have landed there. Beneath the 12th Century Benedictine chapel are remains of a wooden place of Christian worship dating to the 4th Century.'

'As you know, Jeremy, our problem is that the grave and chalice would have been plundered long ago if their location was known to those of the Dark or Middle Ages,' Philip said. 'Glastonbury proves that, found and lost within a couple of centuries, if they ever had them. Arthur's body would have been used as a talisman by a petty lord, just like Alexander's body was by the Ptolemies. Vatican records would show the Grail, if they ever found it.'

'You have studied the legends over many years, Jeremy. How much truth is buried in them?' Ros asked.

'Only tiny suggestions. Cornwall to its credit has more legends than most, more even than the Welsh.'

'Avalon?' she asked.

'We can never know the truth, about Avalon, Camelot or Excalibur rising from the lake. Whatever there was must be hidden beneath a carpet of medieval fantasy.'

Meredith changed her mind. Jeremy is so tired, she thought. He's giving up.

'And yet, Jeremy, not to be impolite, you dismissed the poets, in particular Tennyson. From what I have read he did his research rather well. His meeting with Stephen Hawker, vicar of Morwenstow and a noted Arthurian scholar, was particularly enlightening for him.'

Jeremy drew in breath to think. He did not answer Ros directly. 'What about Dozmary Pool on Bodmin Moor?'

'We took a detour there on the way back from Mason. The "Drop of the sea" or "Douce Maree", "Sweet Lake", according to whichever source, had something: an ancient tinners' village, lots of legends but it is no more than nine feet deep and in 1869 it dried up. There were only Neolithic arrowheads found at the bottom.' Ros pulled back again. 'Short of excavation that produces Excalibur how do we prove any site?'

Ros broke the silence. 'What about the other lake, Loe Lake and the Cober Valley? Tennyson favoured them for the source of Excalibur and Avalon?'

Jeremy was too tired or chose not to answer.

Meredith spoke quietly. 'What about your gift, Ros?'

Jeremy frowned. This was close to poetry and Arthurian fantasy. Facts, woman, facts!

Philip knew that Ros was using her "gift", probably with much greater effect than even he guessed. But she needed time. As Ros had said to him many times, it was not something she could turn off or on like a tap. In the next few minutes Jeremy would try to destroy Justin in his defence of science. Philip deflected the attention

'Leaving aside Ros' feelings for the moment,' he said, 'you would agree that educated speculation can be useful here, Jeremy. For instance Arthur's twelve battles do have references by Nennius and others. How many of them do you think took place in Cornwall?'

'Only one, Guinnion Fort, his eighth, which I would suggest was at Gwenver Cove near Sennen, because they gave thanks at a Christian chapel there. Badon, his 12th, I believe was at Solisbury Hill near Bath in Somerset. Camlann, as we said, was probably at Slaughter Bridge on the Camel River but other possible sites are in Wales and Scotland.'

'With respect, Jeremy, Tennyson suggested Loe Bar,' said Philip. Ros should not have to carry this line of inquiry alone.

'Why don't you two take the Morris and Ros can test her feelings at some of these places?' Meredith suggested.

'Thanks, Meredith,' said Ros.

'Continuing our intelligent speculation,' said Philip.

Careful Philip, you are testing everyone's patience here, Ros thought.

'Why did the dream of Camelot fall apart?' asked Philip

'It collapsed from within. When the outside enemy was defeated his knights grew restless. The search for the Grail was a useful diversion. Ultimately there was a power struggle between the old established regime and new blood in the form of his nephew, Mordred.'

'How does tin fit in, Jeremy?' Ros asked. 'A side reference mentioned a tin ingot found in Falmouth Harbour.'

'In the 19th Century a four-pointed ingot was found in Carrick Roads between St Mawes and St Just-in-Roseland.'

Again she was being steered across the water. A terse, meandering discussion was producing results. Philip picked it up.

'Would it be reasonable to suggest that people who practised such an ancient trade received protection from somewhere?' asked Philip. 'From Arthur maybe?'

Why were Rosalind and Philip grilling Jeremy, thought Meredith? They were not cruel people.

'That is a probable, although there is no direct reference to him. But the Christian links, Arthur's Virgin Mary shield at Guinnion Fort, the visits by Joseph and the boy Christ, are numerous. So we could label the case circumstantial at this point.'

'Tinners and smugglers, Jeremy,' said Ros. She held his eyes. Word of yesterday's altercation at the Orient had reached him. 'Would you like to tell us more about them, past and present?'

Jeremy drew in breath and some energy. His reluctance was evident to everyone in the room.

'They are two separate entities. Until two hundred years ago tin was traded with minimal state interference. The idea of a nation state is comparatively recent, usually seen to begin with Napoleon. Smuggling was a reaction to burdensome taxes. The Cornish were good at it due to their close proximity to France, poor roads and isolation from the rest of Britain. Seafaring is in the Cornish blood.'

Ros waited but Jeremy had no intention of saying more.

'I think we agree that there is some evidence for early Christian links with the miners. From our visit to Geevor mine there is no doubt that the tinners and their families suffered terribly to extract the ore. Oscar was very happy to tell us the truth about a tin miner's life.' She watched the barest flicker in Jeremy's eyes, but he still wouldn't budge.

'We think Christianity, tin and smuggling are linked and have been for a very long time. What is the Tinners Mite, Jeremy?'

Meredith had listened intently. Ros seemed to have a purpose beyond historical enquiry. This was the question. Her eyes were fixed on her husband's face. Eventually he looked at Meredith and could hide nothing.

'The Tinners Mite helps mining families in need, particularly the children. Its funding comes from smuggling secondary metals in the tin-refining process.' He paused and then said directly to Meredith. 'I have helped them for quite a long time.'

'How long?' Meredith asked.

'Thirty years.'

'Why didn't you tell me?'

In the pause there was resignation and relief. 'When the boys left I missed them. As a teacher I taught many children from mining families. Oscar and Peter were bright students who never got the chance our boys had. Their plan was a little disreputable but I approved of their goal. We have helped thousands of children, Meredith!'

'Why didn't you tell me?'

Ros and Philip got up slowly in an attempt to exit the room. But Meredith's raised hand stopped them like statues.

'I didn't know how to. You thought I hated kids, our kids, because I insisted on them receiving a boarding school education.' Ros and Philip did not exist. Jeremy was talking to his life companion. 'I have always loved them as much as you do, Meredith.'

Without her intention the archaeology, the quest, her purpose of linking disparate subjects together, was lost. Ros had opened a box she should not have. Philip was deeply embarrassed. She signalled to him, held up the keys from the table, Meredith nodded and Ros shut the door.

Philip closed the garage and got in the passenger seat. He refrained from Jeremy directions. By the bottom of Dracaena Avenue she had worked out the idiosyncrasies of the Morris and was in third gear.

'Where were you going with that one, Ros?'

She drove for half a mile before she answered. Could she have been less harsh? Was it a feminine thing? That Meredith should not be kept in the dark? 'The miners were Christians from very early. Arthur was Christian. I think Justin was helping the miners.'

'Would you care to tell me who Justin is?'

'He is one of the people I feel when we visit places: Loe Lake, South Cadbury, and Tintagel. If you remember he sat with us in St Just in Roseland churchyard after the flight.'

'And smuggling?'

'Self-help in difficult times? I'm starting to sound like Peter.'

Just before Penryn she took the A39 and then the A394 along the familiar route towards Helston. The day was overcast but mild. It was good to have to concentrate on driving Cornish roads. This was a major thoroughfare but she still kept her distance from the high shaved hedges that hid jutting rocks. When she met large tractors and bigger trailers she became adept at turning into pull-off breaks in the stone walls. Both of them wound up windows when the stench of animal manure from "muck-spreading" in neighbouring fields became unbearable. After nearly an hour she pulled into a parking bay in Marazion within metres of the causeway to the Mount.

As they walked across the stepped walkway Philip did not provide his usual guidebook commentary. They were here to follow feelings, Ros' feelings, so he let her speak.

Ros' vision took in the imposing 15th Century castle-like chapel to St Michael on top of the rock and the protected stone harbour on the western side. The tide was very low so that the height of the "Grey Rock" was amplified. They stopped at the shrine to the Virgin Mary at Chapel Rock before the climb. Inside, her sight touched the antiquities from across the ages but her mind was elsewhere. Until she read the plaque describing the Lisbon earthquake of 1755 which caused a tsunami that devastated this part of Cornwall from a thousand miles away. The tragedy of Lyonesse became a little less "circumstantial". Three world war two concrete pill boxes in the gardens brought back Jeremy and Meredith's stories. Von Ribbentrop, German ambassador to Britain before the war, planned to live here after the invasion. Defence of the realm and Christianity walked together.

In the manicured, terraced gardens of rock and succulents thriving under the influence of the Gulf Stream she wished she had brought her materials and had time to paint. At the highest point they paused at Seagull Seat. Philip noted the hand cut stairs in the stone. Without them this was a near-impossible climb. Arm in arm they looked out at drowned Lyonesse with no trace of forest; only dark rock shelves beneath the blue Atlantic.

After a short drive through holiday cottages along the near-Australian beach of Praa Sands lunch was a pasty and coffee at the Atlantic View Hotel above the Clock Tower in Porthleven. The panorama from the outside tables was across Mounts Bay, more west than before, scenic but taking her no closer to Arthur or the Grail.

As before they followed the road down and along Loe Bar road. This time it was not for height to fly but proximity to the beach. At the end of the road Ros found a grassy bank to park. They "rugged up" as Meredith would say and walked south along the beach. In the blustery wind the sun came out as they stopped in the centre of the mile of shingle that was the Bar itself, blocking the Lake and the Cober River access to Helston.

'You don't need those,' Ros said, looking at the No Swimming signs. 'Just look at the water. It's full of rips and deep eddies. Why would you think of swimming here? It's a desolate place,' she said as she sat down on the sparse grass that crowned the middle.

'Feel anything?' Philip asked.

'Lots. If I saw all the other sites for Camlann I would still choose this one: layer upon layer of suffering, from shipwrecked sailors to the cries of war. Tennyson did his research but I bet it was the poet in him that decided that this was the site of the final tragedy.

"'And there, that day when the great light of heaven

Burn'd at his lowest in the rolling year,

On the waste sand by the waste sea they closed.

Nor ever yet had Arthur fought a fight

Like this last, dim, weird battle of the west.

A death white mist slept over sand and sea:

Whereof the chill, to him who breathed it, drew

Down with his blood, till all his heart was cold

With formless fear; and ev'n on Arthur fell

Confusion, since he saw not whom he fought.

For friend and foe were shadows in the mist,

And friend slew friend not knowing whom he slew;"'

'Idylls of the King: The Passing of Arthur by Alfred Lord Tennyson,' she said after her recitation.

'I'm impressed. Did you feel this from the air?'

'To a degree; but on the ground it's so much clearer. I think Tennyson caught it, don't you? Maybe he tapped into "feelings" as well?'

Soon they were scrambling up the wooded hillside on the northern side of the Lake. The view from the fields above took in the lake, the valley and distant Helston. Even today the land was green and rich despite millennia of farming, mining and harsh elemental storms.

'Could it be Avalon?' he thought aloud.

'I think so. It's peaceful and magical at the same time; new and old maybe.'

After a time of just sitting, him not daring to disturb the atmosphere, she said. 'It's a process of elimination, I suppose, that Jeremy would approve of. Come on. One place left.' She led the way back across the fields and climbed wooden-stepped styles over stone walls until they came back to the car.

§

Meredith sat opposite Jeremy at the kitchen table. There was sadness in the room and not just because of the secret that Jeremy had kept for so many years. Each holiday the boys had come back. There was excitement when she would collect them from the Dell station. But at the end it was at this table she and the boys would look at each other and hold back the tears. Jeremy would not have approved.

Jeremy sat with his eyes downcast, pacing his breathing and milking the heat from his hands cradled around a mug of tea. At intervals he picked up the spoon and stirred interminably before putting it down again. In a few minutes he did it again. He made no attempt to drink it.

Maybe the boys would have been ok, Meredith thought. They might not have turned into yobs. It could have been a different life, not academic but still good. She watched Jeremy stir the cooling tea yet again. It did not need to be a race through boarding school to Oxbridge and then a job.

'They could have been happier with a trade, being careful with their money to buy their first house and then a second. They might have been wealthy before doctors even qualified. And we would have been part of the next stage of their lives,' she said, her passion finally surfacing as words.

'I meant well, Meredith,' Jeremy said. 'But maybe you are right.'

'It's easier in hindsight,' Meredith said. 'We'd all have done different things if given a second chance.'

'Yes,' he said.

§

The A394 up the hill out of Porthleven went through Helston and skirted the edge of Falmouth before passing Perranarworthal and the old tin port of Devoran. Ros was briefly confused on the A39 by two roundabouts in quick succession. The road led south to the narrow farm lane beside Trelisseck Gardens and down to the King Harry Ferry. In minutes the chain had dragged the open car transport to their side of the creek and twelve cars and two trucks, "lorries" to Philip, rolled off. In ten minutes the clanking steel chain had taken them to the B3289 on the other side. Very soon they found a place to park in the secluded lanes of St Just.

'Don't you need to stroll across the headland again?' said Philip hopefully. After that last hour in the car his legs begged for a walk.

'No, this is it. Sir John Betjeman said "to many people(this is) the most beautiful churchyard on earth". Everything in me says it's here.'

They were sitting on the same seat high in the graveyard with views through the palms and sub-tropical shrubs towards St Just Creek. Its full, tranquil waters led out into Carrick Roads and the oceans of the world beyond.

It would be the devil's job to dislodge her from here, he thought. Although with the mention of Justin maybe that was not an appropriate analogy. He had a "feeling" for a change: that this fellow had to be someone religious connected to the place they were sitting in. She was peaceful, silent and he was restless for a solution. Research, archaeological study, flights over this amazing land and plenty of driving had not produced the result. They were near but so far, as somebody once said. Frustration bubbled up.

'I know, Philip, my "feelings" have not finished the job. We are close. As Mr Micawber would say, "something will turn up", and soon.'

After fifteen minutes, 'Let me try something,' she said. 'Hold my hand.'

He did as he was told.

'Do you sense anything?'

'No, give me a hint.'

'Justin is close, talking to me in language I cannot understand. Maybe another man's mind might help me. Close your eyes, relax like you would with your Taekwondo, that meditation stuff you do. Take your time.'

Philip did his best. This might be beyond his rational understanding but Ros was not stupid or a nutcase. He closed his eyes and tried to relax. Slowly, once all the thoughts about missing the ferry, would the weather hold, and how many huge tractors would Ros face on the way back to Clarence Terrace, he did enter a space where there was something. After a time of nothingness, which was his guide that he was meditating successfully, words came to his head unbidden. They were unintelligible for a time until, 'He's speaking in Latin, some doggerel version of the Middle Ages.'

'5th Century Cornwall?' she said.

'Could be.'

'Do you hear the word "Jeremiah"?' she said.

'Yes, repeated a few times.' But for the rest he would need a dictionary. It was fascinating to get a glimpse of her inner world with these people. He felt himself studying the whole thing, trying to be rational rather than just let his mind be open to it. It was like catching a butterfly. If he succeeded he would kill it. But now it was slipping from his grasp. Soon he heard nothing at all.

Ros felt it and let go of his hand.

No doubt she was apologising to Justin for his poor mediumistic behaviour, he thought.

'Sorry, Ros.'

'It's ok. Come on, let's go. We might miss the ferry.'

Was she telepathic too, he thought as they headed back to the car? She was happy for him to drive, enter that narrow street and squeeze into Jeremy's garage with a three point turn.

§

'Ah, well-timed you two. A fellow just came to the door and delivered this. He said it was "fur Phil'p' 'n 'is woman,"' Meredith quoted. She held out a box with several undeveloped rolls of film in it.

When they peered out of the kitchen window there was Oscar looking up from the street. Philip doffed an imaginary cap. Oscar smiled and touched his forelock before he walked along the Terrace footpath towards the Orient Hotel. Philip passed the parcel to Ros. Both guessed at the contents, Ros more accurately than Philip.

In the darkroom Ros lifted the print from the developing solution and pegged it up with the rest. With a magnifying glass she did her best to read out the first two lines of Latin.

'Ego sum, Justin, iustus Rhos in parochia de terra Cornubii. Stannum autem et fossores in vita mea servivi uitae comes fuit Dux Bellorum Britonum Artorius Pendragon.'

'Hello Justin,' said Ros.

Philip spoke the translation. 'I am Justin, Iustus of the parish of Rhos in the land of the Cornubii. In my life I have served the miners of tin and been the lifelong companion of the Dux Bellorum of the Britons, Arthur Pendragon.'

Their fever for discovery was infectious. Whenever Meredith turned up with tea, coffee and sandwiches she felt it. But most of her time was spent helping Jeremy.

'What's that mark on your nose, Jeremy?' wiping it off with her hanky. She frowned when she looked at it. 'Oops I shouldn't have stuck my nose into that one.' He was too sick to realise the enormity of what the miners had given him.

As usual his library was up to the task. Over the next few days Philip and Ros hardly left the room. Philip's task was translation. A piece of cake, Ros might have said, but here she did not dare. Philip explained some of the difficulties but Ros could see that the tiny writing and cramped style were serious problems.

'That's because parchment at this time was stretched and treated sheep or calf skin. It was expensive so Justin would not have wasted any space at all. The photos show individual pages so this was a codex, a collection of pieces of leather clamped on one side like a modern book. Unlike a scroll it could be written on the front and the back, recto and verso, again saving money. Justin believed his account was important.'

Ros noticed that there were considerable differences of colour in the photos, from a cream to burnt custard.

'A large number of animals went into this so there were differences in the hides. But I wonder how the miners preserved the book over the centuries?' said Philip. 'Keeping it out of sunlight would be easy, but what about temperature and humidity? Wrapping it up in material and not too far down might do it: below room temperature and with low humidity. Still it would be difficult. A conservator would recommend a fungicide to stop any deterioration too. I wonder if the miners used arsenic instead.'

Then there was the Latin. The syntax of an English sentence relied on word order. Latin sentences could have words in almost any sequence but the key was the form. Declensions of nouns and adjectives told him the subject or the object for instance. Conjugations of each verb gave him the tense, the mood and who was speaking.

'Amo, amas, amat,' Philip recited, with memories of his Latin teacher, Mr Sporran, an eccentric war veteran whose clothes were permeated with tobacco and alcohol. "I love, you love, he or she or it loves, Present tense." Let's hope Justin's Latin kept the basics of grammar.'

Together they solved the problems: Ros got hold of a full-page hands-free magnifier, with Meredith's help, and transcribed the Latin onto double-spaced paper. Philip recited the sentences out loud, mumbled key words like the main verb, and pored over dictionaries. Ros recorded what she was told. Slowly the English text filled up the space below the Latin.

§

On the drive to Tintagel Ros asked the obvious question.

'Would we have got to this stage without this bit of luck?'

'You have a point but this was more than just fluke. I think people make their own good fortune. They do things that allow fortunate chances to happen. They try and try and try again. And if you look after other people then what you do comes back to you, more often than not. Buddhists would call it karma.'

'In the West it would be "what goes around comes around,"' she said.

But Ros was still mulling over her thoughts. Just after the Tregatt turn off Philip asked, 'Well?'

'There's more to it. We went to Kynance because I saw something. Then we did what fitted our personalities. I am wondering if something or someone was guiding us.'

'Your feelings or?'

'Yes.'

'That it's a two way street?' he said.

'I hadn't thought about it that way. But I don't mind being directed for a good cause, within limits tighter than Peter's. The Comtesse in Cyprus proved that.'

Philip pulled on the handbrake in the hotel car park.

'I did tell you that it is not a gift, more of a curse,' she said.

'More gift today, I think,' Philip said.

§

'Thanks, guys,' Mason said. It was mid-day in the Tides Inn overlooking Tintagel Island. The numbered Photostats in a loose-leaf binder were labelled "Justin's Codex". Over lunch they explained how they obtained it.

'We'd take you to the place tomorrow if we could,' Ros said.

'But then we'd have to kill you,' Philip said with his version of a poker face.

'You and whose army?' Mason threw back. 'But a deal is a deal. Edited it is.'

§

In the afternoon Jeremy was still in bed. Meredith was very tired when they shared a cuppa at the kitchen table: she had been up all night looking after him. The "Justin's Codex", trimmed a little like Mason's, lay beside the sugar bowl.

'Will Jeremy be up for the trip?' Ros asked.

'I will make sure of it. A bit of tonic in his tea might just do the trick? Death warmed up, don't you think?' Meredith smiled.

She was exhausted, Ros thought. Between the two of them who was going to expire first?

§

At one of the outside tables of the Orient Narley and a couple of henchmen sat with pints of Scrumpy.

"Ow 'e be, Phil'p? Feel lik drop o' lappy?'

'Nice offer, Narley, but Peter's inside,' replied Philip. He smiled and opened the door for Ros.

'Shay be a looka. Naw Porthleven built 'at un,' said one of Narley's mates.

'Be lik' tryin' te teach a pig te sing if 'e chase 'at un,' Narley joked.

Peter and Oscar were at the window table with half-drunk pints of Whitbread Tankard and Double Diamond respectively. Philip nodded and pulled up two chairs.

'Another one?' he asked.

Peter raised his hand to say no thanks. 'Naw, I'm brave,' said Oscar.

Philip took the file from under his arm and laid it in front of Peter.

He picked it up and cursorily flicked through the pages.

"Ow be Mr Pasty?' Oscar asked.

'Lik' a Lazarus, Oscar,' Philip replied.

Ros raised an eyebrow at Philip's ability to slip between languages.

'Did you learn enough to make him happy?' Peter asked.

'Yes,' they both replied.

Theirs was the complete translation. The miners had always known and nobody would ever tell.

§

Philip drove slowly with Jeremy in the front, trying not to increase his discomfort with any potholes or excess cornering. Jeremy stayed inside the car as the chain clunked the ferry's path across the incoming tide. Philip pulled up as close to the Lych gate as he could. As he and Meredith unfolded the wheelchair and made Jeremy comfortable Ros drove off in the Morris to find a parking spot. When she walked into the churchyard she distinctly heard the church organ and the choir's rendition of:

"And did those feet in ancient time

Walk upon England's mountains green?"

Philip manhandled the chair down and along the narrow paths. At the spot he pressed his foot on the brake pedals and Jeremy wriggled into a comfortable position. The three sat on the seat beside him. In front was the view of the sunlit, glassy water of St Just Creek. The tide was nearly full. Meredith visibly relaxed into the vista as Ros explained to Jeremy what the Codex said.

Jeremy's eyes appeared to grasp details that he wanted to discuss but his mouth, and now his mind, could no longer put the words together.

'So where are they, Rosalind,' he looked unsteadily across and recognised, 'and Philip?'

They looked at each other. It would be a struggle to hold their emotions together through this. Philip stood up, undid the brakes, and turned Jeremy around to face the hillside. Philip made him secure again and stood behind him. Ros and Meredith joined them. Three metres behind the seat, with a slightly more elevated version of that view, was a small cairn. It had been much robbed for stone in antiquity. Either side of it were two flat, rectangular slabs of Cornish granite. Their age was similar to the cairn so that all markings had long since worn away. Philip doubted if there had ever been an inscription. Shading all three was an ancient Yew Tree. Philip estimated that it was well over a thousand years old.

Jeremy's face showed uncertainty. What was he looking at? Before Ros was able to lean forward to explain a bird landed on the cairn. It was a white dove. Jeremy shook his head. Then his eyes grew brighter in surprise. Two more birds fluttered into his vision and landed, a small Golden Finch on the left slab and the unmistakable colours of a Chough on the right. Across Jeremy's face crept a smile that filled it.

'Tinners take care of their own, Jeremy,' Ros said.

But after a few moments he looked at Ros and then Philip. Tears welled in the corners of his eyes. He looked at Meredith, her cheeks clearly marked by gentle rivers. His face said all the things he had wanted to say for such a long time. Meredith nodded and touched his arm. Jeremy was frightened. He did not want to go.

As Ros watched three shapes seemed to form out of the mist, the kind that covers early morning water. The images of three boys, on the verge of manhood, coalesced into shadowy people. She stepped back and Philip and Meredith instinctively did the same. A slight, fair-haired youth in simple linen toga looked down on Jeremy from his left side. A swarthy, stronger, young man in a longer tunic with faded tassels on the corners stood on Jeremy's right. Ahead, beneath the tree, stood a tall, muscular individual in dark trousers and leather jerkin, with black hair tied in a thin plait at the back. He studied Eashoa intently.

I shouldn't be seeing this, Ros thought. I'm not the right person. Acres of believers have wished this for lifetimes: monks and nuns, hermits and ascetics of every faith, yet it falls to me! There's something not right here but I suppose that's the way it happens. It definitely stresses the atheism. Now I'm sounding like Meredith.

'Hold my hand, Meredith,' Ros said quietly. 'And you, Philip.' Ros then led to a spot so that all three faced Jeremy.

Don't reason, don't analyse, Philip thought. Just accept.

'Meet Justin and Eashoa,' Ros said as the two shades held Jeremy's hands.

Jeremy seemed bewildered. What was happening to him? Until he looked into his palms and then those faces; before realisation transformed his expression.

Then he observed the still figure beneath the ancient tree. Arthur was now considering Jeremy. Their eyes met and Meredith saw recognition in her husband's gaze. Then Jeremy looked at her.

'Yes I can see it all, Jeremy,' she said inside her head. She did not mention one more misty shape peeping around the mottled trunk. He was short, red-haired and with gentle brown eyes.

'Hello, Elvan. You never were one for crowds, were you?' Only Ros heard her thoughts

Time seemed to pause. Jeremy remained very still, in the moment. This was his time and no one, living or dead would disturb him.

Now he was ready. Jeremy's body slowly changed, seemed to divide, so that three wispy figures of vapour, and a fourth smiling observer, rose gently upwards. Just like sea haze their images faded quickly in the sunlight so that they had disappeared within the shade of the tree.

Elvan was last to leave. 'Goodbye, childhood friend,' mouthed Meredith.

Jeremy's body was slumped forward but the soft lines had not left his face. He was content.

'Ros?' Philip said.

'Yes?'

'Eashoa is his Aramaic name. We know him better as Jesus.'

Her Suspension of Disbelief seriously struggled.

§

Jeremy's body was interred at Swanpool cemetery in Falmouth. It was a larger gathering than anyone had expected. On the open lawn were Arthurian colleagues and friends, a few elderly miners with their suited sons, and many former students. Narley and his contingent scrubbed up rather well, Ros thought.

"E be a gud man,' Oscar said to Meredith. She continued to stare into the hole in the soft earth.

'Then why didn't the tinners tell Jeremy years ago?' asked Meredith.

'Cos 'e migh' 'ave told. Justin wouldna' wanted tha',' said Oscar, with no malice at all.

Meredith thought about the words and agreed. Jeremy couldn't resist and she couldn't stop him.

She turned and looked into Oscar's eyes. 'Why trust me then?'

Oscar laughed. 'Tha' be easy. Your da' and granda' were tinners.'

She smiled and nodded.

As she threw the first handful of earth on to the coffin Meredith's thoughts wandered. Jeremy's body would decay here but his heart would beat elsewhere.

§

Mason O'Flaherty officiated at the special meeting of the Cornish Archaeological Society at the Tides Inn. Representatives from the National Trust and the Cornish Tourist Board were present. After speeches and general euphoria over such a find Mason informed the gathering that all proceeds from sales of the book and possible film rights would further Arthurian scholarship in the Duchy of Cornwall. His generous foreword acknowledged the translation by Philip Trevasco, the photography of Rosalind Bernaud and the atmospheric paintings of Meredith Pascoe. Mason's work was a triumph of academic analysis of all things Arthur. On the desk in front of him was a book.

"Fragmentary evidence from the Codex of Justin on the life of Arthur Pendragon" dedicated to respected Arthurian scholar, Jeremy Pascoe.

§

On a fine spring afternoon the sea breeze that crossed Roseland was steady. Isaac stood beside Ros in his field. She held the ribbon high for Philip to choose his time. Hooked in beside him Meredith was doubly excited. As the sails above her rippled and then filled, she tapped the train ticket to Scotland in her pocket, just in case. Tamarisk's expectant eyes were still there when Philip spoke.

'Ready?'

Meredith nodded.

'RUN.'

His first strides took the strain and her goosey steps followed. In four paces they were up. Meredith did what they had practiced and was quickly encased in her cocoon. Her bright eyes looked out over the water. As he built up height they looked down at Ros and Isaac Bolitho, who covered his eyes against the sun.

'That be fir birds tha' un.'

St Just in Roseland churchyard looked as peaceful as ever. Philip held the kite steady against Meredith's animated twists to see things.

'If Leonardo could see us now! It's a miracle Saint Elvan, and probably Justin, would approve of, Philip.'

He smiled and turned the kite towards Carrick Roads. Philip pointed out the Observatory Tower and nearby Clarence Terrace. All the while Ros watched a hawk circle above them, a quiet sentinel.

'Tinners take care of their own,' Philip said as he looked at his companion.

'Denvyth hwedhla,' said Meredith.

'"Nobody tells,"' replied Philip.

GLOSSARY

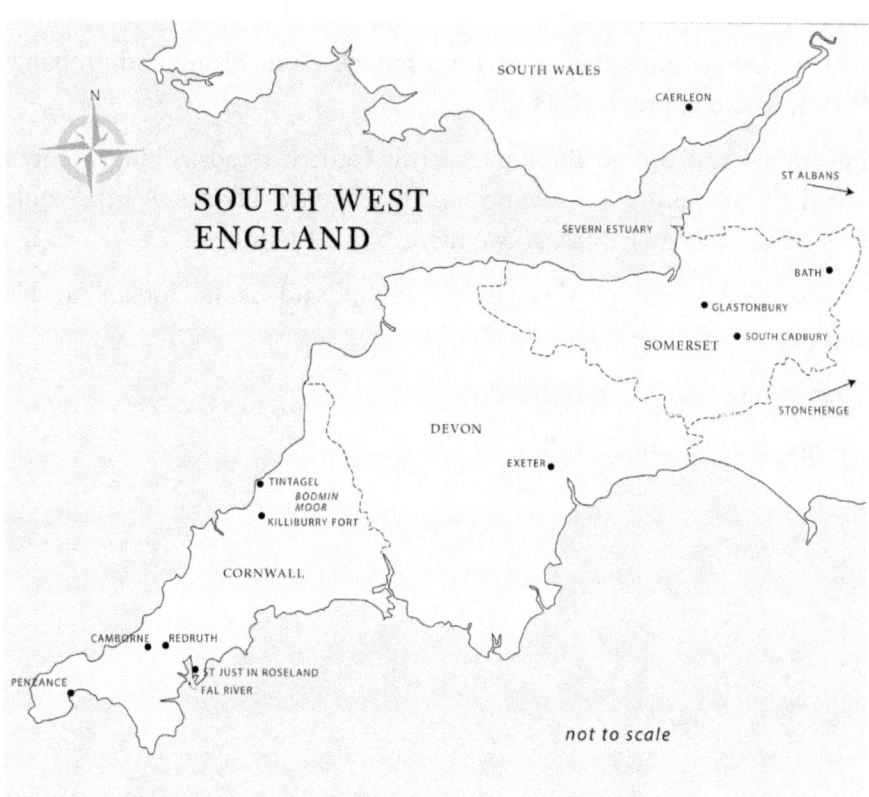

Bath: Aqua Sulis; Badon; Mons Badonicus

Bodmin Moor: Goon Brenn

South Wales: Demetia and Glywysing

Devon: Defnas

Exeter: Isca Dumnoniorum

Fal River: Fala River

Glastonbury: Ynys Wydryn

Killibury Fort: Kelliwic

Severn Estuary: Sabrina River; Afon Hafren

Somerset: Gwlad-Yr-Haf

South Cadbury: Camelot

Stonehenge: Stanheng: Choir Gaur

St Albans: Verulamium

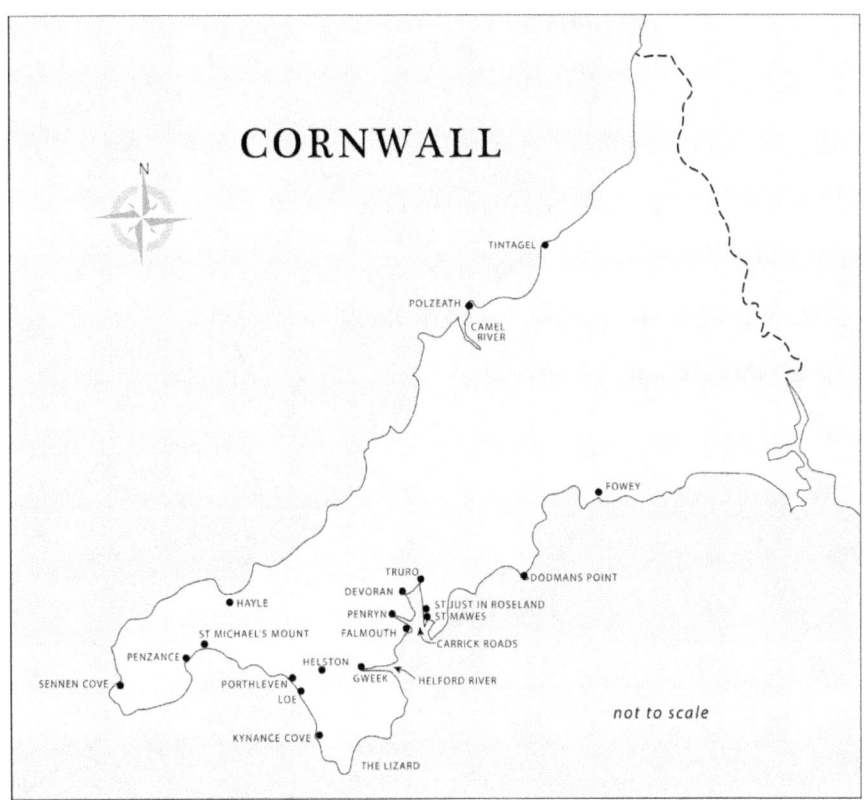

Camel River: Dowr Kammel

Carrick Roads: Rock Anchorage

Devoran: Deveryon

Dodmans Point: Deadman's Point

Falmouth: Pen Dinas (Pendennis Point)

Fowey: Fowydh

Grey Rock in the Wood

Gweek: Gwig

Hayle: Heyl

Helford River: Cerrion; Mahonyer River

Helston: Hellys

Loe: Lake and Bar; Avalon (Affalon);Camlann

Penzance: Pennsans

Penryn: Trelivel

Polzeath: Pentire Hillfort

Sennen Cove: Caer Guidn; Guennon Fort

St Mawes: Lannvowsedh

St Michael's Mount: Karrek Loos Y'n Koos

The Lizard: Ocrinium Promontory

SOURCES

I believe that Arthur belongs to the Cornish, however contentious that is to the Welsh, Britons, Scots and others. Since I was a child I have visited Cornwall and regard it as my homeland. It is a poor country of farmers and fishermen supported by tourism, with a long mining tradition that is largely defunct in the present day. Despite millennia of industry Cornwall is still a beautiful, magical place. As in previous adventures of Philip and Rosalind I have drawn from my own experience. I have tried to maintain accuracy with places and events but the characters are of my own invention.

Even after I chose to accept that Arthur existed I found that his story was a minefield of claims and contradictions. The few facts are buried under legends and medieval romance. Characters who accompany him, such as Merlin and Guinevere, have been so embellished as to be fairy tale. The most likely period of his exploits is called Post-Roman but really belongs to the Dark Ages. I believe that my interpretation is a reasoned balance of researched fact and probable fiction. I hope you enjoy a credible story.

Below are the main sources I have consulted:

Acton V and Carter D. Cornish War & Peace. The Road to Victory and Beyond. Truro. Landfall Publications. 1995

Ashe G. The Landscape of King Arthur.London. Grange Books. 1987.

Ashley M. Arthurian Tales. Sydney. Magpie Books. 1992.

Ashley M. The Giant Book of Myths and Legends. Sydney. Magpie Books.1995.

Ashton G. The Realm of King Arthur. Newport, Isle of White. J.Arthur Dixon.

Barber R. The Reign of Chivalry. New York. St Martins Press. 1980.

Barrowman R C; Batey C E and Morris C D. Excavations at Tintagel Castle, Cornwall 1990-1999. London. Society of Antiquaries. 2007.

Coad J G. Hellfire Corner.London. English Heritage. White Dove Press. 1993.

Coghlan R. The Encyclopedia of Arthurian Legends. Shaftsbury, Dorset. Element Books. 1991.

Day D. The Quest for King Arthur. London. De Agostini Editions. 1995.

Hamilton Jenkins A.K. Cornwall and its People. Newton Abbot. David & Charles. 1970.

Harris H J. Cornish Saints and Sinners. London. Bodley Head. 1923.

Holmes J. 1000 Cornish Place Names Explained. Redruth. Tor Mark Press. 1999.

Idriess I. The Desert Column. Sydney. Angus and Robertson. 1933.

Jackson R. Dunkirk. The British Evacuation, 1940. London. Cassell. 1988.

Jacobsen B C. The Deadliest Blogger: History Page. Deadliestblogpage. Wordpress.com.

Knowles J. The Legends of King Arthur and his Knights. London. Frederick Warne and Co. 1895.

Mallory, Sir Thomas. Tales of King Arthur. Edited by Michael Senior. London. William Collins and Sons. 1988.

Murray's Classical Atlas. Edited by G.B.Grundy. London. John Murray.1967.

Rankin W H. The Man Who Rode the Thunder. Prentice Hall. 1960.

Tennyson A L. Idylls of the King. London. Moxon and Co. 1859.

White P. King Arthur's Footsteps. Launceston. Bossiney Books. 2008.

GLOSSARY OF TERMS USED

Afon Hafren (Sabrina River): Severn Estuary, England.

Afon River: Avon River, near Bath, Somerset, England.

Affalon: Avalon, Vale of Apples, Loe Lake and Cober River (disputed).

Agned Hill: Arthur's Seat, Edinburgh, Scotland.

Angles: Germanic tribe from Baltic shore of Schleswig-Holstein.

Aqua Sulis: Badon, modern Bath in Somerset, England.

Armorica: north west France, including Britanny and Normandy.

Avalon: Affalon, Vale of Apples, Loe Lake and Cober River (disputed).

Badon Hill (Mons Badonicus): Solsbury Hill (disputed), near Bath, Somerset.

Bassas River: river in western Scotland (disputed).

Boderia River: Forth River, Central Scotland.

Brythons: Britons, Celtic tribes of western Britain.

Builth Kingdom: Independent kingdom within Powys, Wales.

Caer Guidn (Guennon Fort): battle site at Genvor (Gwenver) Cove (disputed) near Land's End, Cornwall.

Caerleon: Roman fortress of Isca Augusta, Newport, South Wales.

Calleva Atrebatum: Silchester, Hampshire, England.

Camelot: South Cadbury, Cadbury Castle (disputed).

Camlann: Arthur's final battle. Loe Bar(disputed), near Porthleven, Cornwall.

Cantaware Kingdom: Kent, south of London.

Cassiterides: Tin Islands or the British Isles.

Castle Corbyn ("Crow")(Corbenic): Castel Dinas Bran (disputed) above Llangollen, north Wales.

Cerrion River: Mahonyer River, Helford River, Cornwall.

Clut River: River Clyde in western Scotland.

Coed Celyddon: Caledonian Forest, Scotland.

Cordivicnum: Nantes, France.

Cornovii: tribe living in ancient Cornwall.

Cornubia (Cornu, Kernow): Cornwall.

Cunetio: Mildenhall, Suffolk, England.

Cymbrogi: Celtic tribes of Wales, brothers in arms for Arthur.

Deadman's Point: Dodman Point, Roseland, Cornwall.

Defnas: Devon, England.

Demetia Kingdom: Celtic domain in south Wales.

Deveryon: Devoran, Cornwall.

Din Eidyn: Edinburgh, Scotland.

Din Pentir ("The Rumps"): Hillfort on the Pentire Peninsula on the Camel River, Polzeath, Cornwall.

Dumnonia: south west England, including Devon, Cornwall and parts of Somerset.

Dun Breatann: Dumbarton Rock, River Clyde, Scotland.

Eboracum: York, Yorkshire, England.

Elmet Kingdom: West Riding of Yorkshire.

Fala River: Fal River, Cornwall.

Fosse Way: Roman road from south west England to Lindum(Lincoln).

Fowydh: Fowey, Cornwall.

Franks: tribe who gave their name to modern France.

Frisians: Germanic tribe from coasts of Netherlands, Germany and southern Jutland, Denmark.

Gaul: Roman name for modern France.

Geats: tribe from Gotaland in southern Sweden.

Glein River: River Glen (disputed), Northumberland, England.

Glywysing Kingdom: in western Gwent, now South Wales.

Gododdin Kingdom: Central Scotland, including Stirling, Lothians and borders of eastern Scotland.

Goon Brenn: Bodmin Moor.

Guennon Fort (Caer Guidn): battle site near Genvor (Gwenver) Cove (disputed) near Land's End, Cornwall.

Gwlad-yr-haf: Somerset, England.

Gwynedd Kingdom: north west Wales.

Hellys: Helston

Heyl Estuary: Hayle River and town, Cornwall.

Isca Dumnoniorum: Exeter, Devon, England.

Jutes: Germanic tribe from Jutland, Denmark.

Karrek Loos y'n Koos ("Grey Rock in the Wood"): St Michael's Mount, Cornwall.

Kelliwic (Celliwig): Killibury (Kelly Rounds) (disputed), near Wadebridge, Cornwall.

Lannsiek: Parish on Roseland incorporating St Just Church.

Lannvowsedh: St Mawes, Roseland, Cornwall.

Liger River: Loire River, France.

Lindum Colonia: Lincoln, Lincolnshire, England.

Linnius River: river near Lincoln (disputed).

Lyonesse Kingdom: Land bordering Cornwall as far as Scilly Isles.

Mahonyer River: Cerrion River, Helford River, Cornwall.

Massilia: Marseilles, France.

Moridunum: Carmathen, Wales.

Ocrinium Promontory: The Lizard, Cornwall.

Pen Dinas: Penndennis, Falmouth, Cornwall.

Pennsans: Penzance, Cornwall.

Phoenicia: Lebanon.

Picts: tribe from north and east Scotland.

Port Way: Roman road south west to Salisbury, England.

Powys Kingdom: Central Wales.

Reghed kingdom: northern England and southern Scotland.

Rhenus River: Rhine River, Germany.

Rhodenus River: Rhone River, France.

Rhos: Roseland peninsula, Cornwall.

Rhyd-ruth: Redruth, Cornwall.

Rock Anchorage: Carrick Roads, estuary of the Fal River, Cornwall.

Sabrina Estuary (Afon Hafren): Severn Estuary, England.

Sarmatians: Nomadic tribe of Central Asia, related to Scythians.

Saxons: Germanic tribe from North Sea coastland.

Spinae: Speen, Berkshire, England.

Stanheng (Choir Gaur): Stonehenge, Salisbury Plain, England.

Striveling: Stirling, Central Scotland.

Syria Palaestina: Palestine.

Tarsus: Tyre, Lebanon.

Terynas Ystrad Clut: Kingdom of Strathclyde, western Scotland.

The Lake: Loe Lake, near Porthleven, Cornwall.

Tintagel: Tintagel, Cornwall.

Trelawney: Sir Jonathan Trelawney, 3rd Baronet, Cornish bishop tried for refusing to obey King James 2nd (1685-1688) of England

Trelivel: Penryn, Cornwall.

Tryfrwyd (Tribuit): Junction of three tributaries on the River Frew near Stirling, Central Scotland.

Vallum Antoninum: Antonine Wall, Central Scotland.

Vallum Hadrianum: Hadrian's Wall, southern Scotland.

Verulamium: St Albans.

Werid Estuary: Firth of Forth, Scotland.

Ynys Enlli: Bardsey Island in north-west Wales.

Ynys Wydryn: Glastonbury, Somerset, England.